FORDING THE S

Dubravka Ugrešić

FORDING THE STREAM
OF CONSCIOUSNESS

TRANSLATED BY MICHAEL HENRY HEIM

With an afterword by the author

NORTHWESTERN UNIVERSITY PRESS
EVANSTON, ILLINOIS

Northwestern University Press
Evanston, Illinois 60208-4210

First published in Yugoslavia as *Forsiranje romana-reke* by August Cesarec, 1988.
Copyright © 1988 by Dubravka Ugrešić. English translation copyright © 1988 by Michael Henry
Heim. First published 1991 by Virago Press Limited. Author's afterword copyright © 1993 by
Dubravka Ugrešić. Northwestern University Press edition published 1993 by arrangement with
Virago Press Limited. All rights reserved.

Printed in the United States of America

ISBN 0-8101-1099-7

Library of Congress Cataloging-in-Publication Data

Ugrešić, Dubravka.
   [Forsiranje romana reke. English]
   Fording the stream of consciousness / Dubravka Ugrešić ;
translated by Michael Henry Heim.
      p.   cm. — (Writings from an unbound Europe) (Literature in
translation ; 5)
   Originally published : London : Virago Press, 1991.
   ISBN 0-8101-1099-7 (pbk.)
   I. Title. II. Series. III. Series: Literature in translation ;
5.
PG1619.31.G7F6713   1993
891.8'235—dc2
                                      93-30393
                                       CIP

I

1 In 1983 I spent the month of August in bed with a bad case of sciatica. *What you need is more action*, said my friend Grga over a cup of coffee.

2 In September of the same year I went to Iowa City as a guest of the International Writers Workshop. Kurt Vonnegut mentions the Workshop in his *Slaughterhouse Five*, which fact I learned the following summer on the island of Pag, when I found the novel in the dusty bedside table of my rented room. There were other writers at the Workshop, writers from all parts of the world, but mostly the Third. We lived together on the eighth floor of Mayflower Hall.

3 *This place gives you the feeling everybody in the whole bloody world is a writer*, said Helga, my room-mate. Our kitchen cabinets were stocked with black, long-neglected dishes. *This suite belonged to Wu Cheng and Yuan Chun-chun last year and Ndubisi Nwafor and Abdul Lalif Akel the year before*, said Mary, the 'dorm mother', apologetically. Giving the pots and pans and spoons and forks a tender once-over, I thought of tradition in Eliot's sense of the term and evolution in Tynyanov's. *Writers are like one big family*, I said to Helga, deeply moved, as we scraped our eggs, redolent with the presence of Yuan Chun-chun and Abdul Lalif Akel, out of the frying-pan with ends of bread. *Literature is one big matryoshka*, I said as I chewed. *What's a ma-tryosh-ka?* Helga asked.

4 Our hosts expected us to write, and I fully expected to oblige them, even in our cement ship, which resembled its illustrious predecessor in name only. I didn't write a word. On the wall next to my desk there was a large map of America in colours that reminded me of tutti-frutti ice-cream. I enjoyed watching the rays of the sun stealing through the window and licking the pastel blobs of the states.

5 I made frequent phone calls to my mother in Zagreb. She was always thrilled to hear I was alive. Once she was certain I had died of the heat; once she was certain I had frozen to death; and then there was the time I'd gone down in a plane with a group of writers on their way to Madrid. Our newspapers have a penchant for disaster.

6 One day we went to visit a tractor factory and had caviare with whipped cream for dinner. The businessmen – all tall, greying, and dapper in their navy-blue blazers, grey trousers, white shirts, regimental ties, and matching wives – looked us over in a friendly, if slightly less than all-there sort of way. After dinner our Turkish poet Azim sang the sad songs of Nazim Hikmet and, as he sang, the dining-room's picture window, which overlooked a dark lake, filled with ghosts that turned out to be huge white swans. The swans gazed sadly at the guests and softly drummed their beaks against the glass. Everyone ah-ed in awe. Then the businessmen applauded the poet and the writers applauded the swans.

7 In October I had another attack and went to a West Branch chiropractor by the name of Gene A. Zdrazil. *What you need is more action*, said Gene A. Zdrazil as he stretched my vertebrae with his thumbs.

8 My friends in Zagreb kept sending me long letters about inflation, electricity restrictions and excruciating boredom. I had no idea what they were talking about. Reading their letters made me love my country because it's so small. I felt sorry for it.

9 I've had coffee twice with a woman writer from Denmark who writes novels about reptiles and reptiles only. Even her narrators are reptiles. Then one day in a bookshop I came across a French novel that had a pig narrator. A pig telling his tale of woe from the cradle to the slaughterhouse. *See?* I said to the woman writer from Denmark. *See what?* she said to me.

10 Although after a while the writers began to talk about making love – male writers with female writers and vice versa – for some reason no one took the initiative. Yet they were much more concerned to be recognized as sexual beings than as writers. Azim, the Turkish poet, went out into the hall one night completely naked and wailed, *I am a man*, though nobody had ever thought to doubt it. *The reason is*, Helga said the night we made up our Sex-Appeal Hit Parade of the male writers, *that people may respect writers but they rarely love them.*

11 In November I set off on a trip around the country, leaving my green-and-white striped mug in the kitchen cabinet. In San Francisco I met writers from Brazil, Indonesia, Hungary and Spain. The strange thing was that we ran into one another all over town. Once a taxi-driver told me that every city has its astrological sign. I never found out what Zagreb's is, because, unfortunately, the driver had never heard of it. In the Vegas airport I happened on the East German writer Hans. Together we watched the sun go down. It was much more impressive than the postcards made it out to be. In Los Angeles I went to see some American writer friends who took me to Tijuana. On the way back the border crossing was jammed with cars and Mexicans. The Mexicans were singing sad songs and selling huge white plaster swans. We looked on in a friendly, if slightly less than all-there sort of way and tossed them coins.

12 I spent the Christmas holidays in New York. I lived in Manhattan in the run-down apartment of a woman who had recently emigrated from Odessa. She shared the apartment with her eighty-year-old papa – who spent the whole day sitting in front of the television in his striped pyjamas though he knew no English – and a Siamese cat named Ronechka in honour of the American president Ronald Reagan. I walked all over terrifying, breathtaking New York, thinking about the terrifying, breathtaking things I was going to write about it. I didn't write a word.

13 The taxi-driver who took me to Kennedy Airport had the following to say when he heard my final destination: *Great place – if it wasn't for them Communists!*

14 I got back to Zagreb just in time for New Year's. The city looked tiny, the streets impossibly narrow. The newspapers were chock-full of stories about 1984 and *1984*. With the last burst of

7

energy left from my New York rambles I hit the streets, but before I knew it I was sitting in the dark auditorium watching an ageing Paul Newman in *Bronx Cop*. At the Drina Restaurant after the film I faced a sad-looking array of native dishes and the fact that Zagreb *is* tiny. What I needed was less action.

15 I spent half my salary on postcards with *Greetings from Zagreb* on them. Soon I got a postcard from a writer in Ghana with *Greetings from Accra* on it.

16 In April I went to a writers' conference in Moscow with my fellow writers Saša and Velimir. While we were there, Velimir and I were interviewed by two journalists. First they took a few pictures of us in front of the Hotel Peking, where we were staying, and then said they thought it would be nice if they could take a few pictures of us in front of the statue of Mayakovsky, which happened to be in front of the Hotel Peking. While we were standing there, we noticed an old man walking past and watching us. The journalists told us the old man was none other than Kibalnikov, the sculptor who had done the statue of Mayakovsky. So they took another round of pictures of us, this time with Kibalnikov. We were very small, Kibalnikov was slightly larger (he had climbed up on Mayakovsky's foot), and Mayakovsky was very large. The journalists left without doing the interview. My Moscow friend Vitya maintains that Kibalnikov has been dead and buried for years. It was all highly irregular.

17 In Moscow I went to see Kabakov, the painter, who showed me his unusual magic boxes. One of them contained pictures that told the story of a man who had spent his entire life in a cupboard. The pictures were all black, which makes perfect sense, because they were painted from the viewpoint of the man in the cupboard. That was my favourite box.

18 In May I had a visit from Helga. It was a warm May. At night Helga sat out on my terrace reading *Die Frau und Russland* by moon- and flashlight; during the day she went around saying *Quatsch*, *verrückt*, and *Scheisse*. Then she went back to Berlin. I was sorry to see her go.

19 In May the papers were full of the astronomical rise in prices and catastrophic fall in wages, and a minister of something or other made a statement about swamps and members of the opposition who swam like carp in the swamps and if the swamps were drained we would see whether the carp were still in the opposition.

20 When my friend Nenad asked me to go for a walk with him in the park, he said, *This park is so small that if you don't walk slowly we'll be through it before we know it.*

21 My chiropractor Gene A. Zdrazil sent me a postcard from New York with a balloon on it. The postcard said: *Greetings from San Francisco to you and your backbone. How are your vertebrae doing? Fine, I hope.* The woman writer from Denmark wrote me a letter saying she was hard at work on a new novel whose hero was – a lizard. As I read the letter, I envisioned a *Varanus salvator*, which can grow as long as two metres. I envied her its length.

22 In June I had a visit from Dinu, a Romanian poet, who was on his way to Italy. He told me how happy he was to be a poet from Romania and nowhere else, and said he wouldn't change places with anyone. Regardless. I told him I wouldn't either. Regardless.

23 In June I was back in bed with my sciatica. I had a visit from Ante, who when I told him about my sciatica told me about his spondylitis and gave me a serene demonstration of his cervic vertebrae. *Listen carefully*, he said. I did, and sure enough I could hear them pop.

24 I had a visit from a friend of my mother's. We called her Comrade Zorka, because she had been active in the partisan movement during the war. She told me a dream she'd had. *I dreamed I was in a large auditorium*, she said, *and all the people in the front rows were people I had fought with. They were all covered with medals; they were all generals by now. And there was no room for me. There, you see*, I said to Comrade Zorka. *They discriminate against us even in our dreams.*

25 In July I went to Pag, which is known for its medicinal mud. People taking the mud cure show off their operation scars as they sponge down one another's backs. My back was sponged by a small-town butcher. On the beach I read Le Carré, Canetti, Vonnegut, *The Magic Mountain*, and *The Three Musketeers*. The latter twice through. One night I dreamed I'd made love to my alter ego. My alter ego was ten years younger than I was. *This is pitiful, damn it!* she said afterwards, quoting Porthos. *I respect my elders, but this is too much.*

26 At the end of July I was back in Zagreb, where I found a letter from a Brazilian writer by the name of Carlos, another Workshop crony. He had enclosed a page of xeroxed text, part of which was outlined with a felt pen in red. It said: *The Workshop also had a writer from Eastern Europe, a woman with the unusual name of Dubrufka. She struck me as slightly cuckoo. Every time I mentioned Rio, she brought up a man named Ostap Bender.*

27 One day a poet friend invited me to dinner. During the meal he delivered a long and highly interesting discourse on the importance of good manners. I enjoyed it a great deal. After dinner we made love. *Thank you*, he said to me in his quaint little dialect, *I hope it was as good for you as it was for me.*

28 In August I bought a notebook and wrote, *My hat's running over with characters. What shall I do with the one in my hand?*, firmly intending to write a novel though I didn't know quite what it would look like. *What you need is more action*, my friend Grga said while we were having coffee together. My friend Snježana dropped in one day and asked what I was planning to write about. *Oh, writers, I suppose*, I said, and she said, *But you always write about writers. Good writers can write about anything; only bad writers care about subject matter.* And I said, *The thing is, I love writers; they're so small and pitiful*, and decided then and there to place the as yet non-existent action in Zagreb.

29 The Soviet poet Andrei Voznesensky won our annual poetry prize, the Golden Wreath, at Struga. Our papers have quoted him several times as saying that what is worst for the poet is best for poetry.

30 Early in September I got a postcard from my friend Cule, a Belgrade writer. *Dear Dule*, the postcard said, *I'm fording the stream* of consciousness. *Dear Cule*, I answered lyrically, *My hat's running over with characters. What shall I do with the one in my hand?* The following telegram arrived a few days later: *Fuck it. Stop. You can't do better. Stop. In life or in literature. Stop.*

'How can you prefer stories that are senseless and mean nothing?' the wise Ulug said to the sultans.

'We prefer them *because* they are senseless,' the sultans replied.

Voltaire, 'Zadig, or Destiny'

LUNDI, le 5 mai

LUNDI, le 5 mai

1

José Ramón Espeso arrived at the Zagreb Intercontinental at approximately 6 a.m. The first thing he did in his room was to open the curtains. A grey morning light crept in. Then he went back to his bag to unpack. He hung his suit carefully on a hanger. The click of the hanger against the rod in the closet broke the morning silence. He laid out his neatly folded tie and white shirt on the bed – he was planning to wear them to the meeting – and fifteen copies of his paper, 'Poetry and the Censor', on the desk. Then he went into the bathroom, put down his toilet bag, and took out a toothbrush and toothpaste. He removed the paper cover from the toilet seat and tossed it into the wastepaper basket. He did the same with the cellophane on the tumblers, placing the toothbrush and toothpaste in one of them. José Ramón enjoyed mastering things and space in a hotel room.

He returned to the desk and tested the lamp, turning it on and off. Then he took several picture postcards of Zagreb out of his pocket – he had bought them just after leaving the station – and addressed one of them immediately. He had written a short poem in the train and decided to copy it on to the postcard and send it to his mother, Luisa.

It was just seven when he finished. He checked the programme: *Lundi, le 5 mai, 10 heures: Inauguration solennelle du Colloque et Exposé d'introduction*. The opening ceremonies weren't until ten. He looked around the room, his glance resting on the neatly folded shirt. The grey light had crept under the collar and cast a stingy, barely noticeable shadow. José Ramón decided to go down and have breakfast.

For breakfast he ordered two soft-boiled eggs and tea. He stroked one egg with the ball of his index finger and tapped the top with his spoon. He liked the sound and the ritual of it. He then made a round opening in the shell and carefully extracted the soft contents. When the waiter brought a bowl with curlicues of butter, José Ramón allowed himself a thin slice of thinly buttered bread. He ran his index finger along the edge of the starched white napkin, then along the edge of the teacup and, after taking a sip of tea, counted the number of prongs on the idle fork. If by some chance these objects – the napkin, the cup, the fork – were to vanish, an observer might conclude that José Ramón was drawing magic lines in the air. In fact, however, José Ramón was reviewing lines of the new poem, and the progress of his unconscious index finger along the edge of the starched white napkin more likely than not corresponded to the length of a line, its progress along the edge of the teacup the length of another . . .

As a result of his communist sympathies José Ramón Espeso had served several prison sentences during the Franco regime. And although he still considered himself a communist, neither he nor those around him thought it particularly important any more. Surrounded by the walls of the Carabanchelo, he often imagined the rows of bricks beneath the plaster – their shape, their size, their number. It helped him to structure his inner world and curb his fear. When José Ramón wrote poetry, he perceived the words as he did the bricks. He could feel their roughness or smoothness, their porosity or solidity, their edges, as if he were holding them in his hand, weighing them, and he fitted them together in his poems as if he were laying bricks, building solid walls of words. He became particularly adept at finding a single brick to serve as a key to the whole wall, open it up, yet it was deceptive, required a long, arduous search, tapping, feeling, listening attentively. José Ramón began walling up in his poems the sort of brick-word that, once found, would shift, alter, reverse, or expand the poem's meaning, shed a new light on it, through a crack, from behind. Sometimes there was more than one such word, there were whole lines of them, and sometimes he himself discovered the new meaning only after the fact: it had come about without his help.

At first he did it to evade the censors – he enjoyed the secret, private game of hide-and-seek involved; later he did it for its own sake. The only thing that annoyed him was that critics were lazy and incapable of decoding the word–ciphers. They read the poems as if staring at a wall without the slightest notion that one of the bricks in it might be deceiving them. José Ramón had gone so far as to write commentaries on several poems and store them in his mother's flat.

It was still only half past seven when he finished breakfast. Strolling through the nearly empty entrance hall, he stopped at the reception desk to find out where the Crystal Conference Hall was and learned quite by accident from the amiable man on duty that the hotel had a pool and a sauna.

The sudden possibility of having a swim before the meeting began appealed greatly to José Ramón, and when the young woman at the entrance to the pool told him he could rent a bathing suit, bathing cap, and towel he decided to take immediate advantage of it.

'You have also music, no?' he asked in his broken English, as if he considered a pool without an audio system a rarity.

'Um . . . yes, we have,' the woman said, surprised she had admitted it. The pool was empty, and the only time they turned on the music was when there was a crowd – in other words, almost never. (She may also have been nonplussed by José Ramón's unusual appearance. The old man had put on the transparent nylon bathing cap, and his bald pate shone through it like a fantastic onion dome. In fact, everything about him described a sort of good–natured circle: the nose, the cheeks, the salt-and-pepper beard, the glasses, the paunch . . . The paunch and the onion dome perching on a pair of skinny legs reminded the woman of a picture-book illustration of a less than successful sorcerer.)

The man smiled and said, '*Gracias, señorita*' and waddled off in the direction of the pool. The woman smiled too, then shrugged and put on a cassette that had been given to her the year before by another early swimmer, an American.

José Ramón had three loves: his mother, his poetry and opera. They were quite enough for one life. And when the room suddenly filled with the strains of *Carmen*, he was in seventh heaven. He dived into the water as if diving into the music, just as he dived into music as if diving into water. Floating on his back, he could see the blue sky through the glass roof and count the treetops along the other side of the street, and the clouds and green poplars swam with him, and when Maria Callas's voice flew up to the treetops and rustled them like a breeze, they turned first silver, then dark, and when it flew back down like a shooting star through the glass and the water, José Ramón dived under to catch it.

A few minutes later the young woman peeked out of her booth to see what the unusual guest was up to; she saw him waving his arms, kicking his legs, spouting spray, ducking under, popping up for air, snorting, floating, splashing, then slowly sinking again, leaving only the cap to glide along the surface. He looked like a fat, old, uncommonly happy seal; in fact, the young woman had rarely seen a person so happy.

After a long float on his back he glanced at his watch, flipped on to his stomach, and paddled over to the steps. Watching him emerge, the young woman thought she saw a smile on his face. But just then, as if feeling her eyes on him, he twisted away with a jerk and, in so doing, slipped and fell backwards. Trying to regain his balance, he flung out his arms, but his head came down hard on the edge of the pool. The woman ran up to him with her arms stretched out helplessly, then ran back to the telephone and dialled First Aid with a trembling finger.

'. . . It's an emergency!' she cried into the phone.

'Would you turn down that music, for Christ's sake!' the voice on the other end cried back.

José Ramón's mother, Luisa, who liked exciting, emotion-packed scenes, would have enjoyed this one immensely – had anyone but her son been the protagonist.

José Ramón's personal effects were listed and packed during a routine search of his room in the presence of the young Spanish consul. Noticing the postcard on the desk, the consul picked it up, read it – he was the only person in the room capable of doing so – and placed it in his pocket, which was not altogether in keeping with the rules. He had decided to send it personally to Señora Luisa and enclose his condolences: the consul, like all Spaniards in this world, had a mother.

2

'What do you say to another round, baby?' Vanda moaned coyly, tickling the Minister just below his belly-button.

Baby stroked his worried brow with one hand and patted Vanda's behind with the other.

'No go, baby. I'm late for work as it is.'

The Minister reluctantly crawled out of bed and started gathering his clothes from various parts of the room.

'Then I'll go and make some coffee, OK baby?' Vanda said obligingly, winding her plump charms in a Chinese housecoat the Minister had bought for her in London and sidling off to the kitchen.

'I really love you, baby.'

'I love you tooooo,' he heard Vanda's voice sailing out of the kitchen on the toot of the espresso-maker. Italian. Bought in Trieste the year before.

Oh, that hat! She'd bought a sex manual not too long ago – *The First Hundred Positions* or something like that – and picked the ten best suited to them. Then she copied them out on slips of paper and put them in a little hat she'd crocheted especially for the purpose. And these last few months they had their own little erotic lottery. First the Minister would draw – with his eyes closed, of course – then Vanda. Vanda would always squeal with joy, as if she'd won a million dinars instead of a copulation. Today they'd drawn the missionary position, which, if the truth be known, the Minister found most to his liking or – should we say – loving. You had to hand it to her. She was terrific in bed. She had a heart of gold, too. A few months ago they'd taken the upright position out of the hat because it gave the Minister a sciatica attack. Vanda had torn up the paper and tossed it in the wastepaper basket, and that was the end of that nasty position.

It was nine by the time the Minister had tied his tie and combed his thinning hair.

'Coffee, baby,' he heard Vanda's voice calling from the kitchen just as the telephone began to ring. He gave a start when she handed him the receiver. It had to be Prša. He was the only one who knew about him and Vanda.

'Listen, can you get down here right away?' asked the receiver in Prša's most anxious tones. 'There's been a rather unpleasant accident . . . No, no, nothing like that, don't worry. It's just that I think . . . Yes, I'm at the hotel . . . Right . . .'

Getting into his overcoat, which the solicitous Vanda, his mistress and secretary, had readied for him, the Minister said, 'They need me down at the Intercontinental. See you later.' And so saying, he gave her a peck on the lips.

3

Pipo Fink, a lanky young man in jeans, white tennis-shoes, and Bogart overcoat open just enough to show the *New York University* on his navy-blue cotton T-shirt, was striding across the soft carpet of the Intercontinental when he suddenly halted, made a few hesitant bounces and a brief pan, and, having come to an important decision, set off to the right. Just as he did so, the smooth, polished face of Prša the poet appeared in his viewfinder.

'Where've you been keeping yourself, man?' Prša called out to him in a pointedly hale-and-hearty voice. 'Well?' he said without waiting for an answer and gave Pipo a poke in the shoulder. Before Pipo could come up with something like 'Well, I'm here now,' Prša grabbed hold of him and said, 'Look, there's nobody here yet. What do you say we grab a cup of coffee. Just the two of us.' And he turned Pipo in the opposite direction, the direction in which the Diana Bar happened to be located.

Before he could decide whether he felt like having coffee with Prša or whether he felt like having coffee at all, he was sitting at the bar with a small *cappuccino* sending up smoke signals in front of him.

'You're unbelievable, you know that, man? The rest of us, we get older by the day, and you're so youthful it's disgusting. I mean, look at that T-shirt!'

Prša gave Pipo such a palsy-walsy clap on the shoulder that Pipo began to wonder whether he hadn't mixed him up with somebody else. He didn't remember having exchanged more than three words with him in his life.

'How are things?' Pipo said, as much to prove he could talk as for any communicative purpose.

'Couldn't be worse,' Prša sighed, his face breaking into the furrows of a worried man. 'Catastrophic.'

Faced with Prša's raised eyebrows and dark radiance, Pipo couldn't help recalling the pop singers who got rich quick by 'newly composing' folk music. Our whole society is newly composed, Pipo said to himself. No wonder people have such pitiful role models.

'It can't be that bad,' he said cautiously, by now absolutely certain Prša had taken him for somebody else.

Prša solemnly raised his right hand, spread his fingers in front of Pipo's nose as if demonstrating the number five, and waited for Pipo's reaction.

'I don't understand.'

'Look closer,' said Prša.

'No, really. I don't get it.'

Prša stretched his fingers even more. Four stood upright like candles, while the index finger drooped.

'Is it a trick?' asked Pipo, completely baffled.

'If only it was,' Prša sighed. 'You don't seem to have heard.'

'No . . .'

'You don't know what happened to me?'

'No, I don't,' said Pipo, feeling guilty.

'But you've heard of my performance pieces, my "Culture in the Workplace", haven't you?'

'Oh, yes,' he said, though he hadn't.

'Then you should remember' – Pipo flinched – 'I did it for a light-bulb factory on May Day last year. I had them give me the biggest space they had and turn on all the machines, you know? All the machines and the lights and all. And then I had them give me a mike, a microphone, and hook it up to the PA system full blast, full volume. You know what a perfectionist I am. Everything's got to be just so.'

Pipo knew very little, practically nothing, about Prša, but he nodded and nodded, patiently bearing his boring, synonymically inclined discourse.

'And?'

'They were terrific, those guys, those workers. They put on a real fireworks of a light-show. I don't know how many watts of current, you know, electricity they used, I don't understand those things.

But man, it really worked, that combination of culture and the workplace. You can't imagine what it's like when it works . . .'

'And?'

'And nothing,' he said with a frown. 'While I was reciting my poems, my hand somehow got caught in a – God only knows what it was. Anyway, the shock was enormous. I could've been electrocuted! And this is only the most obvious, visible result.'

'Your finger, you mean.'

'A finger's a serious thing. Our fingers are the tools of our trade. Along with this, of course.' He tapped his forehead. 'If it'd been a leg – just another extremity – or even a thumb, but the index finger!'

'And?' Pipo was disappointed.

'They gave me compensation, disability insurance. They were very fair and proper about the whole thing – you've got to hand it to them.'

He flexed his finger again and looked at it the way a mother looks at her crippled offspring.

'Nothing helps the bugger,' he said bitterly. 'I even tried a spa. It's terrible. And the money it costs me!'

'Money?'

'Don't think they give you a full salary when you're on sick leave. I'm on half pay, old boy. Have you any idea what that means?'

Pipo had no idea whatsoever because he worked freelance, so he nodded sympathetically.

'And then they finally gave me a flat, the bastards,' Prša went on. 'Plenty big and smack in the middle of things, but how many times did I tell them: "Shave off a few metres here and there, just give me something new!" But no. It's catastrophic!'

'But . . .'

'But nothing! Have you any idea what it cost me to renovate the place, fix it up? I wouldn't mind so much if I could pitch in, make myself useful. But with this! I feel like a cripple, an invalid.'

'Still . . .' Pipo tried again.

'Still what? How can you be creative when your finger's in a coma? Oh, a poem or two, perhaps, but a novel?'

Prša was known as a poet, but Pipo couldn't bring himself to ask the obvious question.

'Buy a cassette-player,' he said.

25

'Too late,' Prša replied with a wave of the hand. 'I've finished it. It's coming out this Wednesday.' Then suddenly he snapped, 'Hey, was that a little joke at my expense? Well, this isn't just a technical thing. I mean, it's not like telling a man who's lost a leg to go out and buy an artificial one, a prosthesis.'

'Sorry,' said Pipo, though he saw nothing strange in the idea of suggesting an artificial leg to a man who's lost its home-grown equivalent.

'It's not a practical thing,' Prša said, his newly composed pop-singer face breaking out in a smile, 'it's human; it's not a physical disability, it's a human one. You and me, the two of us,' and he placed an intimate finger in the middle of the *N* on Pipo's chest, 'all of us, we live in a primeval forest, and if man is a wolf to man, then you can imagine what writer is to writer!'

Prša paused and raised his eyebrows to let his point sink in, then leaned forward conspiratorially. 'You must have followed the attacks on me – read them, I mean.'

'On account of your finger?' Pipo asked, sincerely surprised.

Prša made the face of a man who knows he's dealing with an idiot, then the face of a man who has decided to deal with him anyway. 'Some pipsqueak of a poet wrote a long denunciation of me in one of those youth movement papers. You know: a frontal attack, no holds barred. So I said to him, I said, "I want you to understand me, my boy; I want to make it absolutely clear. There's only one thing holding you back," I said.'

And so saying, he raised his famous finger and touched his forehead to indicate a lack of grey matter. He thereby showed a further similarity to the pop singer, who mimes his texts as he sings them, so Pipo played the grateful audience and followed the finger's trajectory.

'"This is what's holding you back, not me. You were born to the sound of the Beatles; I was born to the sound of partisan bullets. We can never be the same."'

'No, you can't.'

'Which is why the snot-nosed little bastard left that rag on his ear. Flew out like a bullet. Know what I mean?'

He would have gone on, but he suddenly noticed someone out of the corner of his eye and said instead, 'Sorry, old boy. Got to go, got to run. It's the Minister. One of the honoured guests dropped dead on us this morning.'

He gave Pipo another friendly poke in the shoulder and said, as if suddenly remembering something, 'By the way, your name – it's Pipo, isn't it?'

'Pipo Fink!' said Pipo. And although it flew out of him like a bullet, Prša was faster. Pipo wiped his face as if he had just been spat at, and thought, 'What a fool I am' and frowned.

'Whisky,' he called to the bartender.

'Right away, Mr Fynke!'

'Hey, you!' he called coolly to Mr Smooth.

Surprised, Mr Smooth turned in his direction, whereupon Fynke whipped out his revolver and sent a bullet through his brain. Mr Smooth crumpled to the floor.

Fynke coolly tucked the revolver into his back pocket.

'Some people have no tact.' He drained his drink at a draught. 'How much do I owe you, Joe?' he asked the bartender.

'It's on the house, Mr Fynke.'

He stopped at the toilet on his way out of the bar. The moment he opened the door, he was confronted with his own face in the large mirror: a young man his height with his blond crew cut, his blue eyes, his jeans, his white tennis-shoes. The only trouble was that, instead of his navy-blue T-shirt with *New York University* on it, this young man was wearing a baby-blue T-shirt with *Berkeley* on it.

'Hi!' said the *Berkeley* T-shirt, all smiles.

'Hi!' said the *NYU* T-shirt, somewhat disconcerted, and slipped into a stall.

4

To tell the truth, the Minister didn't really feel like a minister. How can you be a minister if anyone at all can nag you about anything at all? No, he was a politician, that's all, part of the 'machine'. They'd kicked him upstairs before pensioning him off, and what had they given him? The lowest of the low. Writers. The only good part about it was Vanda, it had brought him Vanda. And Vanda was the best thing that had happened to him in his whole life. During the war and just after it everything had been clear and simple, everything had been – human. Later it all clouded over, and once you were in you couldn't get out, you were a cog in the wheel. He had just finished his apprenticeship at the local butcher's when the war came along and pushed him into the partisans. After the war he actually did a stint as a butcher, but when things started being nationalized he was given special training, first in administration, then in education. That was how it was in those days. Then radio, newspapers, television . . . He had a biography richer than Jack London's! And today's crop – what did they know? Nothing. They had nothing to offer, not even a trade, while he could still make blood sausage with the best of them. And why were those damn writers always after him to be tolerant and accept other people's views? He was their political representative, not their *maître d'*! Of course, they had nothing to do but grind out their completely and utterly useless drivel. Oh, and moan and groan and run down one another and the system, beating their chests and raising their voices against every piddling 'miscarriage of justice'. Now *he'd* put himself on the line for his beliefs; he could have ended up in gaol, he could have been killed in the war. These young people wanted no-risk beliefs. The freedom to say anything they pleased – against the system, of course

– and the right to system-generated status, unemployment insurance, old-age pensions, subsidized housing, trips abroad, high pay – you name it. And what did they give in exchange? A thin volume of poems that they and one or two critics pronounced 'brilliant' because it represents 'culture' and where would we be without culture? Well, the hell with culture. First show me you're a Shakespeare, then talk culture. Where else did they pay you like we do? No country I know. Try starving a little. Weren't artists supposed to starve? Not only did we pay them, we gave them perks like this colloquium. Colloquium! A four-day spree for them and their foreign cronies. Not that our ignorant bastards knew enough of their languages to say two words to them. And what about the foreigners? Who were they, anyway? The ones from the Eastern bloc came to buy their wives bras and panties, and the ones from the West to wash their *ćevapčići* down with plenty of *šlivovica*. Two years ago a self-styled Slavist from Stockholm had kept tugging at my sleeve, asking me about 'the eye'. 'What eye?' I finally asked, and he said, 'I hear you eat sheep eye. Big Yugoslav delicacy.' So we found him one. Someone said he was a member of the Nobel Prize committee. Big deal. Cultural exchange! Our writers foisting their books off on foreigners who regularly left them behind for the chambermaids. At least the chambermaids knew the language. All they really wanted was to force their latest masterpiece on us. And we, fools that we are, we go and publish them. Wouldn't want to miss anything, would we? Got to keep up with the world. But did the world keep up with us? The world didn't give a fuck about us. All right, calm down. Think of your pension. Vanda and the pension. When you retire you'll move in with Vanda and leave the flat and the car and the house by the sea to the snake. The other house too. Everything. To her and to that dimwit, that thirty-year-old rock'n'roller who couldn't get into the army, not to mention the university, the slouch, the sluggard, the good-for-nothing deadbeat. Why didn't I smack him around while there was still time? It was all those damn 'pedagogical values' he now so prized. Open-mindedness, democracy, all that shit . . .

'Oh, Minister!' he suddenly heard as he entered the Intercontinental. 'Minister!' It was Prša, waving his arms like a madman.

'Well, out with it.'

'It's catastrophic! We'll have to rewrite your opening remarks. Or at least call for a minute of silence at the end. One of the guests, a Spaniard, he slipped in the pool and cracked his head open.'

'Oh God,' said the Minister. 'How old was he?' he added, as if the man had died of an illness rather than an accident.

5

Jan Zdražil suddenly felt all the energy drain out of him. He was standing naked in the middle of the bathroom, unable to remember what he was doing there. He felt so weak he put down the toilet seat and sat on the cover. Everything had gone wrong. From the moment when in desperation he had stuck the manuscript in his bag to Zdenka's chatter at the station ('Don't forget panties. You know, the bikini kind'), the icy fear that gripped him each time the train approached a border, and the flash of humiliation when the man at the hotel desk stared long and hard at his Soviet flight bag after handing him back his Czech passport . . . Then in the hotel room the blow he'd felt when he unpacked and found himself face to face with the fact that yes, the manuscript was here with him and, what was even worse, it couldn't go back . . . God, how stupid it all was, how idiotic! And Zdenka! He hadn't known, he hadn't had any idea until that minute at the station: leaning on his elbows at the window of his compartment, looking out at her on the platform, he suddenly realized how he hated her. He realized he hated her with the same strength he'd used all those years to make himself love her. He shuddered at the thought that she might have guessed what he was up to; after all, during the sixteen years of their marriage she had doggedly sniffed out, dug out all his weaknesses, stored them under lock and key in her private pantry so she could always have one handy, always pull one out in time of need. Panties! Don't forget, the tight, bikini kind, she'd said in her usual charming, *double-entendre* way. But what had in the past turned him on – as it did the man at the window next to him, who, when he heard her, grinned a lubricious grin – now disgusted him. He knew things could explode and show a whole new grotesque, distorted face; he only wondered why they'd waited for so long.

There on the desk in the room lay his novel, a genie let out of the bottle. His redemption, his crime. He could all but feel its pulse, hear it pounding. He was gripped with fear again. Get up, that's what he had to do now. Get up, move about, mingle with the crowd, and it would all take care of itself.

For a while he remained seated on the toilet-seat cover, staring at the indifferent tiles. Then, still in a daze, he rose, stepped into the bath, and turned on the water full force. The water was warm. His home was far away. The tiles were blue. The bath was white. Jan was in the bath. The bath was in . . . Za-greb . . . Za-grab . . . Za-grabe . . . Za-grave . . .

6

As Pipo Fink of the bouncy walk approached the Crystal Conference Hall, he was welcomed by a loud babble and a large crowd. Some people were standing, others sitting, yet others milling or making their way to the table where they could pick up programmes, copies of the talks, and head-sets for simultaneous translation. Pipo peeked into the hall and gave it one of his pan shots. At the other end he could see Prša trotting around, talking, waving his arms and scowling, the way people in charge tend to wave their arms and scowl. One man had taken a seat in the front row and was fiddling with his head-set, trying to make out whether things had started yet. A man who trusts his ears more than his eyes, Pipo thought. Prša stopped a gliding waiter and said something with a wave of the arms and a contraction of the brows; the waiter's face remained perfectly aloof. They were used to it; there were functions here every week: a congress of sociologists, a symposium of cardiologists, a convention of Kremlinologists, a seminar of archaeologists, elections for the most valuable athlete of the year, gastronomical extravaganzas . . . There is no difference between a writer, a cyclist and a sociologist. Not from a waiter's perspective at least.

Back in the foyer, Pipo surveyed the terrain for the safest spot. He stationed himself next to a well-developed ficus. Then he switched back to his camera mode, focusing on three tiny, shrivelled old women with thin, grey hair, lacklustre eyes and bobbing heads. Under closer scrutiny they turned into sweet little hens with shiny black feathers and white spots. Children's writers. Periodically hatching lyrical, gaily painted eggs. All my love, chickadees! he called out to them silently, deeply moved, and one of them, as if she had heard him, turned and gave him a blissful smile of non-recognition.

33

Suddenly a mass of muscles blocked Pipo's lens. It was dominated by a protuberant chest and jutting jaw of such inexorable, relentless determination that it took the cameraman's breath away. Ivan Ljuština, the critic, was on the move. Pipo unconsciously clutched at a leaf of the ficus. But just as Ljuština was about to plough into him, he swerved his authoritative body with great dignity. Ox, boar or yak? Pipo wondered, stroking the smooth surface of the leaf with a compassionate thumb. Having reached the opposite wall, the critic turned and started making his way in Pipo's direction again, but Pipo unconsciously took a step to the side, thereby placing himself out of range.

Pipo's internal camera now turned to a small group listening to the famous novelist Mraz. Mraz reminded Pipo of a walrus. He huffed and puffed, twisted his head this way and that (Pipo zoomed in on the tough, wrinkled hide at the back of his neck and counted three fatty folds), waved his flippers, wiggled his fleshy bottom, snorted and honked. For a moment Pipo thought he saw a cloud of steam over his head. His strategic position in the middle of the room and his nonchalant, walrusy good nature combined to give the impression to all and sundry that the real reason they were there was to celebrate his birthday. Or something of the sort. Soon he'll be handing out his latest book to the foreigners, thought Pipo maliciously.

The next group caught by Pipo's kino-eye was a trio of poets whispering confidentially under the cover of a coquettish potted palm. Why do all our poets have oily hair that hangs in noodles over their necks and cheeks, a sickly, grey, and yes, oily complexion, bent backs and tiny, beady, squinty, perfidious eyes? Pipo wondered. The novelists were a healthier lot somehow. The mouselike glint in the poets' eyes made Pipo decide that when he finally got down to writing his *Animal Kingdom* he'd put the poets in the 'Vermin' chapter. Meanwhile a fourth poet had joined the group, a small man in a neat suit and tie. Pipo zoomed in on his sleeves, which were a bit too long, though not so long as to hide a pair of chubby little hands. What was this teddy bear doing among the grizzlies? Pipo thought, and capriciously crossed him off the list of writers, beasts and beings.

Women were in the minority, and most of those present were

young and good-looking, language students from the university brought in to serve as interpreters. They're too smooth and shiny for animals, Pipo concluded, too sleek, too aerodynamic. (Look at her, will you? a friend of Pipo's had said the other day, commenting on a girl in the street. A sight for sore eyes! A regular DC-10!)

Panning again, Pipo registered noisy packs of badgers, crocodiles, monkeys, bears and a lone grey eagle. No wolves, though. Prša went too far when he said a writer was a wolf to other writers; no, a writer might be a mouse or, say, a rat, but not a wolf. Besides, writers made you think of people, and people always made you think of animals, and with that conciliatory thought Pipo stopped his camera long enough to have a good look at the long shot in front of him. In the background he noticed two or three middle-aged women, each seriously leafing through the typed versions of the talks. Foreigners. Translators. Translators were: 1. plain women past their prime (who else would devote so much energy to translating the writers of a 'minor' literature); 2. pale and shop-worn (from spending all their time indoors translating); 3. less than stylishly dressed (because their pay is so low); and 4. modest (because of the very nature of the undertaking). How did they get caught in such a useless and out-of-the-way literature? Pipo wondered. Maybe in their youth they'd had a fling with one or another local writer and, seduced and abandoned, they'd kept translating out of piety to the fling and because, having learned an otherwise worthless language, they might as well do what little they could with it.

'Look who's here!' Pipo heard a voice call out. It was Ena, a.k.a. the Bell-Tower, a journalist and friend from his student days. Ena was tall, almost as tall as Pipo, and was known for her tragicomical ungainliness, which showed more in the way she moved than in the way she was put together. She seemed so surprised at being able to walk that she periodically forgot how to go about it, and her nickname, acquired early in her studies, derived not so much from her height as from her long neck, her small head and her outlandishly large feet. The Bell-Tower had penetrating dark eyes and an unbearably sad expression; she wore her despair – and had worn it as long as anyone could remember – like an old-fashioned brooch. She was a mythical beast – half ostrich, half giraffe. Pipo caught a brief view of Ena's profile. What could a person do with that silhouette, that soul, and those feet? Pipo thought, and suddenly he remembered that he and the Bell-Tower had in the distant past . . . Once or twice only, three times at the most. There were times Pipo thought she was in love with him, the times she snuggled up and wouldn't speak. A kind of adhesive tape.

'What's up?' said Pipo nonchalantly.

'Nothing,' said the giraffe, the ostrich and the Bell-Tower, heading towards the conference hall. 'Aren't you going in?'

'Not just yet,' said Pipo, starting the camera up again. His new perspective – he had a bird's-eye view this time – revealed considerable movement on the right, and he took pleasure in registering the funnel effect of a mass of people flowing out of the frame.

No, this was neither his time nor his place. He just happened to have been born here, got stuck here. He wasn't even a member of the animal kingdom. He lacked the oily hair, the beady eyes. In his dreams he had other plans, he was different. I'm different! he called out mentally to the last human figure to enter the conference hall, after which he switched off his internal camera and went into the hall himself, picking up a head-set on the way. The minute he sat down – in the last row, as near to the door as possible – he set the dial to *English*, superimposed the female English-speaking voice on to Prša's face as he ran through the organizational details, and pushed off on his own.

'I like your house painted white,' said Rose, handing him a Hennessy and pouring herself a Kahlúa Surprise. 'It's like a great white swan lost in snow.'

'Whenever it snows, Rose has a Kahlúa Surprise and comes up with the most poetic images,' William Styron said with a tinge of irony, and threw a few logs on the fire. Then he picked up his Hennessy with those long, delicate fingers of his and asked Pipo, 'Well, how do you like living here in Roxbury?'

'Very much,' Pipo replied. 'I've always dreamed of a house in the country, though I do feel a bit of a bigamist.'

'Bigamist?' said Rose.

'I mean, I love Europe too.'

'Oh, so do we,' said Styron. 'We've been here since 1954 when we bought Alexander Kerensky's house to get away from the barbarity of New York – isn't that right, Rose? – but we always spend summers in Europe.

True, our tastes differ. I prefer Paris, while Rose, with her interest in human rights, has ties to Eastern Europe. And then there's Philip to visit in London . . .'

'By the way, shouldn't Philip and Claire be here by now, Bill? They did say seven, didn't they? The Millers can't make it till later. They're having Galway Kinnell to dinner. And some journalist or other.'

'Philip's chewing away at Zuckerman again,' said Styron, an ironic smile stealing across his pale face, 'trying to make new bubbles out of old gum.'

'I'm not sure you know all our neighbours,' Rose said to Pipo. 'Besides the Millers — Arthur, that is, and his wife Inge Morath — there's Richard Widmark, Dustin Hoffman . . . Tell me, have you met them?'

'No, I haven't,' said Pipo.

'And unfortunately Henry Kissinger and Calvin Klein,' Styron added.

'Klein's put his house up for sale,' said Rose on her way to the window. 'Look at it come down! You'll have a lot of shovelling to do tomorrow, Bill.' She took a sip of her drink and stood gazing out of the window.

'Tell me,' Styron said, turning to Pipo and warming his Hennessy glass with his pale fingers, 'how's your new novel coming along?'

'Harper & Row offered me a $500,000 advance, but I turned them down. I don't want to rush it.'

'And right you are. A writer like you can set his own terms,' Styron said slowly, and then added with a smile, 'After a steady diet of greens American literature is ready for your kind of meaty overkill. That last thing of yours was a major contribution to the literary barbecue. Don't you agree, Rose?'

'Here comes Roth,' said Rose, hurrying off to answer the door instead of the question.

Pipo was wakened by a light touch on the shoulder. He turned to see a *Berkeley* T-shirt.

'Hi!' said the T-shirt in English. 'Mind if I join you?'

Pipo moved over and the young man sat down. Pipo noticed he was wearing a head-set and an almost happy smile. Stupid Yank, thought Pipo. Ready to beam at the most inane introductory remarks. When the young man realized that Pipo was looking at him, his smile broadened. He took off his head-set, gave Pipo another nudge, and offered it to him. This guy's crazy, Pipo thought, but took off his earphones and put on the American's. Suddenly his head exploded with the Talking Heads' latest hit.

Meanwhile the rest of the writers heard:

Comrades, Fellow Writers!

It is a great pleasure and a great honour for me to open this year's Zagreb Literary Colloquium, which will be devoted to the theme of 'Contemporary Literature: Its Trends and Tendencies in the Dialectics of World Events'. Our city, well known for its hospitality, takes particular pride in playing annual host to this gathering of national and international literary celebrities. All of you – poets, novelists, artists – contribute freely of your labours to the cause of peace, breaking down geographic, political and ideological borders to form a neutral ground of the written word where you can wield that proverbial pen which is stronger than the sword . . .

Jan Zdražil, the Czechoslovak representative, duly clicked from channel to channel trying to locate the Russian translation. It came in for a while on Channel 3 ('All of you – poets, novelists, artists – contribute freely of your labours to the cause of peace . . .'), but at that point it faded away, and he sat there helpless, putting on the head-set, then taking it off. Once, when he twisted the antenna-like thingamajig up instead of down, he heard 'May I ask you to stand' come out of the earphones in Russian, and he immediately jumped to his feet and started clapping. Everyone else had stood up too, but for some reason no one else was clapping. Suddenly he felt a tug at his sleeve, and he turned to face the dark, sad eyes of a woman he had never seen before.

7

Things were unusually lively in the lobby after the opening ceremonies. The participants were more at ease now and had started circulating, peering at the name tags on one another's lapels, making friends, forming groups. One of the locals, Ranko Leš, who considered eccentricity a poet's prime responsibility, had pinned the badge to his trousers, just to the left of the crotch.

The French representative, Jean-Paul Flagus, an elderly gentleman with watery blue goggle-eyes, thick, wet lips and a slightly protruding neck that gave him the look of a turtle, had gathered a group of French-speaking writers around him and was talking animatedly, puffing occasional smoke rings from his thick cigar.

'Much as I mourn our colleague José Ramón Espeso, we all know that bizarre deaths are far from exceptional in the artistic world.'

'What do you mean?' asked Cecilia Sørensen, the Danish representative.

'Death by water, for example. Let me pass over water's symbolic nature, interesting as it is, and concentrate on concrete instances. The first that comes to my mind – and doubtless yours – is that of the Chinese poet Li Po, an inveterate tippler, who fell from a boat in his cups and drowned while trying to embrace the reflection of the moon in the water. Or Menander, who, stricken with a cramp while swimming off Piraeus one day, descended to a watery grave. Or Shelley . . .'

'Or Virginia Woolf,' Cecilia interjected.

'Evelyn Waugh had apparently *meant* to die by water,' Jean-Paul Flagus continued, peacefully puffing on his cigar, 'but the school of jellyfish he fell upon kept him from going under. If one can believe W. H. Auden, that is . . .'

'Aristotle is said to have drowned,' the toy poet piped up. 'But then,' he piped down, 'maybe he didn't.'

'Drowning doesn't strike me as particularly bizarre,' said Ranko Leš.

Monsieur Flagus turned and stared at him with a puff and a smile and said, 'Then here is something much more bizarre and something you must have heard of. The Greek poet Terpander choked and died while giving a recitation, because a fig that a member of the audience threw at him flew straight into his mouth and lodged in his windpipe.'

'Pushkin and Lermontov both died in duels,' the toy poet tried again, softly. 'That's no ordinary death.' But as he spoke, he heard how banal it sounded and added, 'And Gorky was poisoned!'

'Right you are,' said Monsieur Flagus, 'but let's take a happier example. Sir Thomas Urquhart is said to have died laughing when he learned that Charles II had been removed from the throne.'

The writers were a bit nonplussed, uncertain whether to take his words as the truth or a joke. Moreover, no one but Thomas Kiely could quite place Sir Thomas Urquhart.

'Well, our poet Miklós Zrínyi was killed by a wild boar,' said Ilona Kovács, the Hungarian representative. 'But that was back in the seventeenth century,' she added, as if it could only have happened then, the seventeenth century being known for its poets and boars.

'You mean *our* poet Nikola Zrinski,' said the poet Ranko Leš, cocking his nose at her as if it were a dangerous beak.

'That's a matter of opinion,' said the poet Ilona Kovács, sighing coquettishly and giving Leš a quick but open once-over.

'Very interesting,' said Jean-Paul Flagus benignly, 'and of course you know that the famous William Thackeray died of gluttony.'

'Francis Thompson committed suicide because he was visited by Thomas Chatterton, who had killed himself two centuries earlier and ordered him to follow suit,' said Thomas Kiely the Irishman.

'What's so bizarre about suicide?' said Ranko Leš, ever protesting. 'You might at least have mentioned Marlowe, who was stabbed to death in a tavern.'

'For not paying his bill!' cried a voice behind his back. Everyone laughed.

'Lionel Johnson', said the Irishman serenely, 'died from injuries sustained while falling off a bar stool . . .' – again the writers burst out laughing – '. . . and James Agee and Robert Lowell died in a taxi.'

'Nothing unusual in that,' Leš interposed again.

'As unusual as dying in a hotel pool,' said the Irishman.

'Another interesting case', Monsieur Flagus continued, calm and collected, 'is that of Sholom Aleichem, who was so deathly afraid of the number thirteen that none of his manuscripts had a page with that number. He died on 13 May 1916, but the date engraved on his tombstone is 12-a.'

The writers felt somehow personally involved in the fate of Sholom Aleichem, and their buzzing died down.

'There are any number of such instances,' Monsieur Flagus went on. 'William Cullen Bryant died in June, as he foresaw in his poem "June". Nathaniel Hawthorne claimed the number sixty-four played a mystical role in his life; he died in 1864 . . .'

'That's not an unusual death; that's a coincidence,' said Cecilia Sørensen coldly, implying either that she was tired of all this talk of death or that she felt it had gone too far.

'All right, then,' said Monsieur Flagus. 'How about Sherwood Anderson, who died of intestinal complications after swallowing a toothpick at a cocktail party? And now, how about calling it a day, because here comes a waiter with drinks.' And in fact a waiter was pushing a cart laden with drinks in the direction of the group. The writers suddenly came to life. When each had a drink in hand, Monsieur Flagus said with dignity and natural elegance, 'I propose a toast to the late José Ramón Espeso.'

The writers drained their glasses. Noticing that Cecilia Sørensen was drinking mineral water, Monsieur Flagus added with a diabolical grin, 'Oh, by the way, did you know that Arnold Bennett died in Paris of typhoid fever from drinking a glass of water? He wanted to prove the water was untainted.'

Once more the writers laughed, and Cecilia Sørensen, clutching her glass of mineral water, withdrew.

8

Troshin and Sapozhnikov were met at the airport by a young woman (Comrade Troshin? Comrade Sapozhnikov? Pleased to meet you. My name is Anja . . . Where did you learn your Russian? I'm studying Russian. I sometimes work as an interpreter) who took them to the bus and bought them tickets. She sat next to Troshin in the bus; Sapozhnikov peered over at her with a helpless, childlike expression, his arms clasped around the leather bag on his lap.

'How did you recognize us?' Troshin asked.

'I don't know. I just knew.'

They always know who we are, Troshin thought crossly, and then was immediately annoyed with himself for dragging out the same old complexes. Yet the wave of shame came over him each time even though he knew the ritual by heart: the girl buys the bus tickets and later discreetly hands them envelopes containing 'special instructions' and the first per diem. The invalid treatment. The border syndrome. Always the same.

Through the bus's tinted glass he watched long, boring streets of housing complexes until at last they came to the Old Town, the cathedral backed by a soft blue hill, a perfect backdrop for a film set in a small Central European city.

'This view must be a favourite on postcards,' he said.

'How did you know?'

'Just guessing,' said Troshin with a smile. 'What do you think, Vitya?'

'Ah,' Sapozhnikov said noncommittally. He was still hugging his leather bag, still staring at her. She wore her hair short, with a long lock left purposefully hanging over her forehead, and sported flappy Chaplinlike slacks, blue-and-white striped stockings, and pink tennis shoes. The only ornament on her broad-shouldered man's jacket

42

was a cheap pin in the form of a small oval mirror. At one point Troshin caught his own tired face in it and, when the girl turned, Vitya's open-mouthed stare. This was Vitya's second trip abroad. He had been in Bulgaria the year before. Things were finally going right for him. Things are finally going right for me, he'd said to Troshin in the plane.

When they piled out of the bus, the young woman proposed they take a taxi to the hotel, 'though it's only a ten-minute walk'. They walked. On the way Troshin kept his professional eye out for the telling first impression. Troshin found that all cities, or at least all cities in socialist countries, have one trait that stands out. In Moscow it is the incontestably enormous number of shops with signs like REMONT CHASOV or REMONT SUMOK, as if Muscovites spent all their time having their broken watches or torn handbags repaired. In Zagreb he was reminded of his favourite authors Ilf and Petrov: a FRIZERSKI SALON at every step, as if the good people of Zagreb did nothing but have their hair done.

'You seem to have a lot of hairdressers here,' he said.

'Why not?' the young woman replied, blowing the lock out of her eyes.

Unlike Ilf and Petrov, Troshin noticed no undertakers.

When in ten minutes they actually did reach the Intercontinental, Troshin thought, 'Zagreb must be tiny.'

'Wow,' said Sapozhnikov, tugging at Troshin's sleeve as they entered the hotel.

The young woman exchanged a few words with the man at the reception desk, then turned to her charges and said, 'Please give this gentleman your passports. Here are the keys to your rooms.'

'613!' said Sapozhnikov.

'610,' Troshin mumbled, catching himself in childish superstition. Six and one is seven. Seven is a lucky number.

'You can leave your things here. They'll be taken up to your rooms. I want to show you the Colloquium office so you'll know where to pick up your per diems and programmes and copies of the talks.'

Sapozhnikov trotted obediently after the young woman, gaping this way and that, and Troshin, just before entering a small room

43

with ZAGREB LITERARY COLLOQUIUM in several languages on the door, caught another FRIZERSKI SALON sign out of the corner of his eye.

'Come in,' the young woman said. 'Franka, I want you to meet our Moscow guests. Fresh from the airport.'

The Franka in question was unusually charming and elegant. Troshin was immediately reminded of an American executive secretary.

'Did you have a good flight? Here are the rest of your per diems. Your rooms are paid for until Friday morning. These briefcases contain programmes and the texts of the talks. We're having a break now; things won't start up again until four. We provide simultaneous translation of all talks into English, French, Russian and German. You can rent head-sets at the entrance to the Crystal Conference Hall, down the hall and to the right . . . Oh yes. Each room has a refrigerator stocked with drinks. You must pay for any drinks you consume, oh and for any international phone calls you make. Excuse me for bringing these things up . . . Well, I think that's everything. I hope you have a pleasant stay. Please don't hesitate to ask Anja or me if there's anything you need.'

The executive secretary's tone, eyes and smile made it clear the conversation was over. Anja had translated softly as she spoke. Troshin couldn't help blushing near the end.

'See you at four, OK?' said Anja when she had finished.

Sapozhnikov forgot himself for a moment and threw her a kiss. She burst out laughing and gave him a friendly wink.

Troshin and Sapozhnikov stood outside the door for a moment, taking their bearings. Just as they set off down the hallway, the door opened and the 'American' peeked her pretty head out and said, 'Sorry, but which one of you is Troshin?'

'I am.'

'There's a reporter from Vienna who's been asking for you. Her name is Sabina Pluhar. I'll let her know you're here.'

'Anyone asking for me?' asked Sapozhnikov, trying to sound witty and encouraged by Anja's hearty laugh. But Franka only smiled and shut the door.

'Hm,' Sapozhnikov remarked and, having finally slung his bag over his shoulder, started playing with his key. They set off again in search of the lifts.

'Who's this Sabina?'

'No idea.'

'A woman on your trail, and you have no idea! You're a sly one, Troshin. Didn't know you had it in you.'

Troshin merely shrugged and glanced over the lobby. The easy chairs were full of sexless septuagenarians dressed in brightly coloured trousers, checked shirts and windbreakers, their eyes roaming absently around the room. A group of American tourists. The scene put Troshin in mind of an elegant menagerie with slightly shrunken animals past their prime. The palms and ficuses only added to the impression.

'What do we do now?' asked Sapozhnikov, uneasily. 'How about a drink?'

'I'm going up to my room,' said Troshin.

'I'll go up too,' said Sapozhnikov agreeably, as if they had come to stay at a *dacha* rather than attend a literary conference.

Sapozhnikov stamped a few times on the springy carpet in the lift and said, 'Pretty posh, eh?'

They were standing side by side in front of a full-length mirror. Troshin was a tall, greying man with finely wrought features; he was wearing a classic grey suit with a light, maroon pullover and a spotless white shirt. Sapozhnikov was short and pudgy; he was wearing jeans, a jeans jacket, and a floral-patterned, open-necked shirt. Inspecting his red face, snub nose and blue eyes, Sapozhnikov raised his hand, scratched his forehead, and smoothed down his thinning, sandy-coloured hair.

'I've lost an awful lot of hair this year, don't you think?'

'It's the fame.'

Sapozhnikov did not seem to catch Troshin's remark. He slowly lifted his nose with his index finger and said ruefully, 'You can see we're bloody Russian from a mile away.'

The lift stopped noiselessly at the sixth floor. Sapozhnikov lingered a moment in front of his door and said, 'You sure you don't want a drink?'

'Go and unpack, will you, Vitya?' said Troshin as he went into his room and closed the door.

Sapozhnikov stood still for a moment or two, then suddenly remembered something important and went over to Troshin's door.

'Hey, Yura!' he said, knocking loudly, 'don't we change our watches?'

'Two hours back!' he heard from Room 610. Sapozhnikov carefully reset his watch and opened the door to Room 613.

9

Sabina Pluhar, student, Russian literature, Vienna, Troshin had noted by force of habit in his pocket diary when the girl phoned him from the lobby.

Now he was down in the hotel bar, sipping a gin and tonic and gazing into Sabina's blank, grey eyes. Scarcely ten hours away from home he was sitting opposite a beautiful young girl who looked as though she'd been reared on nothing but Alpine milk and wild strawberries. (Had he read that somewhere?)

'Have you spent any time in Moscow?'

'Several months. On a grant.'

'So you know your way around.'

'To some extent.'

'And who is the subject of your dissertation?'

'Bibik.'

'Who?'

'Alexei Pavlovich Bibik.'

'I see,' said Troshin with a nod and a smile.

He had grown accustomed to hearing Western specialists in Russian literature bring up Russian authors he himself had never heard of, though it had taken him some time to work through his complex. The breakthrough came when he realized that Western specialists in Russian literature were really only semi-human. That's right. Semi-human. Left-leaning intellectuals of the sixties, left-over idealists of the seventies or the current batch of tourist scholars and phonies. He'd met a Copenhagen postman with a dissertation on Sholokhov, a fisherman's daughter from Iceland with one on 'Gastronomical Motifs in the Novels of Tolstoy', and here was Sabina of the Alps and her phantom of a Bibik. Why hadn't he ever met a Moscow postman writing on Andersen Nexø or a Kamchatka

47

fisherman fixated on Laxness? Moreover, all these 'Russianists' finagled grants to satisfy their scholarly impulses, wangled their way into libraries and archives *our* scholars were denied access to, and ran around after their writers' superannuated widows (some of whom had more than one famous husband) and friends and bystanders, after the writers themselves. They either patiently waited each morning to take their places at the Lenin Library and found out whom to bribe if they needed xeroxing done, or simply paid people to do the waiting, fact-gathering and hand-copying. The mastodon writers were always glad to see them, because they were – foreigners. Sholokhov was surely the first writer the Danish postman had met, while for Sholokhov he was just another Dane. Of course, there were always the gifts: expensive foreign whiskies and cognacs, Levis, exquisite editions of Bosch, Dalí, Malevich, Kandinsky, the smuggled-in writings of Russian dissidents, Bibles, Berdyaev, Solzhenitsyn, Mandelshtam, Tsvetaeva, dictionaries of Russian slang, collections of pornographic poetry, reprints, Talmuds, Torahs, Russian Orthodox mystics, *émigré* newspapers, reports from Soviet courts, prisons and insane asylums, memoirs of defectors, housewives, pilots, generals, homosexuals, painters . . . What was the lure of Moscow? A love of fear? Did they come from their homes all rosy, carefree and vitamin-packed for a taste of something interesting or, rather, dangerous? How quickly they adapted to paranoia as a way of life, babbling on about being followed and bugged (and using the most primitive methods of detection, like leaving cigarette butts in the telephone dial or draping thread over the door), about taking trains to towns outside the official limit in the sweet trepidation of being caught. Over and over they swallowed the same labour-camp stories, copied the same prison-camp songs about Stalin and about Sonka, the personification of Soviet power; they became intimately involved in day-to-day problems, offering aid in the form of coffee, vodka, fruit and shoes from the dollar shops; they took endless pictures of 'typical' Soviet scenes such as wedding parties laying flowers on the grave of the unknown soldier, plump cooks in white kerchiefs, the exotic flea market with its unparalleled collection of freaks, the empty butcher-shop window (especially if decorated with a sign that proclaimed 'OUR GOAL IS COMMUNISM'), the goose-stepping guard in front of

Lenin's Tomb in Red Square, drunkards, slogans, Socialist Realist architecture (Stalin's 'pagodas', the stone ears of corn, the hammers, the sickles, everything the least bit reminiscent of Mukhina, the silver statuettes of Lenin dotting the countryside), the bearded street hawkers of 'dog-meat' *piroshki*, peasants with rabbit-fur *ushanki* pulled down to their eyes, golden-toothed Russian beauties, parks of rest and culture and baroque metro stations – and each of them not only sublimely certain that they were the first to see it all but also, once they have turned genuine grotesqueries into unbearable kitsch, shamelessly forcing their 'authentic', 'ironic' or 'completely unbiased' angle on us, on us *Russians*. And they seemed to take a positive pleasure in the absurdities and monstrosities of a life that was not their own.

Foreigners. He envied them their light, easygoing way of doing things; it came from their personal freedom, something you could not acquire, something you had to breathe in with the air of the country where you lived. He admired the ease with which they entered into conversation with door-keepers, reception clerks, cloak-room attendants, janitors – that ever-present, terror-inspiring band of geezers that constantly aroused Troshin's anxiety. Or used to admire them, admired them until the day he witnessed a skirmish on the streets of Moscow between a no-nonsense policeman and a foreigner and watched the foreigner's self-assurance melt and the familiar, home-grown, humiliated look of fear spread over his face. Troshin knew the mechanisms of fear like the back of his hand, yet it was only after that incident that he realized how tenuous personal freedom, inner freedom, actually was. A foreigner played the tough guy as long as he had his passport in his pocket. Yet some of them stayed on longer than they had intended; some went home irreversibly changed. Changed by what? Among other things by the first opportunity in their lives of being – different.

Sabina Pluhar. Many anonymous young women who had come from Uppsala, Paris, Ann Arbor, Nottingham and Munich to study Russian language and literature experienced their finest moments in 'awful', 'ugly' Moscow: they had been invited to poetry readings, literary salons, theatres, met dozens of fascinating people and, for the first time in their lives, felt they were important, special, even unique. There was always something to do for somebody,

49

something to get out, something to get in. Gabby, Ellen, Viviane, Jane – they all saved 'brilliant' works from the dust of oblivion by smuggling them across the border (unaware, of course, that there were copies galore); they all stuck to the sweet glue of fear and local mythology the way flies stick to flypaper, and had a hard time readjusting to anonymity when they returned home. The only tangible thing they had to show for it all was the senseless thesis on Russian language or literature they had ostensibly gone there to write.

And what did the Russian writers have to show for it? Having a foreigner was a sexual *sine qua non* in his crowd. How many times had he observed his friends and acquaintances showing off their latest catch in the Writers Union dining-room, each an extended geography lesson, a possible invitation abroad, a prospective translator. Making love to a foreigner was more exciting somehow; it was like making love to the Eiffel Tower or Fifth Avenue. If they went on endlessly about how awful their lives were, it was because it raised them in the girls' estimation; if the girls ate it up, it was because it made them, the girls, feel noble. Few of them suspected that it was not so much their sympathy that made them attractive as their passports.

Troshin had never slept with a foreign student. Now a pair of grey Russian-lang-and-lit eyes were gazing into his. A beautiful priestess in the temple of a dead and half-forgotten Bibik. Bi-bik, he scoffed to himself.

'You still haven't told me just what it is you want from me.'

'An interview,' she said matter-of-factly.

'An interview?' asked Troshin, genuinely surprised. 'With me?'

'I support myself as a journalist. My paper is planning a series of interviews with Soviet writers,' said Sabina, a long red nail travelling along her lower lip. And then the upper one. She made it look natural, all the time fixing him with her blank, feline gaze. Troshin actually flinched. Did the eyes have pupils?

'How did you know I was going to be in Zagreb?'

'I found out from the Writers Association here.'

'But to come all the way from Vienna . . .'

'It's my job. Besides, it's not far. I drove.'

'What's the name of your paper?'

50

'*Die Literatur-Zeitung.*'

'I see,' said Troshin, though the name meant nothing to him, and all at once he felt uncomfortable. Two apathetic cat's eyes followed his hands as they went through the motions of lighting a cigarette.

'Cigarette?'

'No, thank you.'

'Have you interviewed anyone else?'

'No, we've decided to start with you.'

'Tell me,' said Troshin by way of procrastination, 'did you meet any writers in Moscow?'

'Kukushenko,' she replied, with the soft sibilant characteristic of the German accent.

'I see,' he said, nodding. Masha Kukushenko, a general's daughter, was known for a salon featuring foreigners 'of cultural interest'. As for the foreigners, they were all duly impressed by Masha's Peredelkino *dacha*, her authentic fireplace, the Italian tile in the bathroom, the constructivist chairs her carpenter so skilfully imitated, the two early Maleviches she hung proudly on the wall and the Kandinsky she carelessly kept under the sofa (never missing a chance to point out how careless she was about it). At Masha's salon Americans could have their bourbon, the French their Courvoisier, and Russians their – otherwise exclusively for export – Stolichnaya. Masha's salon was a major element in her concerted effort to construct an international literary reputation for herself. If Sabina had met Masha, she had surely met other writers. Petrov, for instance.

'Do you know any others?' Troshin asked nonchalantly, wincing slightly at how false he sounded. He was annoyed with himself for being so concerned with which of his colleagues Sabina knew.

'Petrov,' she said simply, though Troshin thought he saw a fine shade of irony cross her face.

She must have slept with Petrov. He got the cream of the foreign beauties. Petrov was the picture of the Russian intellectual, the perfect saint or writer, depending on which happened to be in style. With his sparse beard, blue-green eyes and prominent cheekbones, he was inevitably the centre of attention. At his side she would have met the leading film and theatre actors, gone to all the openings at the Malaya Bronnaya, feasts at the Cinema Club, special screenings: Petrov was a successful playwright and scriptwriter.

Troshin was surprised he felt so jealous.

'And Pirogov,' she added.

'I see,' he said disinterestedly, as he mentally drew the map of Sabina's months in Moscow. With Pirogov she had come to know the 'Russian soul', in other words, a degraded Russian Orthodoxy, home-grown mystics and men of God, fake icons, masses in tumble-down, out-of-the-way churches, neo-Slavophile philosophers. He had doubtless dragged her to dank, semi-clandestine studios to meet either the anonymous artists of enormous tasteless canvases (which, oddly enough, had much in common with their Western counter-parts) or the socialist surrealists, who were not above redoing Dalí, for instance, making Stalin heads rather than Lenin heads dance on the keys of the famous piano. With Pirogov she went to those all-night drinking bouts where everyone tried to outdo everyone else in beating his chest and confessing how low he'd sunk. Well, they *were* a low bunch, besotted nonentities, the lot of them: third-rate poets, black-marketeers, derelicts, con-artists, paranoiacs, last year's wash-outs, and hunters for marriageable foreigners of all ages. Yes, Pirogov had the most attractive itinerary. He was the one Troshin found most odious. But why him? he wondered. What about the others? What about Sovutin? No, he'd emigrated; he doesn't count. Pravdukhin? Bastard and petty informer trading in liberal platitudes. Sokolov? Country bumpkin and Russian chauvinist. Pertsov? Emi-grated, doesn't count. Golubovsky? Committed to a mental hospi-tal, doesn't count. Troitsin? Emigrated, doesn't count. Savelyev? In prison, doesn't count. Tarabukin? Chronically drunk, doesn't count. Mankovsky? Emigrated, doesn't count. Kuzmin? Official, cut-throat, counts a great deal. Sabina had met types, not people. Though at the two poles she frequented there was something happening. In between there was only the grey or, rather, cha-meleonlike layer of the intelligentsia to which he belonged. Or at least liked to think he belonged.

Troshin was fascinated by Sabina's face. Milky white. No expression. A sphinx. Where *were* those pupils?

'And Troshin,' she added, smiling for the first time.

'Troshin?'

'Yes, that's right. I met Troshin too.'

'Now that was clever of you,' Troshin replied ironically and smiled back.

'What about the interview?'

'Where are you staying?'

'Here. At the hotel.'

'What room?'

'710. Just above you.'

'Not today,' he said, glancing at his watch. 'It's too late. I'm tired from the flight. According to the programme, I give my talk tomorrow. How about tomorrow in the late afternoon?'

'Fine.'

Troshin stood up, paid the bill at the bar, and headed towards the door. He could feel Sabina's feline gaze on his back. There was something disconcerting about that girl, something funny, something wrong . . .

10

When, after a few nervous turns around the lobby, Jan Zdražil glanced into the Diana, he was surprised to find two conference participants sitting together at a table. He paused to consider whether he might not join them, but they were so deep in conversation that he decided against it and went up to the bar, where he ordered a coffee. The two were strikingly similar in appearance: both had light hair; both were wearing jeans and white tennis-shoes; even their T-shirts were similar. Both were also a bit tipsy, and they appeared to be playing a game, a kind of verbal ping-pong. Jan had practically no English, yet he had no trouble understanding them.

'Herbert Marcuse,' said the first.

'Angela Davis,' said the second.

'Erich Fromm!' Pipo Fink shot back, remembering how all those years they'd read Fromm like crazy. He had given away untold copies of *The Art of Loving* and Saint-Exupéry's *The Little Prince*.

'Alan Watts!' said Marc Stenheim.

Pipo wasn't sure quite who Watts was, but he returned the ball all the same. 'Suzuki, Zen Buddhism, Hermann Hesse.' He had maintained a repertory of Zen quotes for heavy dates.

Marc let out a rock concert whistle and 'Abbie Hoffman, Jerry Rubin.'

'Rudi Dutschke!' cried Pipo with an elegant European backhand.

'Paul Goodman,' Marc returned.

'Allen Ginsberg!' Pipo slammed. He still had the record of Ginsberg reciting 'Howl' somewhere in the back of his collection.

'Timothy Leary, Carlos Castañeda,' said Marc, delivering a strong drive to the line.

'Bob Dylan,' Pipo returned, grabbing a gulp of vodka and wiping his hands.

'Ken Kesey,' Marc parried with a smooth forehand.

'Jack Kerouac!' Pipo slammed again. He'd read *On the Road* in translation. He'd also read every word Salinger had ever written.

Now it was Marc's turn for vodka and a quick wipe of the forehead, and then, 'Laing!' A perfect serve.

But Pipo was riding high. He'd read Laing too (if much later and, again, in translation).

'Reich!' he responded, though he hadn't read a word of him.

'The Doors!' Marc lobbed for a change of pace.

'Flash Gordon!' Pipo returned with a nice little spin on the ball.

Marc convulsed with laughter, but managed to keep the volley going with a beautiful back-hand 'Black Panthers!'

'Che Guevara!'

'Julian Beck!'

Pipo decided to change tactics, but failed to come up with the English for *Soyons réalistes: exigeous l'impossible* and fumbled a weak *Make love not war* instead, and Marc immediately slammed *The whole world is watching* down his throat.

'Know what we've left out?' said Pipo suddenly, slapping his forehead. 'The most important thing!'

'What?'

'The Beatles! John, Paul, George, Ringo!'

'And Jan Palach!' A ball from another court.

Pipo and Marc turned to see a pale, thin man standing at their table with a cup of coffee in his hand. Pipo looked up at the name tag on his lapel. *Jan Zdražil, Czechoslovakia.*

'Right! And Jan Palach,' said Marc affably. He stood and offered the Czech a seat. 'How could we have forgotten?'

Jan Zdražil suddenly felt very close to them both.

'Do you speak English?' Pipo asked.

'*Po-russki*,' Jan said with an embarrassed shrug.

'I drink, you drink . . . *pyom za Jana Palacha*!' said Pipo, straining to bring back the Russian he had learned in elementary school. '*Ponimaesh?* Understand? To Jan Palach!'

And they all raised glasses of the vodka the waiter had just brought.

Jan Zdražil smiled sadly. Even though his nerves had calmed down, he was on the verge of tears out of sympathy for the Czech martyr. He would have liked to propose a toast to Joan Baez, whom he greatly admired, but he was afraid it would seem inappropriate.

Pipo was a bit put out at the Czech for having interrupted the game. He and Marc had entered the university in '68, with the minor difference that Marc had experienced what Pipo had dreamed. Or, rather, what Pipo had *followed*, always behind. By the time things reached him, he saw his past in them, something over and done with, though at the moment they took place he was unable to recognize them as the present. Or something like that . . . He'd made his first trip to London after London was out. He'd been late for Paris too. And went with his mother. On a package tour. By which time the in-crowd had weighed anchor and moved on to India. Or at least hopped on the train to Belgrade to be part of the riots. While others were living in communes, he lived at home; while others were growing marijuana on their balconies, his balcony groaned under bottled cucumber plants.

'Gone with the wind,' said Pipo with a distraught wave of the hand.

'*Gone With the Wind*,' said Marc with a broad smile.

'Vom Winde verweht,' *said Rudi Dutschke. Pipo threw a worried glance at Greta and shook Rudi's hand.*

'*The struggle goes on,*' *he said firmly. Rudi didn't hear him or made believe he didn't. He turned towards the window.*

'*It's snowing in Århus,*' *he whispered and lowered his eyes.*

All three sank into memories after their joyful though short-lived meeting-of-the-ways on the now dusty map of the sixties. Pipo thought how popular the word *joy* had been back then, no matter what it meant. And what's replaced it? Where have all the flowers gone?

'I really don't know how to say this . . .' said Jan Zdražil to Pipo.

'Go ahead,' said Pipo, proud that his Russian was holding up.

'You see . . . well, I have the manuscript of a novel with me. *My* novel. Six hundred pages. It's a ridiculous situation to be in. Ridiculous. I can't go into it now. The problem is, I can't take it back with me. To Czechoslovakia, I mean. You understand, don't you? I took it with me in a moment of desperation and managed to

get it out, but if they caught me taking it back in . . . well, I won't
go into details, but I'd be lost, done for – know what I mean?'

Pipo translated Zdražil's rather vague formulation to Marc, who
responded with the simple and friendly, 'Oh, a dissident.'

'No, no!' said Zdražil immediately, troubled by the word and the
speed with which the American had labelled him. No, they didn't
understand. How could they understand? How could he explain it
to them?

'You want me to take your novel and give it to a Czech publisher,
an *émigré* Czech publishing house in the States, is that it?' asked
Marc helpfully.

'Yes. I mean . . . no. I'll let you know when you . . . All you
need to do is take it there. Or it can stay *here*, actually.'

'No, no,' said the American. 'I'll take it home with me. No sweat.
Only – you've never seen me before. How can you trust me?'

'I have no choice. I'll be going back on Thursday, and . . .'

'OK,' said Marc.

'Then I'll give it to you tomorrow morning,' said Zdražil with a
sigh of relief.

Pipo breathed his own sigh of relief. Interpreting from one foreign
language into another, especially Russian, which he barely knew,
was wearing him out. Besides, it bothered him that the Czech had
hit it off so well with the Yank and had a six-hundred-page novel
under his belt, while he, Pipo, had nothing. But Zdražil looked so
happy and grateful that Pipo and Marc couldn't help ordering
another round of vodka, after which Pipo, moved almost to tears,
began singing:

> Let me take you down
> Cause I'm goin' to
> Strawberry Fields.
> Nothing is real
> And nothing to get hung about . . .

But the bartender came over and asked him, politely, not to sing,
adding that the bar was closing.

Shortly thereafter the man at the reception desk of the Zagreb
Hotel Intercontinental looked on indignantly as two obviously
drunk young men stripped to the waist and exchanged T-shirts,

then undid their shoe laces and exchanged running shoes, grinning at each other all the while. Just as he was about to ask them to be quiet, one set off for the front door, the other, humming and reeling slightly, for the lift.

Meanwhile Jan Zdražil was stretched out in the semi-darkness of his hotel room, staring at the bluish light seeping through the window, staring and mumbling:

> Down pours the rain through the twilight,
> This night will be all but endless;
> When the wolf turns sheep-minded,
> It's time to lock gates and windows.

11

Jean-Paul Flagus looked up questioningly at Raúl. Raúl nodded and shoved open the heavy door. They found themselves in a dark hallway shot through with the stench of urine.

'It's on the second floor,' Raúl said apologetically, 'and the lift is out of order.'

They trudged up to the second floor. Raúl rang the bell. A dim light shone through the glass door. Jean-Paul Flagus tapped his elegant walking-stick on the floor with impatience. Raúl shrugged and rang again. A human shadow crossed the glass and slowly slid open a peep-hole, revealing two green eyes through thick spectacle-rings that bored into the visitors out of a grey, stonelike face. After a certain interval the lock clicked and the visitors were admitted.

'Good evening,' said Raúl in accented Croatian.

The spectacled figure merely nodded morosely and withdrew, leaving the visitors to fend for themselves.

The only light in the rooms came from antique chandeliers. The visitors peered into a large hall crowded with tasteless green arm-chairs. It had a piano in one corner and a number of enormous photographs on the walls. Jean-Paul Flagus waved in the direction of the photographs, and Raúl reeled off a series of names: 'Kovačić, Šimić, Preradović, Reljković, Nazor, Gaj, Mažuranić, Krleža . . .'

'Writers?'

'Yes, sir.'

'This one too?'

'Their late chairman.'

'I see.'

The room reeked of stale tobacco. Jean-Paul Flagus separated the filthy curtains with his stick. The huge windows looked out on the gloomy main square.

Level with Flagus's eyes, a neon owl was raising a wing. Flagus waited for it to raise the other. The owl stubbornly insisted on raising only one. The clock in the square said twenty past nine.

The visitors went into another room. It was furnished more modestly and was equally devoid of people. In the third room they found the same grey stone face that had opened the door for them. This time it was standing behind a bar, but its green eyes were still boring into them through thick spectacles. Next to it, at the bar, stood – or, rather, rocked back and forth – a woman wearing what looked like a cross between a Superman costume and a jogging suit: red bottoms, a green cape draped nonchalantly over the shoulders and running shoes. She turned, glass in hand, and observed the visitors with great interest.

Jean-Paul Flagus and Raúl took a table. The face behind the bar did not flinch.

'Mozart!' the woman shouted suddenly after some time had gone by. The stone face flinched.

'Two teas,' said Raúl. The man shook his head no.

'Two coffees, then.'

'The machine is out of order.'

'Two chuices,' Raúl said, for some reason mixing up *ch* and *j*.

Again the man shook his head no.

'Guell, guat have you got?'

'Spritzers.'

Raúl gave a perplexed shrug of the shoulders, which the man took for an order, and shuffled off to fill it.

'What would you say to our inviting the lady at the bar to join us?' asked Jean-Paul Flagus with a smile. By the time Raúl had stood, however, she was making her way to the table.

'Good evening,' said Raúl while the woman took a seat and planted her glass on the table. 'Tell me please, is this the Writers Club?'

'It is,' she shot back, 'and please stop torturing yourself with Croatian. As you can hear, I speak perfectly decent French.' Then she half-asked, half-stated, 'You're with the Colloquium?'

Jean-Paul Flagus nodded amiably and enquired, 'Excuse me, madame, but where are the writers?'

'Writers? We have no writers. No writers, no literature. *Life*

60

writes the novels in this country; nobody gives a damn about literature.' And so saying, she tossed off the rest of her drink.

'But tell me,' Jean-Paul Flagus asked after a hearty laugh, 'is there any other club, restaurant or watering place where writers tend to gather?'

'Writers, writers! What's this fixation with writers?'

'All right, then. Where the local . . . bohemians meet.'

'You can't have bohemians if you have no writers.'

'Spritzers,' said the frog man, placing two glasses on the table. 'And your bill.'

Jean-Paul nodded, and Raúl took out a credit card.

'We don't take cards,' the man muttered through his teeth.

'Put it on my account, Mozart. And cut the crap, will you?'

The man nodded and went back to the bar, where he slipped back into his frozen frog mask.

'Thank you, madame,' said Jean-Paul Flagus amiably. 'Permit me to introduce myself.'

'Don't bother. I'll never remember you anyway. Foreigners never stick around this town. They're always passing through.'

Jean-Paul Flagus observed the unusual woman with interest. '*À votre santé*,' he said in his language.

'*Živjeli*,' she said in hers, and tossed down another glass.

'Might I invite you to a little party this Thursday at the Hotel Intercontinental?'

'Writers again?'

'I'm afraid so.'

'I may come,' she said, and shouted, 'Another spritzer, Mozart!'

'Excuse me,' Jean-Paul Flagus said, standing, 'but we must be going. What is your name, if I may enquire?'

'Just call me Tarzan!'

'Thank you, madame,' said Jean-Paul Flagus. '*Au revoir*.'

The woman paid no attention whatsoever to their departure, but the bartender saw them to the door and nodded. The moment they were on the landing the lock clicked and the shadow vanished.

'Are you certain that was the Writers Club, Raúl?' Jean-Paul Flagus asked as they made their way down the unlit stairs.

'This was the address they gave?'

'It looked more like a mortuary to me,' muttered Jean-Paul Flagus.

'Perhaps they gave the wrong address,' said Raúl once they were out in the street again.

'It doesn't matter, Raúl,' said Jean-Paul Flagus. 'It was worth it to find out that in Zagreb Mozart is a bartender and life does all the novel-writing.' And he laughed his hearty laugh.

12

Dear Peer,

I do adore planes! Did you know that? They give me the same thrill no matter how often I go through the rituals. I can hardly wait to find my seat and fasten my seat-belt. I'm always the first, and I go to with such gusto that the passengers around me rush to follow suit. Anyway, I buckle up, and – I'm a good girl – I pay close attention to the stewardesses' puppetlike routines, turning my head in whatever direction they point, even if I never quite understand the message behind their charming background gurgle. But my childlike excitement comes to a climax when they start handing out the plastic trays. I look forward to mine the way I used to look forward to my Christmas stocking. I examine each of the goodies with great glee: the little round bun, the slice of ham, the lettuce leaf, the cold Wiener schnitzel, the tea biscuits . . . I release the plastic knife and fork from their cellophane wrapping, the salt and pepper from their sachets, and with the greatest of concentration and heartiest of appetites devour every last morsel until at last I come to the *pièce de résistance* of any meal fit for a doll: the chocolate with the maraschino cherry in it. My elation does not begin to wane until I spit the stone into my hand (where I can lick it with my tongue without anyone seeing) and hide it in my napkin just before the stern stewardess comes to take the tray away. But I've been good, says my eager face to her indifferent one; I've eaten everything on my plate. I ask for a blanket even though it's not cold. I wrap myself up in it, enjoying its fluff against my cheek and clutching one of the corners. I can never fall asleep without a piece of material in my hand; it serves as a security for my return. *Don't forget your blanket, Cecilia*, I hear my grandmother's angelic voice hovering over me, *or you won't come back from your dreams*. I give a tug on the corner of the blanket and inhale my own breath mixed with the heavy scent of wool, and off I float, back to the womb, dreaming of the thrilling moment when I was cast out into the world. Yes, fear of flying is definitely womb-related . . .

We got in late, so I took a taxi to the hotel. The city looked rather gloomy from the back seat, but the hotel room is perfectly pleasant. I'm reading Handke's *Wunschloses Unglück* in bed; I bought it for the plane. A

51-year-old housewife takes a lethal dose of sleeping pills, dons a sanitary belt and towel and lies down in bed with her arms crossed neatly over her chest. I was deeply moved by that detail, the unconscious rituality of it, and by the terribly feminine quality of the apparel (a sanitary towel!) she chose for her encounter with death. A woman taking her pathetic, worn-out sexuality to the other world, ready for heaven or hell with her towel . . .

I turn out the light. The hotel room is flooded with a dense darkness. I curl up and purr like a cat, catching images out of the dark like warm, stuffed mice, sniffing them, nibbling at them, shuffling them here and there with my hand. I close my eyes, certain they won't run away: I have hypnotized them, they can't move. Now I feel full. I can let them go. And as they shyly creep back to their boxes, I sink into sleep . . .

The only celebrity here is Thomas Kiely. He's stopped drinking and for the last five years has been working on a novel. Susan Sontag isn't coming, unfortunately. I've read her paper on Sigrid Undset, whom no one here has ever heard of. I've also met two young local woman writers, Tanja and Dunja (I just love those Slav names, don't you?); they're the only ones with human faces. Thomas has asked me to have dinner with him.

Love,
Cecilia

64

MARDI, le 6 mai

1

'Tell me, baby, that poet, José Whatshisname, was he famous?' Vanda asked, pressing her cheek against the Minister's upper arm.

'How should I know?' the Minister answered. 'Maybe back where he lived. In Spain.'

Vanda mumbled something like *Hm* and said no more. She loved the rich and famous with the never-ending devotion of the poor and anonymous. She knew everything there was to know about them, or at least everything available in the domestic yellow press. She identified with them through and through – that is, through thick and thin. When Joan Collins announced to the world that she was undergoing a slimming cure, Vanda ate only hard-boiled eggs and water for three days. (On the fourth she fainted.) When the forty-year-old Linda Evans announced she was going to have a baby, Vanda, who was forty-seven at the time, was pregnant for two whole days. When Richard Burton died, she sided with Elizabeth Taylor and explained to everyone why she and Liz couldn't go to the funeral and sent an enormous bouquet of white roses instead. When a local pop singer received an exorbitant tax bill, Vanda railed at the authorities for three days, yet when her neighbour, who was living on a meagre pension, complained about how prices were skyrocketing ('They give us just enough to die on!'), Vanda was offended ('All you can talk about are the bad things!') and recalled how unfairly public opinion had complained of the allowance paid to Prince Charles and Princess Diana. That's what Vanda was like. Moreover, she told the lives of the rich and famous with such sincerity and verve that whether the Minister liked it or not her 'scandal-sheet claptrap' ended by having an effect on him. At a recent meeting he'd caught himself bringing up Fassbinder, and although he immediately bit his tongue (What am I doing? Vanda's claptrap again! That morning she'd told him, 'Know what, baby? That crazy Fassbinder was a homo. Died of it, poor thing!'), there was a big article in the paper about Fassbinder the next day because a reporter who happened to be at the meeting interpreted the reference as the Minister's way of hinting that the public was not well-enough informed about the latest in German cinematography.

Vanda's passion had its positive side: her zeal ('You mean you *know* him, baby? Know him *personally*?') was good for the Minister's self-respect. But it had its negative side as well: if the celebrities in question were local politicians, the one aspect of their private lives open for all to see was their death. And death always and without exception made Vanda think of one thing and one thing only.

Whenever the headlines proclaimed the death of a public figure (even an increase in electricity rates seemed less irritating when juxtaposed to the loss of a beloved leader), the Minister would start gearing up, but if they happened to be watching the evening news together, he had no time: an item concerning the death of an official provoked instant erotic rampage. At first the Minister was concerned about her reaction ('If this leaks out, it will mean a full-fledged scandal!'), but he also found it titillating ('I'm still going strong!'), and after a while he not only grew accustomed to Vanda's memorial services, he came to look forward to them. Unlike Vanda, however, he tried to keep a certain dignity about him, if that is the right word, and he played his part with greater reserve than usual. After all, the men in question were often his close colleagues. And it tended to happen more and more often and with less and less regard to the criteria: some nobody'd kick the bucket and the first thing you know he was on television with his date of birth and outstanding achievements.

After the wave of excitement had passed, at about the time the weather report came on, Vanda would break into sobs and for some reason, still weeping and wailing, put on not only the clothes she had been wearing but a layer or two more. Whereupon, looking for all the world like a soldier in full battle dress, she would announce, 'I don't know what's got into me, baby. I don't know what's wrong.'

The Minister would comfort her and help her off with the extra clothes – he loved her when she cried – and as he undressed her, her guilt feelings would turn to concern: 'What's our poor country coming to, baby? With all these people dying, there won't be anyone left before long.'

This unusual ritual was Vanda's way of re-establishing her equilibrium: by over-dressing she overcame the sexual being in her; by shedding the excess clothes she became a social being again. Pondering Vanda's slightly kinky behaviour, the Minister came to appreciate her instinctive grasp of the relationship between Eros and Thanatos. Vanda was all compassion and sacrifice. Whenever a public personality died, her noble nature identified with the victim, and the only way she could show her empathy (short of committing suicide!) was to travel down the sweet, cathartic tunnel of what the French call *la petite mort*.

Vanda's hand began to move. The Minister had a feeling he knew the direction Vanda's psyche had taken. He was not mistaken.

'How about a minister's position for José, baby.'

She said it so beautifully, so mournfully, with such restrained passion that even though he couldn't stand poets the Minister had to give in. She said it so beautifully, so mournfully that he didn't notice she had made a slip of the tongue. Instead of *missionary* position, she said (and right she was, in fact) *minister's* position.

2

The morning session went off according to plan, though people looked a bit sleepy, and the ranks had already begun to thin. The first speaker had been the ebullient Silvio Benussi on contemporary Italian poetry. He was followed by Josip Grah, a monotone, who spoke on dialects in modern poetry with a marked emphasis on his own Čakavian dialect. He gave so many examples that the interpreters could not possibly keep up with them and the foreigners present experienced long intervals of silence in their earphones. The more ambitious among them, like Benussi, kept twisting the dial, hoping to find something; Cecilia Sørensen, the Dane, kept twisting a strand of her blonde locks, then putting it in her mouth and nervously nibbling on it; Thomas Kiely, the Irishman, had draped one arm over the empty seat next to him and was using the pencil in his free hand to raise and lower the glasses from his nose, as if he were sending signals; and Victor Sapozhnikov, hoping perhaps that his earphones made him invisible, was having a little nap. Only one unidentified grey-headed individual in the first row was taking assiduous notes.

Prša was sitting at the table on the podium flanked by the writer Mraz, who was chairing the panel, and Małgorzata Uszko, a Polish critic well on in years.

Josip Grah finished his talk without anyone noticing, but before he could leave the podium the Czech writer Jan Zdražil, clearly agitated, ran up and took his place. Prša raised his hand in an attempt to signal it was not his turn, but the Czech grabbed the microphone and wailed, '*Soudruzi! Pánové! Spisovatelé!* . . .'

Only then did the writers lift their heads and see a pale, thin man breathing heavily and shouting, '*Lidé! Ukradli mi román! Moje životní dílo!*' The earphones immediately began to buzz: *Man hat mir meinen*

Roman gestohlen! Mein Meisterwerk! . . . My novel's been stolen! My masterpiece! . . . *On m'a volé mon roman! Mon chef-d'oeuvre!* . . . *U menya ukrali roman! Moy shedevr!*

At first the room was silent; then a din broke out. Prša tore the earphones from his head and jumped out of his seat. He rushed over to the lectern and, while whispering something in the Czech's ear, used one hand to push the microphone away as if it were a bomb that needed defusing and the other to hold the poor man up, as he had more or less collapsed into Prša's embrace. Leading him off the podium, Prša glanced out over the audience and with a gesture that betokened rich experience in organizing conferences or waiting tables he made it clear to all assembled that there was nothing to worry about, he had the situation under control, they were to carry on as if nothing had happened. The panel chairman, reading him loud and clear, immediately called the next speaker. The bomb had been defused.

Ivan Ljuština, a local critic who was planning a heavy-artillery attack on local prose, poetry and plays, made his way to the podium amidst commentary on the Czech's predicament.

'Crazy, he's crazy.'

'And if he's telling the truth?'

'You can see straight away the man's paranoid.'

'His *masterpiece*? Well, well.'

'Don't you think we ought to call a break until this thing is . . .'

'He doesn't know what he's saying. His nerves are shot.'

'I don't think so. I don't know why, but I trust the Czechs.'

Only two faces showed quiet concern. One belonged to the American Marc Stenheim, the other to the journalist Ena the Bell-Tower.

The moment Prša and Zdražil had left the room Ivan Ljuština launched into his tirade, and the moment Ivan Ljuština opened his mouth two women made a show of rising and marching out. Cecilia Sørensen, the Dane, followed suit.

3

Pipo had trouble with time. Time in general. The big clock in the sky that people set their lives by. Perhaps he'd tripped or stood agog for a moment and lost step. Perhaps he'd forgotten to wind himself up one morning. You don't always notice those things at once.

Then from one day to the next he realized his friends were living another life. An invisible barrier had grown up between him and them: they had all found jobs and wives, made kids, fallen into a way of life, a sort of mechanical social game; they all had their moorings, their doctors, their barbers and hairdressers, their tennis partners, their dinner parties, their weekend getaways and summer holidays, their loans, their meetings, their cottages and flats, their mistresses, their triangles, their goodbyes and reconciliations. They all knew one another, knew what to expect from one another. All except Pipo.

Pipo didn't know what was happening or why. He just stood there with his mouth open and watched it all sail past. Moreover, as time went on, the *action* around him seemed to pick up speed. Sometimes his friends reminded him of pin-balls popping out of a hole the moment they landed in it, while he himself was a lazy ball, caught in a hole, waiting for another to come along and knock him for a loop, send him off in some giddy new direction. And more and more often – the gap seemed to widen year by year – he felt completely abandoned down there.

Friends were always glad to see him: It's our Pipo! And he was. But he wasn't either. Because he was different too. Then it would start: Say hewwo to Unca Pipo! Hewwo, Unca Pipo! And then: Say hello to Pipo, monkey-face! And when one of those monkey-faces, the fourteen-year-old son of close friends, gave him a look that clearly said, '*Another* old fart!' Pipo got scared. Scared because he'd

72

always felt more monkey-face than old fart and now the genuine article had put him in his place. Could the Dustin Hoffman character in *The Graduate* really be thirty-five by now? When his friends stared out at him from a bunker of wives, kids and jobs, he kept sniffing for a scrap of misfortune or dissatisfaction to prove that he, Pipo, had the upper hand.

His colleagues were no better. Writers played their own social games – meetings, clans, trips, bars, magazines, critics, quarrels, claques – and Pipo took no part in them. It wasn't that people had anything against him; it was just that no one had anything *for* him. In fact, there were times he felt he didn't exist.

One day he dropped in on a friend who wrote a popular TV series and found him drowning in a pile of newspaper clippings.

'What's all that?'

'This? Oh, reviews and things. I have my clipping service send them over periodically so I can see how I'm doing with the press.'

Pipo signed up with his friend's service. A week or two later he received a clipping about a certain Petar Fink who had robbed a cash register in a provincial supermarket.

As each new ego-building routine came to naught, Pipo would wander from pillar to post.

One pillar was a project for 'a major work' – oh, not something that would change the world necessarily, but at least an *I'll show them* kind of thing. He would move his desk over to the window and stare at the street for hours on end, daydreaming. When the local retired population began standing at the window and staring back, Pipo decided to – or, rather, wondered whether it mightn't be a good idea to – install the kind of glass that would let him look out and keep them from looking in. But then he gave up and moved his desk back away from the window and stared at the wall. At first he maintained his discipline and stared at the wall from behind the desk, then he moved to the couch and stared (at the desk), and soon he was wafted off to sweet oblivion on giant sheets of paper covered with imaginary jottings.

Once that pillar began to develop cracks, Pipo moved on to the post, in other words, he left his room (left his room!) and opened up to the outside world, determined to take an impassioned stand, to *do* something. He would carry on ridiculously long discussions with his neighbours on the increase in gas rates (Am I mad? What's wrong with me?), calling the electric company the worst names and threatening to write them nasty letters (he actually did write a letter once, but received no reply), overreacting to every article in the papers, every spot on television, flying into a rage over the inefficient management of a cement factory in some godforsaken backwater, throwing fits over an irrelevant interview with a pop singer, and taking up arms against litter in the streets, corruption in government, the regime's economic policy, local ruling cliques, central planning, vegetarianism, the legal system, dogs, people . . . everything! He'd show them!

And what did his mother say when he carried on with his raving in the kitchen? 'Gosh, Pipili, I had no idea. I'm fit to be tied!'

Then Pipo's film would rip and the shutter come down click! over his lens. *Pipili*! How could she still call him that! And *fit to be tied*! Where did she dig that up? (And what did it come from, anyway?) Why was she fit to be tied, for God's sake! Or, rather, of course she was fit to be tied.

Once he noticed the cracks in himself, he began noticing them in other people as well. And all of them approaching the age of forty. Mid-life. Pipo swore to himself he would not let it get the better of him; he would circumvent the crisis somehow. He would avoid the trap of his former-rock-musician, current-economist friend who had periodic attacks during which he wrote long letters to Mick Jagger begging him to take him on. The cracks in question would form at the border between desire and possibility, and while Pipo had plenty of desires he couldn't quite put his finger on them. All he knew was that he hadn't grown up yet and was tired of being stuck where he was, bound to the post – or was it the pillar? – like a punching-bag for life's daily workout.

The workout began early in the morning, that is, at ten, when he tended to wake up.

'Pipili! Want some coffeeeee?'

Still half asleep, Pipo could feel Jessica Lange, light as a feather, snuggled against his smooth, well-developed shoulder under the blanket. And then, pow! his mother's nasal, old-lady-sweet 'Pipili' – the button that set off the countdown: 35, 34, 33, 32 . . . and so on, until he shrivelled into a tiny ball with a wrinkled face and half-blind eyes, holding his breath as if preparing for a dive, then ducking back into the warm, dark-red nothing, and finally re-emerging as a bright and shining mama's boy.

'Yes, Mother!' Pipo shouted back, thereby dooming Jessica Lange to eternal banishment.

Pipo yawned and glanced at his watch. Twelve. Then he saw the Berkeley T-shirt and pair of Nikes lying on the floor. The Yank! He'd overslept their meeting!

He jumped out of bed and made a beeline for the bathroom.

4

During the break Jan Zdražil was on everybody's lips. Once more a
lively group had formed around Jean-Paul Flagus.

'If what our poor friend claims is indeed the case,' said Monsieur
Flagus mysteriously, his watery eyes wandering from face to face,
'we can be certain the culprit is either a woman or a dog.'

'And why can we be certain?' Cecilia Sørensen, the Dane, asked
sarcastically.

'Because history shows it to be true,' said Monsieur Flagus,
smiling and lighting a thick cigar. 'And not only history.'

'But why dogs?' asked the poet Ranko Leš.

'Why women?' asked Cecilia Sørensen with a withering glance,
which he returned with a flick of his beaklike nose.

'Surely you know the case of John Warburton, the famous
eighteenth-century collector of Elizabethan and Jacobean drama
manuscripts, who left his collection in the care of Betsy Baker, his
cook, and lost all but three to kindling and cake-tin linings. The
three remaining volumes are now in the British Museum.'

'Death to Betsy Baker!' said Thomas Kiely, raising his glass and
clinking with everyone but Cecilia Sørensen, who had failed to
respond.

'Then there was the time Thomas Carlyle gave John Stuart Mill
the first volume of his *History of the French Revolution* only to have it
burned by Mill's servant girl, who took it for rubbish.'

Monsieur Flagus blew a few smoke rings, glancing from one of
his audience to the next.

'After the death of Sir Richard Burton, the English translator of
The Thousand and One Nights, Burton's wife burned his version of
the *Kamasutra*, deeming it too obscene for publication.'

'That's enough of your male-chauvinist anecdotes!' cried Cecilia

Sørensen in high dudgeon. 'Have you ever thought how many women in history were deprived of the chance to get near a desk, to say nothing of writing burnable books! What are a few petty manuscripts compared with the women who've ended up in the madhouse or with their heads in the oven!'

'Do continue, Monsieur Flagus,' said Ranko Leš with another flick of the nose to Cecilia Sørensen.

'With the women or with the dogs?' asked Jean-Paul Flagus with a smile.

'With the women,' answered the toy poet. Cecilia Sørensen gave a snort and stalked off.

'Once, in a fit of rage, the wife of William Ainsworth hurled her husband's all but finished Latin dictionary into the fire. It took him three full years to recap what he had lost.'

The writers were clearly touched by the assiduous lexicographer's plight.

'And here is a case', he said, searching the lobby for their Danish colleague, 'that proves that men *are* occasionally at fault. Edwin Arlington Robinson lost a long poem he had meant to include in his *Captain Craig* . . .' – and here his eyes narrowed into slits – '. . . and found it again in the brothel where he'd left it.'

As the writers laughed, the toy poet thought bitterly that he'd never be the *raconteur* Jean-Paul Flagus was, never have his charm or elegance.

'What about the dogs?' asked Ilona Kovács, the Hungarian.

'Just recall the legend of Sir Isaac Newton's dog, Diamond, who overturned a candle on his master's desk and caused a fire that destroyed a number of important papers. And John Steinbeck's dog Toby, who tore *Of Mice and Men* to pieces. Two months later Steinbeck wrote a new version and never missed an opportunity to credit Toby for his critical acumen.'

'Bravo! Bravo!' cried Ilona Kovács. She was obviously a dog-fancier.

Now that Jan Zdražil was forgotten, things began to liven up. Thomas Kiely brought up the case of Joyce's typist, whose husband apparently threw a chapter of *Ulysses* into the fire; the toy poet recalled the suitcase full of manuscripts Hemingway lost in a train while in France; Ilona Kovács the case of Molière's servant, who lined a wig with his master's translations of Lucretius. Then gradually, imperceptibly, they turned to the more juicy topic of who had stolen what from whom. Leš immediately took the lead. It turned out *he* was the one from whom the most had been stolen and copied.

Jean-Paul Flagus regained control just before it was time to go back to the meeting. 'We were unfair to our Danish friend,' he said. 'Dogs and women are not the main culprits by any means; manuscripts disappear because those in power wish them to disappear. Going back to 213 BC, we find that the Emperor Shih Huang-ti ordered practically all books burnt. And why? So that history might start with him. Shih Huang-ti had many followers, and . . .' – he added with a smile – '. . . has many still.'

5

Jan Zdražil and Prša the poet were having a serious talk amidst piles of xeroxed talks and briefcases stamped with the Colloquium's logo in the small, stuffy room that served as the event's hotel head-quarters. They were being assisted by a rather cowed student of Czech whom Prša had called in to interpret when Slav solidarity broke down.

'But my novel's been stolen!' the Czech repeated, wringing his hands, his face pale and bathed in sweat, his eyes filled with despair.

'Not that again! Look, who needs your novel, anyway? You did say it was in Czech, didn't you?'

'I can't be sure anyone needs it,' the Czech replied modestly. 'Nobody's read it yet.'

'Well, nobody'll have time to read it here. You can make a few copies when you get home, and send it out to people.'

The Czech suddenly seemed to have all the air knocked out of him. He lowered his eyes to his shoes.

'That's the trouble,' he said in a dull voice. 'It was my only copy.'

'Your only copy!' Prša cried, incredulous, and glanced over at the student.

'His only copy,' she confirmed softly.

'You see, I . . . it's so hard to explain . . . I hid the copy I had . . .'

'Hid it? Where?'

'In the washing machine.'

'Where?!'

'In our old washing machine. In the basement. We've got a new one now. Zdenka made a down payment of . . .'

'Who's Zdenka?'

'My wife.'

'Oh. Well, go on,' said Prša, assuming the tone of a well-meaning police inspector.

'Anyway, the new washing machine broke down . . .'

'I don't see what that has to do with anything.'

'The thing is, Zdenka tried to get them to come and service it, but you know how they are. You can pester them from here to kingdom come. So Zdenka did a load by hand, and . . .'

'And?' Prša threw a worried glance at the student, which she correctly interpreted as concern for the Czech's mental health.

'And then she remembered there was one cycle on the old machine that still worked: Wring Dry.'

'Look, would you come to the point? I don't understand a word of this.'

'Zdenka didn't know I'd hidden the manuscript in the old machine . . .'

'What are you anyway? Some kind of Švejk?'

Zdražil was too busy wringing his hands and wiping his forehead to catch the allusion.

'You should have seen what that six-hundred-page manuscript looked like.'

'Hey, wait a second! Whatever made you hide a manuscript in your washing machine? What made you put it there in the first place? And why in heaven's name did you bring your only copy here?'

The Czech sat up a bit straighter and said, 'I'm afraid I can't say.'

'Aha! So that's it! Writing novels against the state!'

Again the Czech chose to ignore Prša's remarks. 'I can't say because I don't really know. A stupid impulse. I was at my wits' end. And when I got here, I realized I couldn't take it back.'

Again he started searching for that straw, and again he lowered his eyes and muttered, 'Now there's nothing left but suicide.'

'Suicide!' shouted Prša, looking over at the student for confirmation. 'You mean kill-yourself suicide?'

'*Ano.*'

'"Yes," he says,' said the student.

'Not on your life! You can save that for home, for your own country. You have no idea of the complications it would mean for us here: consulates, embassies, police, lawyers, doctors, reports, transporting the body! Catastrophic! No, it's out of the question!' He turned to the student. 'Make sure you get that all in. You can't imagine the trouble we had with that Spanish guy yesterday! And he didn't even do it on purpose . . . I mean . . . it was just an accident.'

'*Ano*,' said the Czech quietly.

'"Yes," he says,' said the student.

'And all because of a novel! Really! Grow up!'

Suddenly the Czech pulled himself together and looked Prša in the eye so proudly that the poet had to pull in his horns. 'That novel was my life's work,' he said.

But that got Prša going again. 'Ha! We all have our "life's work"! Prove it!'

The Czech's face fell again.

'Listen, forget the whole thing. Forget the whole thing or you'll be committed.'

'But I mean what I say.'

Prša was at the end of his tether. 'Look,' he said to the student, 'maybe you can talk some sense into him. There's nothing we can do for him. The hotel manager has interrogated the maid. She is the only one with a key to the room and the only one allowed in. She never even saw a manuscript. Tell him to calm down and stop imagining things. I have neither the time nor the patience to take the matter any further.'

And so saying, Prša opened the door. Zdražil and the student went out into the corridor dejected. Before closing the door behind them, Prša took the Czech's hand and shook it firmly. Then he raised his eyebrows and gave him the kind of look usually reserved for goners.

6

'I can't tell you how pleased I am you accepted my invitation, Monsieur Prša,' said Jean-Paul Flagus with a friendly smile and a raised glass. 'To your health!'

'Thank you. To you.'

Prša's French wasn't holding up too well.

'Perhaps you'd prefer me to switch to English or German?'

'No, no! What for?' said Prša as nonchalantly as possible. He knew neither English nor German.

'I must repeat how glad I am you were able to make time for me in your busy schedule. You have my admiration. Planning it all, setting it all up, seeing to so many people – my hat's off to you. You do bear the lion's share of the responsibility, don't you?'

'Oh, it's nothing really. And don't believe everything you see. It's really an illusion, a Potemkin village, understand?' He had unconsciously spoken louder and louder, until in the end it sounded as though he were speaking to someone hard of hearing.

'I'm afraid I don't quite.'

'What I mean is the whole thing's a fake, a fraud! Nobody's willing to lift a finger for our poor culture. It's so . . . provincial.' And he stood and gazed into the distance like the provincial landowners in Russian novels.

Jean-Paul Flagus heard him out with the patience of a dignified elderly gentleman.

'By the way,' he said after a short pause, 'a distant relative of mine, Gustave Flaubert, once remarked that the backwater of Yonville is as interesting as Constantinople. *Mutatis mutandis*, Zagreb is as interesting as Paris.'

'Well, your relative was wrong,' Prša said, annoyed, but then did a double take. 'Hold on! Did you say just now you were related to Flaubert?'

'I did. Is that so strange?'

'His nephew, did you say?'

'Distant relative. What of it?'

'If I had relatives like that, I'd shout it from the rooftops.'

'You think so?' said Monsieur Flagus with a smile. 'You might well conceal it. It's not easy living in a shadow, even if the shadow is a hundred and fifty years long.'

Prša pictured a 150-year-long shadow towering over Monsieur Flagus.

'You're right. It has its good and bad points.'

'Now that we're on the subject, could I possibly have a look at some of his works in your language?'

'I'll make sure you get them.'

'Thank you. My assistant Raúl is at your disposal.'

Prša was impressed. Bringing a personal assistant all this way. Must be a big shot. Or filthy rich, with all those royalties. Flaubert's shadow had a golden lining.

'By the way,' Jean-Paul added, 'I liked the talk that young man gave today. It had a caustic, uncompromising tone to it.'

'You mean Ljuština? Don't believe a word he says. A phoney if there ever was one. You can buy him for a drink!'

'Is that so? And the gentleman who spoke so movingly about dialects? A revelation!'

'Grah? He's catastrophic! Provincialism at its worst. And completely out of date. Nobody abroad has read a line of our *mainstream* literature, for God's sake, and he goes on about *dialects*!'

Monsieur Flagus nodded, smiled, and said, 'What about your famous novelist? You know who I mean. A nice man . . .'

'No, no. He's catastrophic too! Not a drop of talent! Pure ravings. "The hit-man of the written word" – that's what I call him.'

Jean-Paul Flagus observed his interlocutor carefully. Prša was highly flattered: Flaubert's venerable gold-lined shadow hung on his every word. He suddenly felt the need to lay bare his soul to the man and was sorry his French was so weak.

'Literature is stronger than its assassins, Monsieur Flagus,' he said, himself moved by his passion. 'If I didn't believe in the power of literature to resist, to overcome those who attack it, I would not be devoting my life to it.'

'Right you are, my boy,' said Monsieur Flagus. 'Let us drink to the invincibility of literature. For why else are we here?' And he smiled and raised his glass.

7

'Bar-bi-tu-rates,' the strange foreigner repeated.

'But I've told you,' a washed-out blonde replied, 'we don't sell barbiturates over the counter.'

The foreigner wrung his hands, then took out a handkerchief and wiped his pale, sweat-drenched forehead. The washed-out blonde observed him carefully and, without taking her eyes off him, called into the back room, 'Lidija, come out here for a minute, will you?'

Out came a washed-out brunette.

'Ask him what he wants,' the blonde pharmacist said to the brunette pharmacist.

'*Doyouspeakenglish?*'

'*No*,' the foreigner said and shook his head.

'*Sprechensiedeutsch?*'

'*Nein.*'

The man looked sadly over at the two women and ventured, '*Po-russki?*'

'*Nyet*,' they said, shaking their heads in unison.

For a while the foreigner's face registered unadulterated despair, but then it brightened, and he grabbed his forehead with one hand and made a hideous face. Then he looked over questioningly at the women.

'Headache,' said the blonde, and for some reason grabbed her own forehead, made a face and looked over questioningly at the man.

'*Ano*,' said the foreigner with a nod.

'What'd I tell you?' said the blonde, taking out a box of headache tablets and placing them on the glass counter.

Meanwhile the foreigner made another face, rolled his eyes and pointed to his stomach.

'Nausea,' said the first pharmacist to the second as if she were an interpreter.

'Shall I give him something for his stomach?' asked the brunette. The blonde, not taking her eyes off the foreigner, nodded her assent. The brunette found what she was looking for and put it next to the other box. She was about to make out the bill when the strange man made yet another face and bent over pointing to his back.

'Backache?' the blonde said softly to the brunette and then turned to the foreigner and said out loud, 'We don't sell that over the counter either. Understand?'

But the foreigner kept bending over, puffing out his cheeks, clenching his jaw.

'I can't take this any more,' said the blonde sympathetically as the foreigner's pale face turned redder and redder and the veins at his temples started showing.

'Know what's wrong with him, girls?' interjected a portly cashier who had been sitting at the cash register doing some accounts. 'He's constipated, that's what.'

The brunette immediately took out a third box and put it on the counter next to the other two, and the foreigner straightened up with a grateful smile. The brunette made out the bill. The foreigner went over to the cashier, paid it and held out his hand. The cashier gave him a surprised look, but shook it. The foreigner returned to the brunette with his receipt, picked up the boxes and stuffed them into his pocket. Then he extended his arm over the counter and shook first the blonde's hand, then the brunette's, and left the pharmacy content.

'You know,' said the blonde to the brunette, 'my grandmother was Czech, and I never learned a word of the language.' And the two of them stood there as if hypnotized, staring out after the foreigner who had by then disappeared.

8

'What do you write?' Marc asked Pipo. They were sitting in the Kavkaz Café sipping the local grape brandy. 'Fiction or poetry?'

'Uh . . . fiction,' said Pipo. Pipo Fink had one and only one book to his name, but it served him as a kind of internal blanket. He *felt* himself a writer.

'And is it enough to live on? I mean, what you earn from it.'

'Well, yes,' Pipo answered, and blushed. (It was a lie. He lived with his mother on the pension she started receiving after his father had died. He did write for children's television, but he looked down on his TV scripts though they provided him with a bit of pocket money and a bit of status at home. No one asked what Pipo did; Pipo was 'the TV personality'. It was always good for a few points over coffee with the neighbours: 'Pipo?' his mother would say. 'Burning the midnight oil as usual. In fact, it was three by the time he got to bed last night.' At which point the neighbours would shake their heads in wonder, and Pipo's honour was saved. Which was all that mattered, because beyond the confines of the house where he lived no one cared a hoot about his employment record.) 'In a way.'

'Well, I can't live on what I earn as a writer,' said Marc. 'My stuff isn't commercial. So I do kids' shows – TV – on the side. I'd starve otherwise.'

'My stuff isn't commercial either,' Pipo said quickly. 'Hey, how do you like the *loza*?'

'Great stuff,' said Marc, taking another sip. Then all at once he turned serious. 'Hey, do I strike you as, like, alienated?'

'Alienated? No. Why do you ask?'

'All Americans are alienated.'

Pipo was so thrown by Marc's fit of alienation that he couldn't think of anything to say and so ordered another round of *loza*.

'Do I strike you as anti-intellectual?'

'You? What are you talking about?'

'All Americans are anti-intellectual. That's why I went to law school after graduating in English. And while I was in law school I did three correspondence courses: gourmet cooking, truck driving, and underwater fishing.'

'But what for?'

'Just the way I am, I guess,' said Marc with a shrug. 'I've got five books out too – two novels and three collections of stories.'

'You're a superman!'

'Think so?' Marc asked, clearly unsure of himself.

'Look at me! I barely got *one* degree. I can make coffee and a hard-boiled egg, and I don't know which end of a fishing pole is up.' What he couldn't bring himself to say was that he'd written only one book. It was too late for that.

'Yes, but you're a European!'

Pipo's mouth fell open. He'd never dreamed of being European as a plus. Just then he spied Ivan Ljuština the critic and Ranko Leš the poet sitting at the next table, and the thought that they might want to come and butt in on him and Marc made him so childishly jealous that he suddenly stood and said, 'Let's go.'

'Go? Go where?'

'Anywhere.'

'What's wrong with here?'

'That's the way we do things. We're always going somewhere else.'

Marc downed the rest of his *loza*, stood up, and followed Pipo out of the Kavkaz.

Meanwhile, the following conversation was going on at the table next to theirs.

'Who was that?'

'Some yokel from New York. You can tell by the way they dress.'

'And the guy with him? Fink, wasn't it?'

'Fink it was. Remember that piece of shit he came out with two or three years ago? *The Life and Works of Pipo Fink*, he called it. You reviewed it.'

'I did? Maybe. Wonder what the Yank sees in him?'

'What difference does it make? America's out. Has been for ages. That guy and Fink – they're just leftovers from the sixties. You saw the Berkeley T-shirt, didn't you? No, no. America is definitely out.

'You think so?'

'I know so. Europe is in! *Mitteleuropa!* And we're smack in the *mittel.* Austria-Hungary on the march! On the march to trend-dom! It's all in the nose. You've got to have a nose for these things or you can wave bye-bye to the choo-choo of history. When it comes to culture, America's the sticks, the pits. Who cares about America these days? Apart from a handful of illiterate teeny-boppers, that is. How can you compare Miller and Mailer to the likes of Musil and Mahler, to the likes of Freud, Kafka, and Krleža – to mention only a few? No, plastic culture is dead, instant culture is buried!'

'The reason I love America', said Pipo with great verve as they were walking to the next café, the Zvečka, 'is that there you can be anything you like – or everything. You take off for – I don't know – Rocksprings, Texas, and get a job in a McDonald's off the freeway, and the minute you're bored you hitch out to Long Beach, California, where you give lessons in deep-water fishing, but you're bored again, so you split for Aspen, Colorado, where you're a ski instructor, and come the call of the wild you move on to Greenville, Smithville, Connellsville, to the mythical Tombstone if you feel like it, and soon there you are back in New York, in the Village, in your Bleecker Street loft, writing up a storm.' Pipo got so carried away that he seemed to have jetted into Zagreb from Stateside for a quick *loza.*

'I don't live in the Village,' said Marc. 'I live in Brooklyn.'

'All right, you live in Brooklyn, but you know what I mean, don't you?'

'Sure, sure,' said Marc, 'but *you* can be anything you like too, can't you?'

'I most certainly cannot! It's not a matter of individual choice; it's a kind of energy, an all-encompassing, day-to-day kind of energy, if you know what I mean. I see it in your movies. Everything's always surging, foaming, bubbling over. You pull a metal tab and whoosh! an ordinary beer is alive with energy. Whoosh! you dig? Press down on a Big Mac and what do you feel? Elasticity! Even your fries are crispier and crunchier. And Kentucky Fried Chicken! So round and full and firmly packed. A whole lot sexier than . . . say, that redhead over there. And then, all you Yanks are into exercising, jogging, aerobics. Everything about you is firm, erect. America is one big adrenalin-powered *perpetuum mobile* yo-yo, one big never-ending, come-one-come-all orgasm. See what I mean? You won't find that here. Our rhythm's all off. It's like the difference between one of those new giant-screen, high-resolution colour monitors and a black-and-white console from the fifties. Just look around you . . .'

Pipo motioned towards the crowd of young people hanging out in front of the Zvečka, leaning on parked Hondas and Kawasakis, blinking in the sun like lizards and showing not the slightest inclination to move.

'What are they doing?' asked Marc, obviously untouched by Pipo's views of America.

'Cruising, rapping.'

'What I wouldn't give for time to cruise a little, rap a little,' said Marc, finishing off his *loza*. 'That's what makes a real writer!'

'Like in Harlem,' said Pipo, who had never been to America. 'But I'd much rather do my cruising and rapping in Harlem. See the difference?'

'No,' said Marc sincerely.

Maybe it was the difference between the movies and real life: the only America he'd ever seen was on Zagreb screens.

'Let's go,' Marc said to Pipo.

'Go? Where?'

'Anywhere. Didn't you say that was the way you did things?'

On their way to the Blato Café, Pipo thought how much he liked this Yank, how he'd taken to him from the start and wanted to tell him everything there was to tell about himself, and he thanked his mother ('Thank you, Mama,' he whispered to himself) for putting him in an English-language kindergarten and making him take courses and even private lessons in English.

90

'You have no idea', said Pipo, as they sat over their fourth *loza*, 'what on-the-road writing meant to me. I wanted to be our Kerouac. So I figured I'd take to the road and have a go at it. Well, no go. Our roads weren't up to it. Or my rickety baby Fiat. And where would I go? Virovitica? Know what I mean?'

'I think so,' Marc said, not quite able to picture a baby Fiat and completely in the dark about Virovitica.

'There's another problem,' Pipo went on. 'Nobody here uses *ich-Erzählung*. Well, almost nobody.'

'What's *ich-Erzählung*?' asked Marc.

'It's when you write in the first person, using *I*.'

'Oh. That's all I ever do.'

'You didn't need to tell me that. I knew, I knew. We don't do that kind of thing. I can't sit down and write the way Vonnegut writes so elegantly: *I'm just a coot from the Cape and I smoke a pack of Pall Malls a day*. Or whatever it was. If I wrote *I'm just a coot from Virovitica and I smoke a pack of Dravas a day* I'd be the laughing stock of Zagreb. Disbelief suspended to breaking point, if you know what I mean.'

'Of course,' Marc nodded automatically.

'Or if I wrote *Today I ran across Pero at the Blato*,' said Pipo, inspired by the appearance of said Pero at the door, 'all Zagreb would wonder who Pero was and probably decide they were Pero themselves. Know what I mean? It's our inferiority complex. We're hicks. So when I write that I ran across Pero it doesn't sound at all like Vonnegut's intimate, confidential pow of a first person. Maybe only Vonnegut would care – if he could read it – that I ran across Pero at the Blato.'

Pero must have had an inkling he was being talked about, because he passed right by their table. Pipo waved.

'I'm sure he'd care,' said Marc. 'Hey, isn't it time to split?'

Next stop the Corso Café and another round of *loza*.

'Another thing,' Pipo began at once – he was wound up, he couldn't stop – 'another thing is that we're still up to our necks in Socialist Realism. The subconscious kind, I mean.' And so saying he looked around as if Socialist Realism were standing behind him, breathing down his neck.

'Nothing wrong with that,' said Marc. 'I'm a realist myself.'

91

'You're putting me on!'

'No, really.'

'But what does it mean to you? What do you write about?'

'The seamy side of life in all its gory detail.'

'The refuse dump of life? That sort of thing?'

'How'd you guess? Know what I called my latest book? *The Garbage Pail.*'

'Fantastic!' cried Pipo, green with envy. 'That's what I've been saying all along. You've got everything you need! What a country!'

'Right.'

'Right you've got everything you need or right what a country?'

'Both.'

'You mean you love your country?'

'Why, yes.'

'You must be out of your mind! Nobody loves their country. What have you got a country for if not to hate it? Know what I mean?'

'No,' said Marc.

'It's very complex. Like a mother–son relationship.'

'But I love my mother!' said Marc.

'You don't understand!'

'All right, then. Tell me why you don't love your country.'

'Because – it's very complex, I told you – well, because it stinks of onions and *ćevapčići.*'

Marc asked what *ćevapčići* were, and as soon as Pipo had finished his description of the grill and the meat Marc said he was hungry. So off they went to a restaurant. And while they were drinking their *loza* – their *loza* aperitif this time – Marc pulled a small pair of binoculars out of his pocket (he'd clearly had enough talk for the time being) and trained them on the nearest trees.

'What's that?' Pipo asked, feeling suddenly abandoned.

'Binoculars.'

'What for?'

'Bird-watching.'

'Bird-watching?'

'Bird-watching,' Marc said, and without removing the binoculars from his eyes he took a small book from his other pocket and laid it on the table. It was *A Guide to European Songbirds.*

'How can you tell a bird's a songbird?' Pipo asked.

'By the book,' said Marc, still perusing the trees and bushes.

There's a Yank for you, thought Pipo, furious. Instead of sitting and waiting quietly for his *ćevapčići*, what does he do but pull out a pair of crazy binoculars and ogle the fauna. Pipo was especially hurt for his fellow European songbirds, as if he were one himself: the Balkan sparrow, say. Americans have it easy: they assume that just because you order something it's going to come. So Marc was all relaxed and Pipo was all nerves: he had constantly to be on the look-out and make sure that the waiter didn't spit in the soup or charge you for two portions, that the pigeon parading along the fence didn't take it into its spiteful head to make a mess on your table, that the plaster peeling off the wall didn't choose that very moment to bonk you on the head, that cars didn't enter the crossing before the light turned green, that the nearest skyscraper didn't suddenly crumble, that your electric bill was accurate, that the woman in the post office did in fact stick the stamp you bought on your envelope, and that there really was a second street on the left when the man on the street you asked for directions said you couldn't miss it (and in nine out of ten cases there was no 'second street on the left', which was nine cases too many!). If Marc was relaxed and Pipo's leg was swinging a mile a minute under the table, it was because all Pipo's energy went into 'making sure'. You couldn't even be sure the damn bushes would turn green in spring; they could just stay as they were and screw you, Pipo . . . How could an American understand that?

'Hey, let me have a look,' said Pipo, and Marc handed him his binoculars. The only living flying creature Pipo could discern was the pigeon parading along the fence. And then behind a nearby bush he spied a ghostlike figure staring out at him through the same binoculars.

'I must be drunk,' said Pipo. 'I'm having visions.'

'By the way,' said Marc, 'our friend the Czech had his manuscript stolen today.'

'Really?' said Pipo, though despite his sincere concern he could not stop himself from falling on the onions-smothered *ćevapčići* that had just arrived.

Marc, his mouth soon full as well, could only mumble 'Mm' in reply.

The man at the Intercontinental reception desk frowned at the sight of yesterday's cut-ups. Drunk again. First they stood for ages at the house phones; then they came over and enquired whether a Mr Zdražil had gone out; and even after he pointed out that Mr Zdražil's key was not in its box they went back and tortured the phones again. But at last they gave up and staggered off in the direction of the bar.

9

Troshin sat comfortably ensconced in an armchair, his legs up on the radiator. He was slowly sipping cognac from the sample he had found in the refrigerator in his room. Mission accomplished, he thought. He had delivered the boring paper expected of him, a perfect imitation of Soviet literary criticism – on aesthetic pluralism in contemporary Soviet literature, on thematic diversity, on the technological revolution with a knowing aside to ecology – leaving village prose and the rich humanist tradition for Sapozhnikov. He was proud of his ability to mimic the clichés and took a certain pleasure in reading 'Another one of those Russians' on the faces of his audience.

He enjoyed sitting in the semi-darkness looking out at a city he did not know. And had no desire to know, for that matter. He loved hotel rooms. This one was quite luxurious, as they went, and completely without identity. He loved the absence of identity.

For some reason Troshin was reminded of a man named Ginzburg, a writer he'd met in Leningrad some fifteen years ago. This Ginzburg had been an active member of the literary scene in the twenties, writing stories and plays, even shooting a few short films. He disappeared during the purges to surface again, apparently somewhere in Central Asia, after the war. Then, in the sixties, he was 'discovered' by the literary crowd, the memoir hunters. Though taciturn and distant, he took a shine to Troshin and asked him to his flat. Troshin was amazed at what he found: one enormous room completely bare except for a wardrobe, a desk, two chairs, and a bed made with military precision. No paintings, no books – nothing to indicate a long, rich past. Just a small photograph of a young woman hanging over the bed. And there he stood, in the middle of the room, with one hand deep in his cardigan and the other constantly pointing at the ceiling. Thinking back on it now he had the feeling that the old man was reaching for an invisible silk cord that would some day descend and slowly pull him up with it.

He smiled at the image. Then he stood, went over to the refrigerator, took out another one of the bottles and returned to his chair. He'd often felt like fading away, disappearing, pulling up stakes and switching cities, careers, people, yet the greater the desire grew, the vaguer it became. It was especially strong when he travelled, when, like now, he was protected by the apathetic walls of a hotel room. In moments like these he had no identity whatsoever. The people downstairs didn't care in the least whether he was Troshin, Ivanov, or the man in the moon. They'd probably never heard of him and certainly never read a word he'd written. His only identity was as a representative of his country, and he'd let Sapozhnikov do the representing. He was better at that sort of thing.

Why in God's name was this childish dream of an invisible cloak so strong in a 47-year-old writer with two marriages and a relatively successful career behind him? Why had he always reserved the right to vanish? Because he was an observer. Lyuda had once said to him, 'You're not one of us, you know that?' And she was right. He had never belonged, truly belonged, to anyone or anything. Not that he didn't want to. No, he was incapable of it. There had always been something urging him to stand aside, stand apart, refuse to join, maintain a dim sense of himself as an individual . . .

Yet it was with Lyuda he'd tried hardest to belong. He'd slid into his first marriage like dough into a mould, and she, Lyuda, was that mould. Lyuda brought 'real life' into his existence – and with a vengeance. She was impressed with his being a writer. Besides, it meant all kinds of privileges that seemed important to those cut off from them: holidays at special writers' resorts, good food (caviare, smoked salmon, luxurious meals at the Writers Union restaurant), glamorous parties, opening nights, foreign films off limits to native audiences, interesting people, and, most important, access to foreign travel. Lyuda loved the trinkets he brought back from his trips abroad, and she held on to long-since-empty English tea tins and French perfume bottles because they made her, well, different. Lyuda taught him how to buy a Japanese colour television set, how to get a plumber in, how to find decent cooking oil, beef and sausages, windscreen-wipers, gold, valuable antiquarian books and of course the indispensable, 'mythical' fur coat.

Then one day he realized he wasn't living life any more, life was living him. He said he broke it off; she said he drifted off. 'You've drifted off once and for all,' she said to him, and applied for a divorce.

Maybe he had in fact *belonged* while he was with Lyuda. But what made him think about it now? Was he getting old? Was there something wrong with his clock? His mother had once said to him, 'Yura, there's something wrong with my clock. I keep winding it and it keeps going backwards.' And as she said it she pressed her gnarled hand to her heart.

'Yura! Yura!' came Vitya Sapozhnikov's voice through the door.

Troshin picked himself up and opened the door.

There he stood, swaying slightly. He put his finger to his lips and slipped into the room carrying a white plastic bag.

'Psst!' he said, emptying the bag of a bottle of colourless liquid, a jar of pickles, some tinned fish and a loaf of bread.

'Where did you find the pickles?' asked Troshin with a smile.

'What about this, eh?' said Sapozhnikov, brandishing the bottle, which was no longer full. 'See this?'

'What is it?'

'Alcohol. Pure alcohol. Well? How does that grab you?'

Sapozhnikov staggered into the bathroom and emerged with two glasses. He filled them both to the brim.

'Cheers, pal! Bottoms up!'

Sapozhnikov emptied the glass at one go, made a terrible face, exhaled, tore a piece of bread from the loaf, put it under his nose, and sniffed. Then he collapsed into the armchair.

Troshin left his glass untouched.

'Can you believe it, Yura?' he said, opening the fish. 'Pure alcohol! They sell pure alcohol in the pharmacies! The real stuff! I didn't believe it when Tarasyuk told me back in Moscow.' He dunked the piece of bread in the oil, then gently removed the fish, piece by piece. 'Know who else found out about the alcohol? Guess! The Czech! Our fellow Slav! I caught him sneaking out of the pharmacy. Hey, don't you want any?'

Troshin shook his head.

'An . . . cho . . . vies. Anchovies,' said Sapozhnikov. 'What do you think it is? Some Indian variety? Anchovies.' By this time his mouth was full. 'Hey, tell me something, Yura. Tell me why they don't like us.'

'Who they?'

'Everybody!'

'Can't you be more specific?'

'It's hard to say. The Czech wouldn't look at me, our hosts are polite and no more, and that Hungarian bitch just stares. Well, they can screw themselves,' he concluded with a hiccup. 'The only one I like is the American.'

'Why him?'

'We had three vodkas in the bar today.'

'I didn't know you spoke English.'

'You don't need English to drink vodka. I said *sehr gut* to him, he said *khorosho* to me. Great guy . . . Come on, Yura. Bottoms up. Looks like you and me are going to spend a lot of time together.'

He got up and, just about maintaining his balance, took a deep breath, clicked his heels and downed half a glass. Then he expelled the air from his lungs, seated himself with great solemnity and pulled a pickle out of the jar, gawking at it as if it were a newly discovered genus.

'There's something I've been meaning to ask you, Yura.'

'Ask away.'

'Are we the first socialist country in the world? Well, are we?'

'We are, Vitya,' said Troshin as earnestly as he could. 'We are.'

'Well then, why are all the others doing so much better?'

'What others, Vitya?'

'All of them. Every damn one of them.'

'They may be doing better, Vitya . . . but they're not first.'

'What a man, Yura! What a mind! That never would have occurred to me. Yes, you're a sly one, Vitya. There ain't no flies on you! If they hadn't given us separate rooms, we could drink . . .' And in mid-sentence he started snoring, his head drooping on his chest.

Troshin lit a cigarette and began pacing the room. Poor Vitya. This was only his second trip abroad. He was still vulnerable. Crossing the border was for some a serious (though hard to put

98

one's finger on) insult. There were even those who turned down the opportunity. He'd known a professor of ancient history who had never been out of the country and reached an age when he stopped wishing to travel. And then he was told he'd been included in a delegation to Greece. Greece! The old desires came back to life; *he* came back to life. But when he got to the airport, he was told his name wasn't on the list. It was an error, an error on the part of the airport officials, but an error too late to rectify. The old professor went mad.

Troshin had experienced the insult many times himself, and he knew how hard it was to take. But he knew how much harder it was to renounce. Several years before, on a trip to Hungary, he and the entire Soviet delegation had ambled through the streets of Budapest hiding samples of mohair – blue mohair, pink mohair, green mohair – anything they could take home to wives, mistresses or sisters, because those were the years when mohair was the rage and showed up everywhere in the form of sweaters, scarves and funny-looking rumpled winter caps. (In winter the women in the streets looked like so many tropical birds.) Anyone searching them would have been at a loss to know why each member of the delegation was stuffing his pockets with wool. Could they have belonged to a secret sect?

Then there were those who'd never been abroad. Troshin had a friend, a 'quiet' dissident, who lived in a cramped, out-of-the-way room with his wife and three children but had a map of Paris on the wall. He knew every street by heart in all but the most outlying districts.

Vitya's spree was a helpless protest against the insult known as 'crossing the border'. As soon as they crossed the border – not only Vitya, *all* Soviet citizens – the complexes began to make themselves felt. They were defenceless. Between the exit date and the date of re-entry they were subjected to the financial humiliation of accepting their hosts' per diems, their own currency being worth literally nothing outside its borders, and the psychic humiliation of realizing that they themselves were of no use to anyone and therefore virtually worthless as well. The moment they re-entered, everything came back together again. Vitya, in his usual self-confident, self-satisfied way, would tell everyone where he'd been and what he'd seen, embroidering a few things, of course, and suppressing a few others. That he'd tried to sell his camera, for instance, so he could buy his wife a pair of shoes and himself a pair of jeans.

Sapozhnikov was sleeping the sleep of the drunk. Troshin dragged over the other armchair and draped Sapozhnikov's legs over it. He decided to go out for a walk and wake him up when he came back. He put on his shoes and opened the door quietly, but out in the corridor he changed his mind and set off for Room 710, the room just above his own.

At that moment Sapozhnikov's body twisted slightly, and a telltale thread of mohair emerged from his jacket pocket. Pink mohair.

10

'Who is it?' came a voice after a long, insistent knock.

'It's me. Ena.'

'Are you alone?' asked the voice after a long pause.

'Yes, I am.'

Ena waited patiently, lighting a cigarette, pacing the corridor. Just as she was about to give up, the door opened. Instead of the face she had expected, however, she saw – no one. She entered with a feeling of dread.

'Shut the door,' the voice said. It came from the bathroom.

'It is shut,' Ena shouted in the direction of the bathroom. All she got for an answer was a rush of water.

The room was stuffy; the windows were shut, the curtains drawn. Ena opened the windows. The bed was crumpled. An Aeroflot flight bag lay open in the armchair. Next to it were two neatly folded shirts, a bag containing some dirty socks, and a plastic case with a toothbrush, a tube of Floura toothpaste and a metal soap-dish. A Colloquium briefcase filled with Colloquium papers lay on the bedside table next to a box of cough-drops. *Hašlerky*, Ena read on the box. She took one, unwrapped it and popped it into her mouth.

The noise of the water coming from the bathroom had not diminished. Ena lit another cigarette and paced the room. Then she leaned her elbows on the window-sill and peered out at the evening lights. When she got to the end of the cigarette, she decided enough time had gone by and went up to the bathroom door.

'Mr Zdražil?' she said loudly.

All she could hear was the monotone whish of the water.

She knocked, knocked again and shouted, 'Mr Zdražil, do you hear me?'

Again she heard only the dull, insistent whish.

She looked around the room as if looking for help, then steeled herself, took a deep breath and pressed the handle. There, on the toilet bowl in baggy pyjamas – the bottoms of which rested in a heap on the floor – sat Jan Zdražil. He was as pale as a sheet and in tears.

11

Slowly, almost cautiously, he pressed his lips to Sabina's. They were
cold. Her breath was as fresh as a child's. A scene from his childhood
suddenly flashed before him. He must have been thirteen. Before his
first lover's tryst he locked himself in the bathroom and practised by
covering the dull bathroom mirror with kisses, slowly, almost
cautiously, pressing his lips to the cool, smooth surface. His eyes
half shut, he made small, warm, misty circles, dreaming of Olya or
Natasha – he couldn't remember which – and suspecting even then
that behind her stood a long succession of unknown women's faces
overlapping one another like a pack of cards. Had he – standing
there, innocently, on tiptoe, his eyes lowered, his head raised – had
he somehow kissed all his future loves?

Sabina's mirror-cool kiss had brought Troshin back to his childhood, but his eyes were now wide open. He seemed to be searching
for that thirteen-year-old behind Sabina's face.

Naked, Sabina was dazzling, her skin whiter than white. His eyes
slipped down over her blonde, straight, childlike hair, the fine line
of her neck, her perfect round breasts, her oval thighs, the pink
circles of her toenails.

She mounted him placidly and rocked her pelvis slowly, evenly.
Intense as his pleasure was, for the first time in his life he felt no
need to touch the object of his desire. He observed her instead. For
a while the long fingers of her carefully polished scarlet fingernails
traced gentle circles round her nipples, as if they were a membrane
stretched precariously over milk, but all at once she flung her arms
back to her neck and let her head swing slowly, upside down,
distracted. When the light from the window caught her hair, the
absent face of Troshin's pale rider seemed surrounded by a halo.
Then she let out a soft sigh, dropped her head on his shoulder –

103

nearly licking him like a cat but never quite looking at him – and rolled out of bed. She immediately went into the bathroom. Through the open door Troshin heard the tinkle of urination. He surreptitiously twisted his body so as to watch her sitting on the toilet bowl. First he noticed she was rubbing her feet together; then he thought he saw that fine ring of light above her head again.

Lithely, noiselessly, Sabina slipped back into bed. She immediately fell into a peaceful sleep. Troshin lay motionless for a while, afraid to move. Then he quietly climbed out of bed, walked around it, and observed Sabina's breathing like a spy. God, she was beautiful! There must be something wrong, some error somewhere. She had taken the initiative. When he appeared at her door (having dutifully phoned from the lobby) and said stupidly, 'I've come for my interview', and she had brushed up against him, he knew the interview had been merely a pretext. But a pretext for what? She took him simply, naturally, without shame or pretension. Why him, though? Why a middling, middle-aged writer, a total unknown outside his country with wrinkles and patches of grey to boot?

Troshin slipped into his shoes and tiptoed towards the door. Just before he reached it, he stopped and turned. Sabina was sleeping the peaceful sleep of a child. Suddenly Troshin had a strange vision: the white queen. Was Sabina's the last face in the succession that had looked out at him from the mirror of his parents' flat at 54 Trubnaya Street?

104

12

Dear Peer,

This town is just a blob on the map, say Tanja and Dunja, and I'm beginning to think they're right. A boring Central European Oblomovka. The streets are sleepy; the people have pale, mean faces and crawl along like dazed flies. Today I sat in a nearly empty restaurant and watched the man at the next table. He was eating some meat with great concentration, gnawing away at the bones, leisurely stripping them clean with tiny bites like brush strokes until they shone with a greyish gleam. Each time he finished off a bone he would hold it up to the light of the window and examine it as though it were a precious stone, and if it failed to pass muster he would nibble at it a bit more. Then, satisfied at last, he would set it aside on a special plate, forming a gradual pattern evident only to himself. The last bone he held up – it was small and round, like a bird's shoulder-blade (if birds have shoulder-blades) – fairly sparkled in the light. At least I imagined it did. In any case, I was seized with a desire to stand up, go over to his table, take his wrist, nibble on his thumb, kiss the skin between his thumb and index finger, take the round bone into my mouth, and slip it under my tongue like the wafer in Communion. And just then I saw a scene out of my childhood. I used to put buttons in my mouth, the kind with four little holes and a raised edge, and make believe they were fruit drops. My tongue still remembers their cool, smooth surface. I used to love sticking my tongue into the holes, running it along the edge, ducking the button under it, keeping it there until my mouth filled with saliva. The button wafer. Why did I do it? I don't know. Why am I writing this to you? I don't know. Sitting there in the restaurant, I surreptitiously tore a button off my blouse and popped it into my mouth. I enjoyed the thought that for a second and at a point whose name and nature I'd never know our paths had crossed, mine and my neighbour's, while he sat there oblivious, performing his ritual, delivering a secret bone message as indecipherable as the message in an ancient ornament.

After our dinner yesterday Thomas and I went to his room, politely felt each other's erotic pulse, and went our separate ways. The main thing I retain of the encounter is the image of his big round balls. One's erotic memory inevitably registers details that unjustly (or justly?) mask the whole. It is a haunted attic of smiles, sighs, smells, looks and body parts – never whole individuals. Parts of me are scattered throughout various erotic attics as well . . .

At the morning session one of the writers claimed that a manuscript of his, a novel, had been stolen. He kicked up quite a rumpus about it, as if his *biography* had been stolen. I'm starting to see myself as a puppet filling in the empty squares (picture a crossword puzzle) of a model female (feminist) biography. Maybe the feeling I can't shake – a feeling of the fragility of all things – isn't a psychotic fear after all; maybe it's the ultimate reality. The fear that if you take off a glove your hand will go with it, the fear that if you roll up the blinds the cityscape will go with it . . . Remember the day you jumped out of the car to wipe off the windows and I screamed the minute the rag touched the glass? I was terrified you'd wipe my face away. Well, now I know: if some day someone pulls the right string, I'm going to cooome uuundooone.

Love,
Cecilia

MERCREDI, le 7 mai

1

The Minister hated 'poets'. They respected him. They were attracted by his antipathy. (Poets are like children. There is only one thing they cannot stand. Antipathy.) Prša was a special case. A bastard and sycophant like the others, true, but one who peddled his wares honestly, even gave an occasional factory reading.

The reason the Minister so despised poets was that poetry for him was like the mumps or the measles, something you got over when you were young. Besides, the only poetry that ever meant anything to him were the lyrics of the hit tunes he grew up with. Vanda would squeal with delight or giggle as if tickled whenever he sang 'Be My Love', 'Your Dainty Little Hand', 'You Only Love Once', '*Bésame mucho*', 'Domino', and other favourites of his youth. He didn't need self-styled poets shoving their creations in his face. The few books of poetry he'd been forced to read at the pedagogical institute had left no trace on him. What good were they? In fact, he took a dim view of literature in general. With one exception: Andrić. Andrić had won the Nobel Prize; he was world famous; that counted for something.

Sometimes the Minister gave his poets a dose of their own medicine. Not long ago one of them had come to him wailing and moaning about how he had nowhere to live, how he had a wife and children to support on all but non-existent royalties and so on and so forth, and the Minister had glanced up at the poor poetic creature and said as calmly as you please, 'What do you expect? We're all pawns on the chessboard of life.' That shut him up all right!

And now this Czech! Another day, another scandal!

'You won't believe this, baby, but he's locked himself in his room and won't answer the phone. And yesterday, right in front of Prša, he threatened suicide.'

109

'Why would he want to kill himself?' asked Vanda. 'A Czech.'

'How should I know? They're a bunch of babies, those poets.'

'But he must have had a reason, baby,' said Vanda compassion-ately, putting her arms around him and planting a noisy kiss on his biceps. She was trying to think of the reasons why famous people – not necessarily Czechs – had committed suicide, but the Minister pushed her away and scratched the place she had just kissed.

'He claims somebody stole a novel he wrote. His masterpiece, he says! Another lunatic! Why don't they watch who they invite?'

'But that's a perfectly good reason, baby!' said Vanda, nibbling on the Minister's ear.

'If he goes through with it, the shit'll really hit the fan!'

'How will we know?'

'Prša's up there banging on his door this very minute.'

Vanda pictured the fat Czech (for some reason she was sure he was fat) taking off his tie (a blue tie with red stripes), fashioning it into a noose, throwing it over a light fixture, testing whether it would hold, and then . . .

'Baby,' Vanda whispered, all goose pimples, her hand inching down to the Minister's wand, but finding a limp blob in its place.

Vanda was disappointed. She loved everything connected with those unmentionables. They lifted her out of the everyday world into an erotic Disneyland where male wizards turned her into something she felt closer to her true being. She loved the magic transformation of that silly little fleshy blob into a smooth, pink, shiny wand; she loved breasts puffing up like balloons, nipples springing out of hiding, wombs widening in wonder at its approach. They were the only toys we grown-ups have left, she thought, and lately they seemed more and more inclined to break in her hands. She turned to the wall and with her thumb in her mouth wondered when it would be time to throw the toy into the well.

'He won't do it, baby,' she said softly.

One glance at Vanda's sad, sagging backside did the trick. Embracing her from behind, the Minister set them off on a long, sweet, jolting ride in their own rickety train, clinging to each other while the steam spurted forth, choo-choo, and the smoke-stack puffed, choo-choo, and the water bubbled and boiled, choo-choo . . .

110

'Oh-ah, oh-ah,' went Vanda, panting rhythmically like an old steam engine. 'Choo-choo, choo-choo,' went the Minister, stoking her fire. And little by little the little engine made its way up the big, big hill until 'Oh-ahhhhhhhhh!' went Vanda and the phone rang, announcing their arrival at the station. The Minister jumped off on to the platform, and Vanda, all warm and glowing, stuck her thumb back into her mouth as if to keep the last bits of pleasure from escaping.

'He's alive, baby,' the Minister called out from the entrance hall, and the moment he hung up his deep pink wand hung down.

'For God's sake,' the Minister muttered, though the referent was not clear.

2

'Ena, Ena,' Jan whispered into Ena's neck. 'Where are you?'

Jan's warm breath brought her back from the place her mind had wandered to. She had been thinking that life seemed to be contracting, that there was less of everything. Maybe it was the onset of the ageing process. She had noticed the first signs on her body: one wrinkle, then another, the muscles in the face slackening slightly, her mouth puckering as with tart berries, the loss of the drop-of-a-hat smile. Not that it worried or upset her; no, she felt she was observing it all from within, where the other Ena remained intact. The only thing she really missed was tenderness, that touch of a hand roaming over the contours of her body for no reason, with no goal. Lately it happened less and less and lasted only as long as the chemistry of arousal. She was afraid her hunger for it would become a tribulation, and recalled what the father of her daughter had once said: You'll need a bathrobe to wrap yourself up in one day when you're cold. Her ten-year-old daughter was definitely not bathrobe material, and at thirty-six she was growing increasingly sensitive to draughts.

'Ena, where are you?' Jan whispered.

'Here,' she said softly and turned towards him.

'Ena, Ena,' Jan whispered, kissing Ena's fingers. He crawled up her arms with his warm lips, pausing at the shoulder to inhale her fragrance.

'God, you're beautiful . . . lovely . . . inviting. Ena, Ena. You're all silk, you're my lily, my waterlily, my tropical liana. I love you.'

Ena listened to Jan's melodic Czech with a smile on her face: he was the answer to her dreams, her twin. Everything was right, everything meshed perfectly. Twins recognize each other at once – in their faces, their voices, their gestures. She knew it the moment she chanced (chanced?) to sit next to him, the moment she first gazed into his eyes and tugged at his sleeve – he looked so confused, so lost – to come and sit with her.

'And what am I?' he laughed. 'Just a *knedlík*.' She laughed with him. Then, with the help of sign-language, he told her about how when the elderly woman sitting next to him in the train learned he was Czech she pointed at him and said the only Czech word she knew, '*Knedlík*.' Dumpling.

As Jan laughed, he pictured Zdenka, himself and their four girls as a family of pale-faced dumplings. But the seemingly outlandish image wasn't so outlandish after all: their relationship owed its very existence to a closely related foodstuff.

Once, when Zdenka was five and Jan was four, they 'made pies' together: Jan carefully pressed the top of a tube of toothpaste into Zdenka's bare bottom until little puffs of pink flesh popped up on it. The game continued until their parents caught them at it and gave them both good spankings. But soon Zdenka moved away to Prague and he forgot all about her.

Ena listened attentively, curled up in bed and smiling. Although she caught no more than the general drift of his Czech, she decided not to ask about individual words. Jan sat with his legs tucked under him, completely involved in the story.

They met again in the spring of '68 – he a shy provincial, a first-year student, she a Prague sophisticate and full-time teacher. It wasn't long before Zdenka asked him with charming tongue in charming cheek, 'Want to make pies?' And they did. Maybe a little birdie had told Zdenka the Russians were about to invade and Czechs were in short supply.

Jan was talking fast now, like someone given permission to speak after a long silence and afraid of having it taken from him. At first Ena strained to understand; then, overcome by the sheer force of what she soon recognized as a confession, she gave up and simply held his hand, looking on in silence as it poured out of him.

They had married immediately because Zdenka immediately got pregnant. The poet and the nursery-school teacher. He had a book of poems by then, but it was no great shakes and was published in the provinces, and if he gave the words 'nursery-school teacher' an ironic twist now, at the time he was well aware she was more self-possessed and more experienced than he. In matters of 'pie-making', for instance, he had ventured no further than the toothpaste-top stage. Be that as it may, he rushed through his studies and got a job in a publishing house. A second book followed, then a third, and soon he'd gained acceptance as a poet. Zdenka enjoyed being married to a literary man, or at least she said she did, and he enjoyed hearing her say it. But then things started happening, important things, and he began to waver. Zdenka, who had a fine nose for such things, sensed what was going on inside him, and punished him for it with a second pregnancy, and a third, and a fourth. She became more and more domestic, running an idyllic household and piling one family ritual on another: shopping, cleaning, getting ready for winter, going on outings, picking mushrooms, giving birthday parties, visiting relatives . . . She dramatized every aspect of married life, demanding his full participation in each bout of diarrhoea, each case of measles. She kept him under constant surveillance, catching every absent gaze, bringing him back in ways he had to accept. He had to accept everything she did because he had begun to feel guilty: her laws were the laws of life; his guilt was his manuscript, his novel. At first he dreamed it; he would wake up in the middle of the night regurgitating words, sentences; he would retrieve whole chapters from his memory and type them up noiselessly in his mind, filling page after imaginary page. Only then did he begin to write – by day on the sly at the office, by night in the bathroom at home – afraid of his colleagues, afraid of Zdenka, afraid of himself. He felt like a maverick who had spent years underground putting together a bomb he knew no one would use. But what could he do? The novel was his redemption, his revenge, his self-respect. Good God! People spent year after year in gaol, and he spent year after year in the maternity ward; people were out striking, and he was out buying sauerkraut; people went off to Police Headquarters never to return, and he and Zdenka and the girls went off to the countryside for Sunday walks. On the August day the Russians marched into Prague he and Zdenka were honeymooning on the Black Sea, and on the May Day the Czechs wrote anti-Soviet slogans and burned flags he was painting the fence at his in-laws' weekend cottage. In other words, Jan went on 'making pies'. His first daughter, Jana,

114

was born on 21 January 1969, the day Jan Palach set fire to himself in protest against the invasion; his last, Lucie, was born on 7 January 1977, a day of mass arrests in the wake of Charter 77. No one bothered Jan; his file was as pure as the driven snow. Who was right: Zdenka, with her well-honed sense of self-preservation, or Jan, with his constant, insidious desire for self-immolation? She had made him a model paterfamilias, and he hated her for it. It was the perfect crime. No one would ever know; no one could ever prove a thing. Perhaps she had destroyed the manuscript on purpose, knowing the harm it would do.

By this time Jan was choking on his words, shaking feverishly, half mumbling, half groaning. Ena took him in her arms and patted him as if burping a baby. Each time he tried to talk, Ena smothered the words in kisses. Jan responded gratefully and in kind. Finally, he buried his head in her lap and whispered a prayer: 'God, please bring my manuscript back! It's the labour of a lifetime!'

Ena did what she could with her body, her breath, the beat of her heart. She believed that unbelievable story of a stolen novel, a washing-machine wife, and daughters born on politically significant days.

'Where are you, Ena?' he whispered, kissing Ena's stomach.

'Here.'

Jan sat up and took Ena's hands in his. He gazed at her for a long time, kissing the tips of her fingers, pressing her hands against his cheeks. 'I wanted to kill myself,' he whispered. 'You've given me a new lease of life.'

'Is that what you wanted to kill yourself with?' she asked with a compassionate smile, pointing at the empty pill boxes on the bedside table.

After a short hesitation Jan took a cellophane envelope out of the drawer. It had a white pill in it.

'What is it?' asked Ena, turning it this way and that.

'I don't know. I found it on the floor yesterday. Someone must have shoved it under the door.'

'Do you think it's poison?'

'*Ano*,' said Jan solemnly. 'Cyanide.'

'But who would want to hurt you? And why?'

'I don't know.'

Ena gave Jan a long, hard look, then went into the bathroom.

'Well, that's that,' she said, jumping back into bed to the sound of the flushing toilet. Now his story sounds even more preposterous, she thought, gazing silently at him. There were only two possibilities: either he was crazy, which she didn't believe, or someone was playing a dirty joke on him, which seemed equally improbable.

'It's like a dream,' Jan muttered, 'like something happening to another person. What do I do now? Tell me, what do I do?'

In either case the best thing for him is to get out of here, thought Ena. 'You go home,' she said, 'that's what. But first we get dressed and report the stolen manuscript to the police.'

'*Ano*,' he nodded helplessly.

'You probably have some shopping to do before you leave. Gifts for your wife and the girls?'

'*Ano*,' he said, suddenly pale.

'It's not your wife's fault, Jan, or yours for that matter. There are times when being a coward is harder than being a hero.'

'*Ano*,' he nodded. Then, looking up at Ena with a mixture of resignation and horror, he said in a dull voice, 'Panties. That's the most important thing. The tight bikini kind.'

Again he ran his fingers over Ena's eyes, nose and mouth. He was like a blind man trying to fix their contours in his mind. Then he put his arms around her in a tender embrace. She could feel the beat of his overworked heart and pressed against him as if trying to melt into his body or surround it, defend it with her own.

3

Pipo and Marc were sprawled out in armchairs near the main entrance of the Intercontinental. It was early afternoon, and Pipo was enjoying his morning coffee. Through the glass doors they watched a group of writers filing aboard a bus parked in front of the hotel.

'It's like watching a goddamn newsreel,' said Pipo with a sarcastic sigh. Ranko Leš had just leaned down from the top step to take a plastic bag from Ilona Kovács, the Hungarian, who then coquettishly scrambled in after him.

'They're going to a meat-packing factory to sneer at the workers,' Pipo grumbled, 'because some idiot thinks it's his job to be the link between arts and industry.'

'The missing link,' Marc said placidly.

Next to board was Silvio Benussi, who for some reason kept stroking his beard, then Thomas Kiely, the Irishman, wearing round, thin-rimmed glasses and hunching round, thin shoulders like his great master James Joyce, whose photographs he had studied meticulously.

'Wouldn't it be cool if the workers beat them up?' Pipo muttered. 'Put them through the meat-grinder?'

Then came the famous novelist Mraz, whose stomach stuck out so far in front of him that the bus seemed likely to tilt when he got in. Nothing happened.

'But they won't beat them up. No, they'll be tickled pink to knock off for a few minutes while Prša passes out unsold copies of his book and they pass out gift packets of sausages and hot dogs, with a few decaying pâtés thrown in.'

Marc took a sip of orange juice and watched the clumsy Russian, Sapozhnikov, approach his comrades clutching a camera.

'I can't stand it any more!' Pipo protested, more to the lobby than to the bus and more by way of working off his hangover than anything else. 'To think we once had a Krleža! Let reality take over, and what do you get? A bunch of Mato Lovraks, that's what! A bunch of Mato Lovraks scribbling their way through just enough paper to earn a sausage a day: that's where our literature's at!'

'Who is Krleža and who's Mato Lovrak?' Marc asked, following the progress of the elderly Polish critic Małgorzata Uszko up the bus steps.

'Krleža is like . . . No, you haven't got anyone like Krleža. And Mato Lovrak is a children's writer, something like Mark Twain, only much, much worse.'

'I wouldn't mind being Mark Twain *or* Mato Lovrak,' Marc said serenely, watching two lean, stooped, dark-eyed youths get on the bus.

'Well, I'd rather be Erica Jong!'

'Why Erica Jong?' Marc asked apathetically, watching Prša, who was watching the writers get on the bus.

'So I could write about who discovered which of my erogenous zones and who I gave erections and ejaculations to, and what kinds of orgasms I had and with whose help – that sort of thing. And so I could look out from the cover of my thick, beautifully designed books in bookshop windows the world over and appraise my audience, both male and female, look out at them with my eyes half shut and my mouth half open, touching some phallic symbol or other – a pillar or a telephone receiver or a pencil stump . . .'

Now the French delegate, Jean-Paul Flagus, was mounting the steps. He was followed by his swarthy amanuensis.

'When you get down to it,' said Pipo spitefully, 'what I'd like most of all is to be rich and famous.'

Finally Prša himself climbed aboard, looking here and there with a worried face, making sure everyone was present and accounted for, no one running up at the last minute. Suddenly he waved, apparently motioning someone on, and Pipo, afraid he was waving in his direction, slouched down further into his chair and covered his face with a palm frond. But soon the toy poet came in sight. Prša pounded him on the back like a coach welcoming his star player in from the field, and after a final worried glance towards the imaginary camera hidden in the real palms near the hotel entrance he nodded to the driver and the bus set off.

'And to be loved as a writer and a person. And to be envied! I don't get any feedback. Emotional, material or otherwise. I'm nothing to them.'

'Bullshit,' said Marc calmly and stood up. 'Hey, wait for me here, will you? I'll be right back. Or even better. Go ask about the Czech. At the desk.' And off he went to the lifts.

'Why is he so hooked on that Czech?' Pipo muttered to himself. '*You* go and ask if it means so much to you.' But he picked himself up and went over to the reception desk.

'Mr Zdražil appears to have checked out,' said the man at the desk.

'Appears or has?'

'He handed in his key and left with his luggage.'

'Hm,' said Pipo.

'Hm,' said the man at the desk.

Pipo glanced in at the Diana Bar, saw the blonde Danish woman sitting at a table with Ivan Ljuština the critic, instinctively nodded at them, and then went and collapsed into his chair. He ordered another coffee, lit a cigarette, and soon he was panning the bushes on the other side of the glass. The puny bushes. Fit only for a TV screen. The whole damn place was on a pitifully small scale. You could walk through the centre of town in twenty minutes; the nearest mountain took an hour and a half to climb; you were likely to meet all the people you ever knew in the space of a morning. No glitz, no glitter, no serendipity. Any chance that chick getting out of the taxi would saunter up to Pipo and say in a Lauren Bacall alto, 'Got a match, buster?' None whatsoever. The chick went straight to the reception desk. Pipo followed her through his viewfinder, then panned back to the bushes. Inhaling, Pipo Fink observed the puny bushes . . .

Inhaling, Pip Fynke observed the glittering lights of Manhattan.

'How was it?' she asked sweetly.

'I split,' he replied, his eyes fixed on the lights. 'Can't take the crowds, if you know what I mean.'

'What about Jessica?' she asked.

119

Pip caught the edge in her voice and smiled. She didn't notice, because she was facing the other way.

'What's it to you?' he asked, still staring out at the city lights.

'Tonight she's that much more of a star, and it's all your doing.'

'Oh, I'm just another screen writer,' he said calmly.

'Why not write something for me? Something that will make people sit up and take notice?'

'Because people sit up and take notice as it is,' he said in a deep voice, as if talking to the lights.

'Come over here, darling,' she said in her most velvet, seductive tones.

Pip calmly put out his cigarette, then turned slowly to face her. Her bright eyes were shining like embers in the dark. His hungry glance moved up her slim, smooth thighs, her trim waist, her apple-shaped breasts, her long neck, her luxuriant shiny hair . . .

He walked over to her slowly, placing his lips on her elegant pink knee at the very moment Brooke Shields' silky pleading voice came out of nowhere saying, 'Do it to me, baby.'

'Well, what'd you find out about the Czech?'

Pipo stared up at Marc, annoyed that he looked so rushed and serious. He was carrying an Adidas bag.

'He's checked out. Or appears to have.'

'Shit!' Marc said through his teeth. 'Hey, let's split. What do you say?'

'Fine,' said Pipo, getting up. Marc set off at a brisk pace; Pipo followed obediently. Marc jumped into a taxi that was waiting at the entrance.

'Hey, where are we going?' Pipo shouted.

'You tell me!' said the taxi-driver.

'Anywhere but here,' said Marc.

'Then let's go to my place. You can see how I live.'

He gave the driver the address.

'You could've walked, you know,' the driver groaned.

But Pipo didn't hear him. He was busy worrying whether his mother had gone to visit his aunt or changed her mind again.

4

'Tell me,' said Inspector Popović, raising his voice slightly, 'what is your . . . relation to the gentleman?'

'None,' said Ena, blushing.

'Did you see the stolen object or witness any action that might be regarded as incriminatory?'

'No,' said Ena, embarrassed.

'Then I must ask you to wait out in the corridor.'

Blushing again, Ena the Bell-Tower did as she was told. Jan Zdražil gazed mournfully after her.

Inspector Popović took a deep breath and lit a cigarette. Good. Now they could get down to business.

'I want you to take this pen and fill in the following information: surname, given name, home address, date of birth, reason for stay in Zagreb, place of residence in Zagreb, approximate time and place of theft, possible suspects, oh, and a precise description of the stolen object. Pre-cise, understand?'

'Yes, sir!' Jan Zdražil replied briskly, encouraged by the inspector's ash-grey uniform, navy shirt and tastefully matching tie, black socks and shoes, neatly shaven face, and a pair of glasses that betokened a certain intelligence. Everything did in fact go smoothly. Until he came to the pre-cise description of the stolen object, that is.

The problem was, he wasn't sure how best to summarize the plot, yet he felt a plot summary essential to his deposition. After all, Zagreb could be full of greenish folders containing six hundred typewritten pages bound with white ribbons. But how to condense six hundred pages into a few lines? 'The novel takes place in a Prague publishing house,' he wrote – and got bogged down. Then he decided even that was unsatisfactory and crossed it out. How could he explain that the point of the novel was to give an accurate picture of the process whereby a masterpiece was ruined, maimed, with the assistance of a small, perfidious and terrified band of politicians, editors, reviewers, critics, bureaucrats, typesetters . . . He himself was one of them; he knew how it worked from the inside. He'd begun as a copy editor, correcting spelling errors; then he was told to eliminate that once innocent but in the post-invasion context now loaded word *temporary*; soon he was blue-pencilling whole passages, sniffing out sedition like a well-trained hound, digging behind words, breaking up sentences, and finally, as a full-fledged editor, altering endings and characters, cutting episodes and chapters. He didn't need to go so far, but he was drunk with power and started taking the initiative. The more vicious he grew the more guilty he felt, and the more guilty he felt the more vicious he grew. He would wake up with nightmares of a gigantic, savage pencil deleting, deleting, deleting. The thing that had finally brought him to his senses – and this was something he couldn't tell Ena – was that a writer he was jealous of and whose novel he'd purposely mangled had gone and hanged himself. He had killed a man. That was when he decided to write his own novel. The novel would be his pillory and therefore his redemption. And now all possibility of redemption was gone. He would kill himself, all right; he would find a way. He couldn't go back, couldn't go back to the duplicity of it all; he couldn't stand it any longer.

His heart was pounding; he was in a cold sweat; he felt himself sinking into the slough of despond. He looked up at the inspector, who was staring into a drawer of his desk – reading, Jan thought. And suddenly he realized, realized for the first time how selfish he'd been: he'd written the novel for himself and for himself alone. Its only purpose was to cleanse his hangman's hands. He had never thought of the harm it might do to Zdenka or the girls. Perhaps fate had intervened.

Jan pushed the form over to the inspector.

'Finished?' the inspector asked, looking up and shutting the drawer. 'Good. Sign here . . . Right . . . This is your copy. We'll let you know as soon as we find it, OK?'

'OK,' said Jan Zdražil half under his breath.

'Did anybody here know about your novel? Besides you, I mean.'

'Yes . . . I mean, no,' Jan mumbled.

'I see,' said the inspector, standing and holding out his hand. 'Well, goodbye.'

'Goodbye,' said Jan and turned to leave.

'Before you go,' Inspector Popović called out to Jan Zdražil, 'tell me, what's the title of your novel?'

'*The Story of My Life*,' Jan said placidly.

'Oh,' said Inspector Popović and suddenly broke out into a long, hearty laugh.

Jan Zdražil followed suit, and was soon wiping tears away with his sleeve.

5

The head of the Sausage Division was on hand to greet the writers in front of the factory. On their way to the main shop he said a few introductory words about the varieties and quantities of products his division turned out, but he made it clear he had no intention of boring them or squelching whatever poetic inspiration they might derive from the visit by flooding them with facts and figures. The writers were relieved, especially the locals, who had been subjected to many such visits and knew what to expect.

As they entered the shop, the workers burst into applause and gathered round them. The division head explained to the workers that the visitors were writers and, the pen being mightier than the sword, very important people. He told them how proud he was that their factory and their division had been chosen for this great honour; he said that he was certain they too were thrilled to meet live writers, because workers loved good books as much as anybody; he was especially glad to welcome the Minister, who had done so much to bring culture to the masses, and in particular to the workers, and to promote amateur groups of all kinds, and he knew the Minister would be happy to hear that the Sausage Division had its own folklore group and its own amateur theatre and that one of the workers was also a well-known naive painter . . .

Several times during the division head's speech Prša leaned over unobtrusively and whispered, 'Good, Jura, enough . . .', and finally Jura asked the Minister to say a few words. The Minister said he was especially glad to be here with the workers, the revolutionary bedrock of our society, because he himself had started off as a worker. He was also glad to have the opportunity to tell them about a new book by Comrade Prša, a writer who for years had written with the working class in mind, that is, had done everything to make his works accessible to men and women like them and had now reached the pinnacle of a career devoted to bringing together the arts and industry with a novel entitled *The Golden Finger*. The Minister then pointed to several packages the bus driver had lugged in after the writers and said that they contained fifty copies of *The Golden Finger* autographed by the author and that he hoped they would find their way to the factory library or, if the factory had no library, that they would serve as a basis for inaugurating one.

Next Prša himself came forward to announce that in consideration of our foreign guests who do not speak our language he would forgo reading excerpts from the novel and recite a few short poems instead. He also asked the workers to give a special round of applause for the distinguished foreign delegation, which included a descendant of the famous French novelist Gustave Flaubert. The workers applauded. Then Prša recited his poems. He recited them in a strong, staccato voice as if setting the tempo for a march or making a point in an argument. The poems abounded in one-syllable words like *blood*, *knife*, *dust*, *bone*, *fear*, *fist*, *bile*, *war* and *wolf*. Ilona Kovács, the Hungarian, who had lost all the colour in her face the moment they entered the shop, perceived the words (which she could not understand) as porcupine quills the poet was trying to spit out. Prša himself contributed to the effect by the anguished look in his eyes and twists of his mouth. At one point Ilona Kovács seemed about to go limp in Ranko Leš's arms, but someone ran up with a glass of water just in time.

The workers duly clapped when Prša finished his poems. (One of the workers was particularly taken with the line *My eye-tooth gleams in the dark with blood lust*, and spent the rest of the afternoon shift scaring the daylights out of any woman in sight by creeping up on her and reciting it.) Then the packages of his novel were opened and everyone could see how beautifully designed it was.

At that point the Minister went off with a man in a white smock to look over the operation, and the writers and workers were left to fraternize. Of all the writers, the workers liked the elderly Pole, Małgorzata Uszko, best. She was the only one who went up to them and tried to get a conversation going; she gave buttons and pins to some, shook hands with others. The writers couldn't understand this strange behaviour in a woman who was otherwise nondescript in every way. After a while, however, Mraz the novelist also began making overtures to the workers, asking about the products they made, and when they pressed a sampling of their wares on him he did not refuse. Ilona Kovács, as white as a sheet by now, was leaning her full weight against Ranko Leš. Leš gallantly offered her his handkerchief, which she gratefully accepted and waved in front of her nose.

Just as the visit seemed to be coming to an end, Jean-Paul Flagus asked if he could be allowed a few words. Luckily the English interpreter, a pretty young student who had volunteered to accompany Thomas Kiely, turned out to have some French as well. Monsieur Flagus began by thanking the workers, on behalf of the foreign writers, for their kind welcome, went on to say what a deep impression the visit had made on him, and then launched into a subtle exposition of why he considered writers and workers brothers. The interpreter didn't quite catch it all, so what came out was that writers produce spiritual food and workers meat. Monsieur Flagus then pointed out that the Germans, who are known for the love they bring to their culture, manufactured a car at the turn of the century called the Goethemobile in honour of their great poet Goethe. Then there are the famous Schillerlocken, that is, fish fillets, which the Germans, again delving deep into their cultural heritage, named after their immortal poet Schiller. As for the Austrians, they are known the world over for their delicious chocolate Mozart-Kugeln or Mozart balls, named after their famous composer Mozart, and we French have our Chateaubriand, that fine cut of steak, which we, as a nation proud of its literary tradition, named after our fine poet and novelist Chateaubriand. Then Monsieur Flagus took the liberty of proposing that the meat packers should follow suit and name one of their products after a famous writer, and given today's opportunity he saw no reason why this – and here he picked up a sausage – fine specimen of a sausage shouldn't be named . . . Prša.

The proposal met with stunned silence. Prša himself reacted with raised eyebrows followed by a noncommittal frown: he wasn't sure whether to interpret it as an insult or a compliment.

All at once the division head, Jura, stepped forward and, after telling the interpreter to be sure and give an accurate translation of the point he was about to make, said that they were members of a society which prided itself on self-management, where no decision came down from above, where every proposal had to be sent before a workers' council and considered collectively.

Then a worker said that although they had never been asked to name products before, she saw no reason why they shouldn't. The names the products now had were stupid, and they, the workers, could certainly do better. She didn't particularly care whether the sausage in question was named after a classical writer or the comrade here who'd just read them his poems, but she thought it was a good idea in general.

'Right! Good for you, Ankica!' the workers shouted.

The division head nodded and scribbled something on his pad.

There followed a lively discussion over which classical writers might be paired with which sausages, but someone always had an objection based on national and other such delicate considerations.

Finally one worker broke the deadlock by suggesting that the very mild frankfurter for children and diabetics they had just started producing be named after the international children's classic *Winnie the Pooh*. But someone immediately objected to the 'pooh' part, and someone else pointed out that Winnie wasn't the name of an author.

At that point the worker who had been cheered earlier as 'Good for you, Ankica' spoke up again and proposed that the new frankfurter for children and diabetics be named after the *title* of the book they had just received as a gift: *The Golden Wurst*.

'But the book is called *The Golden Finger*!' a few voices called out.

'I can read!' said Ankica. 'But you can't call a frank a finger!'

They all agreed that Golden Wurst was an excellent name for the new frankfurter.

Meanwhile, there had been some stirrings among the writers as well. Leš whispered that he could just see the headline of the review in tomorrow's paper: PRŠA'S GOLDEN WURSTS. Although Mraz the novelist looked upon the whole business as a farce, he was upset that the only author put up for a sausage was Prša, and hid his annoyance by gobbling up one sample after another. Prša himself kept raising his eyebrows and frowning noncommittally, as if he were an innocent bystander, but in the end he went over to Jura, the division head, and whispered something in his ear. Jura then asked the guests to pick up the gift packets that had been prepared for them, and the writers, having done so, filed out slowly. Again Małgorzata Uszko was the most active among them, shaking hands with practically the whole afternoon shift before leaving.

The bus trip back to the hotel was exceptionally lively. The local writers crowded together in the back seats, having a good laugh at what had gone on at the factory.

'Think of taking a long, sharp knife and lopping off an end of *Crime and Punishment* bloodwurst.'

'Or reading an article in the paper about Zagreb hospitals reporting over forty cases of Krleža poisoning!'

Thomas Kiely, the Irishman, was asked by his new interpreter friend whether he'd enjoyed the visit.

'I . . . I don't know, really,' he replied. 'You see, I'm a vegetarian.'

While Silvio Benussi dozed, his neighbour, Victor Sapozhnikov, quietly inspected the contents of the gift packet.

Mraz the novelist sat next to the elderly Polish critic Małgorzata Uszko, who was blithely looking out of the window, trying not to notice Mraz's highly noticeable hiccups.

'Excuse me,' he said after a long while.

'*Nie szkodzi*,' she said politely and turned back to the window.

Ilona Kovács, as pale as ever, sat next to the poet Ranko Leš with her head resting on his shoulder.

'Never in my life have I seen so much meat,' she said in a frail voice.

'It was all so socialist realist,' said Leš. 'At least that's how the foreigners will see it.' He had obviously stopped thinking of Ilona Kovács as a foreigner. 'There should have been more performance, more theatricality, if you know what I mean. More outrage, more blood.'

'Right,' said the toy poet, trying to stick his head between them from the seat behind. 'More blood.'

'By the way,' said Leš over his shoulder to the toy poet, 'now I know what Prša's ready-made poetry has always reminded me of!'

'What?' asked the toy poet.

'Instant hash!'

Prša and the Minister sat together in the front.

'Catastrophic!' Prša whispered to the Minister. 'An utter fiasco!

Sabotage – that's what it was! You should have heard him go on, that Frenchman. How can I look anybody in the eye after this?'

'Look, if Mozart can take it, so can you.'

'But those are nice little chocolate balls, not wursts, not wienies.'

'Wienies, balls – what's the difference?' said the Minister.

'It's all Ljuština's fault really. If he'd come and said a few words about my novel the way he promised, things would have got off on the right foot.' Prša looked up at the Minister for approval, but the Minister's eyes were shut. He appeared to have dozed off.

Ljuština! Of course! Prša now had someone to vent his fury on. Whatever had possessed him to ask Ljuština to talk about the book? He had a monopoly on criticism as it was, the traitor. A right-wing, petit-bourgeois type if ever there was one. He'd seen him polish off a twelve-pound lobster (that somebody else paid for)! He was a clever one. Wrote reviews like machine-gun fire, but used his wife as a cover (her father was a Party bigwig), and to play it even safer he stuck to first novels, oh, and women. True, Prša himself wasn't too happy about women messing around in literature, but even he considered Ljuština's stance a cop-out. Besides, Ljuština hated workers almost as much as women: you wouldn't catch him touring a factory; no, might get some grease on his Burberry. He should have known! And suddenly it dawned on him: Ljuština was a perfect candidate for his file!

He swung his head round, afraid he'd blurted out the word, but Monsieur Flagus, who was sitting a few seats behind him, merely gave him a polite nod (to which he was obliged to respond), and further back the local riff-raff, totally oblivious to him, were having a grand old time (he could imagine at whose expense). He turned round again and stared straight ahead.

For some time now Prša had been haunted by thoughts of the obituaries he would write if certain of his fellow literati were to up and die. At first he tried swatting the thoughts like flies, but they kept coming back, even growing in intensity. He'd be sitting at a meeting or in a café with a colleague's smiling countenance before him and all he could think of was the man's obituary. One day he finally admitted the thrill it gave him – and started a file. At first he marked it only with a big O in the upper right-hand corner, but when Nada left him and moved back to her parents with the kids, he heaved a sigh of relief and added *BITUARIES*. It was his secret, his solitary voice. Everybody's got some weak point, some flaw, he reasoned: some people pick their noses, for instance. So now every time a colleague insulted him, intentionally or not, he automatically started a new page in his head (surname, given name, and so on) and could hardly wait to race home and open the file. He used the obituaries to exorcize the hatred constantly building up in him.

Prša's existence was fuelled by hatred. He saw himself surrounded by enemies, the lone champion of freedom, fatherland and mother tongue. The Writers Association had about three hundred registered members, and Prša's file had reached the hundred and fifty mark. Since he'd started it, a number of its denizens had in fact died, and there was Prša, ready and waiting. In time newspapers automatically called on him for 'lit obits'. No one saw anything out of the ordinary in it; on the contrary, it was interpreted as concern for his fellow man. Which in a sense it was.

Prša continually updated the file. Some entries were simply personal reminders (*Lent M.M. fifty thousand*), others were more political in nature (*leftist, chauvinist, liberal, nationalist, Stalinist, clericalist, Russophile, apolitical, shows Fascist leanings, supported the Cominform, shows anarchist leanings, Americanophile*, etc.); recently he had taken to summarizing each person's character in a single word (such as *blabbermouth, pushover, money-grubber, skinflint, glutton, sex-fiend, hypocrite, mud-slinger, back-biter, megalomaniac, egocentric, milk-sop, toady, tippler*) and was working at boiling it down even further to his favourite one-syllable mode (*rat, jerk, scum, beast, louse, twit, wimp*, etc.). When he had nothing better to do, he would plot his subject's political and personal axes on graph paper, hoping to establish regular correlations. Not that he set great store by the results, but it was curious that, say, Russophiles tended to be gluttons and rats, chauvinists sex-fiends and scum, liberals skinflints and twits . . .

And now it was Ljuština's turn, he thought as the bus pulled up in front of the Intercontinental. He could hardly wait.

But the moment the writers set foot in the lobby, word began to spread that Ivan Ljuština, the literary critic, had been lured into one of the foreigners' rooms to be seduced – no, raped – by a group of unidentified persons and that as a result of injuries sustained during the attack he had been whisked off to the nearest hospital. And in fact, Franka, the elegant private secretary, immediately ran up to Prša and whispered something in his ear.

'No!' a pale Prša exclaimed, his mouth falling open. He was overcome by a strange combination of fear and power: someone had turned his rancour into reality. 'I'd better give this some thought,' he said to himself with a shiver. But first he raised his eyebrows and headed for a phone.

6

'Bastard!' Dunja hissed through her teeth, glaring at Ljuština with her hands on her hips and her legs spread wide. The literary critic lay naked and spread-eagled on the bed, his arms and legs firmly bound to the bedposts with sheets. A fifth sheet served as a gag.

'Dirty bastard!' She turned to Cecilia and Tanja, who were looking on, and said, 'See him? See the bastard?'

The critic's eyes flashed as he tried to kick free, but all that came of his pains was a series of savage grunts.

'Hear him? Wants to tell us something. Want to tell us something, bastard? Well, go ahead! We're waiting! Get it off your chest, you bastard!'

'Bastard this, bastard that!' Tanja interrupted. 'Can't you come up with anything more original?'

'Any suggestions?' Dunja cried, furious. 'And by the way, you're not much help just sitting there.' She switched into English for Cecilia's sake. 'What do I do now? Spit on him? What's left if you can't even rape him like a normal person?'

At the word 'rape' the critic's exposed pendant retreated even further into its little fleshy sack.

'Bastard!' she spat, and then sat down herself and lit up a cigarette.

'Look, let's get down to business,' said their Danish cohort. 'We haven't got all day. Are we going to rape him or aren't we?'

'He won't let us!' Dunja howled. 'Besides, the thought of touching that . . . that . . . water buffalo makes my stomach turn!'

'You seem to forget why we're here,' Tanja remarked calmly. 'The abomination in question has for the last few years systematically discredited our activity as writers.'

'Right on!' shouted Dunja, and Cecilia nodded in solidarity.

'Did he not speak of our works as kitchen literature? Did he not

132

write that "given the gossip-based nature of the female imagination, a biological category that cannot be overcome", a woman can never be a novelist?'

'He did!' Dunja roared. 'You did, didn't you, you bastard!'

'And did not the selfsame individual,' Tanja went on mercilessly, 'did not the selfsame individual state that gossip is woman's basic relationship to the universe and that women's writing represents "the lava of babble as it issues from kitchens the world over"?'

'See, Cecilia? You're included!'

'Then I say we should torture him accordingly!' Tanja concluded.

'Accordingly?' asked Dunja and Cecilia, looking puzzled.

'Accordingly,' Tanja replied calmly. 'With kitchen utensils!'

'Yes, yes!' cried Dunja vindictively. 'Let the bastard stew in his own juice!'

'But here in the hotel . . .' Cecilia began.

'Tanja's place is two minutes away.'

'Even so,' said Cecilia, twisting a curl between her fingers, 'I can't quite picture . . .'

'Picture a meat-grinder,' said Tanja, looking her in the eye.

'Yes, a meat-grinder!' cried Dunja, clapping her hands and throwing the critic a nasty look. He'd started grunting again. 'Or an electric knife – if you're up for castration.'

At the word 'castration' the critic let out a mighty roar, and giant beads of sweat sprang up on his forehead.

'I object,' Cecilia said. 'They could throw us in gaol.'

'Then how about running a grater over him and pouring on the pepper?' said Dunja. 'Or giving him a corkscrew tattoo.'

'No,' Cecilia objected again in no uncertain terms. 'We need something quick and easy.'

The women sank into thought.

The man held his breath.

'I know,' said Tanja, breaking the silence at last. 'I'll be back in five minutes.' And with that she left the room.

'Want something to drink?' Cecilia asked on her way to the refrigerator.

'Sure.'

Dunja stood up, stretched, went over to the critic, and gave his nose a good strong tweak. 'What an animal,' she said. 'Sweating, snorting, rolling his eyes . . .'

'Here you are,' said Cecilia, handing her a glass. 'Don't give any to him,' she added, motioning in the critic's direction.

'That bastard?' she snorted. 'Not on your life.'

Soon Tanja reappeared carrying a plastic bag. Dunja and Cecilia looked at it, disappointed. Tanja took out two jars and placed them on the table with a meaningful look in her eye. The labels said 'MUCILAGE'.

'Glue?' said Dunja. 'Are we going into the carpentry business?'

'Cecilia was right,' said Tanja as she prised open the jars. 'We need something quick and easy. And shame is far worse than the worst pain we might inflict on him.' She took a balloon out of the bag and tossed it over to Dunja. 'Blow this up, will you? Meanwhile, the two of us will prepare the abomination for the procedure.'

She handed Cecilia one of the jars and picked up the other herself. The two of them then poured the sticky contents over the naked critic, who looked on horrified and helpless.

'This . . .' Tanja said, wrapping the critic's pendant in a handkerchief, 'we shall leave untouched for the moment.'

At that moment the naked critic lost consciousness.

'Look, he's fainted,' said Cecilia, a bit concerned.

'He'll come out of it, the abomination,' said Tanja calmly, setting aside her empty glue pot and taking a penknife out of her bag. Then, knife in hand, she held a pillow over the sleeping critic's body and made a series of neat slits. Out gushed streams of tiny, white feathers. She continued until all the pillows were empty and the critic's body was completely coated.

'Abomination's the word,' said Dunja, sputtering with laughter. 'The abominable snowman!'

'Hm,' said Tanja, looking over the critic's feathered body. Then she took a piece of string out of the bag, tied the inflated balloon to one end and held the other out to Cecilia and Dunja. 'Volunteer?'

'I don't mind,' said Cecilia, and tied the other end to the critic's fleshy sack. Just as she was finishing, the critic opened his eyes and yelped in pain.

'Now blow!' Dunja squealed joyfully. And all three blew as hard as their guffaws would allow.

134

Up went the balloon, up went the string, and out from the feathers peeked the critic's pendant. The women clapped; the critic blushed. Then he lowered his eyes and moaned again in pain.

'Mission accomplished!' Tanja declared, brushing excess feathers from her dress.

'I'll meet you down in the bar,' said Cecilia. 'I just need to phone the reception desk and report that my room's been broken into.'

'Super!' said Dunja. 'Maybe I can rustle up a photographer. There've been a few reporters around covering the Colloquium.' And she and Tanja left, all titters.

Cecilia stood immobile for a moment, then walked over to the phone and lifted the receiver. Then she put it down again and sank into a chair. The room was oddly still. She put her feet up on the other chair, lit a cigarette, and glanced over at the feathered object and its satellite balloon. Then she rose and undid her skirt, letting it slip to the floor. Then she went up to the bed and popped the balloon with her cigarette. A pair of terrified eyes followed her every move. Then she snuffed out the cigarette and languidly unbuttoned her blouse. Slowly, hesitantly, a fat red pistil rose up out of a bed of soft white feathers.

7

Thomas Kiely, Ilona Kovács, Ranko Leš, Silvio Benussi, the toy poet and Jean-Paul Flagus had squeezed around a table in the Diana Bar to discuss the as yet undocumented rape of the critic Ivan Ljuština.

'It's balderdash,' said the Italian Silvio Benussi, 'sheer gossip. I'm beginning to wonder whether someone isn't purposely spicing up the programme with scandals: first Espeso, then Zdražil, and now this Ljuština fellow. Though technically speaking, a man can't be raped . . . Not by a woman, at least.'

'Didn't some Finnish woman write a novel on the subject?' asked Thomas Kiely.

'Märta Tikkanen,' said Ilona Kovács. 'I saw the film version. I've heard there were plenty of men raped in the camps in Siberia. In fact, every time a man happened into the women's barracks . . .'

'Tell us about it!' said Ranko Leš, cocking his beak at her. 'It's got potential.'

'No, no, I couldn't,' she giggled. 'All I can say is it's a matter of technique.'

'I am reminded of the Greek poet Sotades,' said Monsieur Flagus calmly, 'who was bound, placed in a barrel, and hurled into the sea, and all for an objectionable satire.' He lit a cigar, blew a smoke ring and surveyed the assembled company with his watery glance. 'Or, if you find it more to your liking, take the Arabic poet Tarafa, who was burned alive for a couplet criticizing the king.'

The writers found neither one nor the other particularly to their liking: both Sotades and Tarafa were too far removed to arouse their compassion.

'The English are past masters at that sort of thing,' said the Irishman, coming to life. 'Early in the seventeenth century a poor printer who dared publish a book by Robert Parsons was first hanged, then disembowelled and quartered. A certain Alexander Leighton was put in chains, then tossed into a rat-filled pit, then whipped and – after his ears and nose had been chopped off – branded. The same thing happened to William Pryne, whose plays the king found distasteful, though he was branded first and only then deprived of his ears and nose . . .'

'*Jaj istenem!* Please! You're making me sick!' cried Ilona Kovács.

'Well, the Italians are no better!' Silvio Benussi inserted, taking advantage of the Irishman's annoyance at being cut off. 'Lodovico Castelvetro, as I'm sure you all know, killed a man for defending the poetry of Annibale Caro. And Nero – well, I'd best not go into that . . .'

'Gorky was poisoned!' the toy poet piped up, true to his Gorkimania.

'Oh, the Russians!' cried Ilona Kovács. 'The Russians are the worst, the lowest of the low.'

'Have you ever stopped to think how many writers have been in prison?' said Ranko Leš. 'Wilde, Cervantes, Diderot, Villon, de Sade, Genet. Wilhelm Reich was sentenced to two years in a Federal penitentiary – and died there. That was in 1956, almost yesterday!'

'Plenty of heads have rolled in France as well,' the Irishman said to the Frenchman.

'Right you are,' said Monsieur Flagus with a smile. 'One can't even begin to count them. Taken in the proper historical perspective, then, the modest if piquant punishment our Zagreb colleague received – assuming, of course, it was the result of his critical activities – deserves a certain recognition.' He raised his glass and said, 'I give you today's victim!' and, after a long draught, added, 'There's not a writer worth his salt who has no enemies, mind you. I daresay each of you can recall wanting to take a critic and/or colleague and . . .'

'Bite his ear off!' shouted Ilona Kovács, clearly with someone specific in mind.

'Step on his toe!' the toy poet ventured.

'Impale him on a spike and roast him over a slow flame!' said Ranko Leš, true to his Balkan origins.

'Cut off his head with a carving knife!' said Silvio Benussi, true to Mother Goose.

'Brand, hang and quarter him!' said Thomas Kiely, true to his own account.

'There, you see?' said Monsieur Flagus with a smile.

Just then Prša came into the bar. When he saw the writers, he waved and smiled. 'It's all a hoax,' he called out on his way to their table, 'a piece of cheap gossip! He's at home with a migraine. I've just spoken to him on the phone.'

Everyone looked extremely disappointed. The toy poet leaned over to Leš and whispered, 'I remember reading somewhere that Euripides was torn to bits by a band of women. Is that true? Or is it just another piece of cheap gossip?'

As if in direct response, Jean-Paul Flagus started reciting with his inimitably discreet charm:

> . . . *the whole horde*
> *of Bacchae swarmed upon him. Shouts everywhere,*
> *he screaming with what little breath was left,*
> *they shrieking in triumph. One tore off his arm,*
> *another a foot still warm in its shoe. His ribs*
> *were clawed clean of flesh and every hand*
> *was smeared with blood as they played ball with scraps*
> *of Pentheus' body.*

8

Jan Zdražil stood leaning against the window of the Budapest train.
Next to him on the seat lay his Aeroflot bag, six hundred pages
lighter than when he had come, though now boasting two pairs of
yellow panties with the word 'Thursday' emblazoned across the
front (the only ones Ena and he could find on such short notice). He
looked down at Ena, who was standing on the platform, looking
for all the world like a rangy, disconsolate bird. Although he'd
found and lost her in the space of a day, he had the feeling he'd
loved her all his life. Things had unfolded and refolded so fast that
Jan couldn't yet tell whether he should be happy or disconsolate.

The train set off. Ena lifted her bag to her breast and hugged it
with both arms. One of the bag's inner pockets hid a white tablet
wrapped in cellophane. Was it real or was it not? She would find out
some day. When she was freezing.

9

Vanda had all sorts of erotic aces up her sleeve. Her favourite was a game called 'Imagination'. At least that was what *she* called it. She liked it because it gave her a chance to cultivate her artistic tendencies, use fine words. It wasn't the Minister's favourite: the Minister liked his language (and his sex) as straightforward as possible.

The game, like all perversions, was born of satiety. Vanda would lean her head on the Minister's shoulder, half-close her eyes, and, languidly playing with his ear, whisper, 'Imagine this, baby . . .' Whereupon she would purr out bawdy little stories she made up as she went along.

Once upon a time a Minister was lying stark naked on his bed when suddenly he heard a tap, tap, tap on the door. Who is it? the Minister called out, and before he knew what was happening, in came two jet-black Black women, and they were stark naked too. Well, the Minister didn't blink, didn't say, How do?, didn't even enquire about the elections in Nigeria; he just asked, Can I get you something to drink?, and they answered, Fine, and as soon as they'd finished drinking she moved straight to the essence of the story, that is, the bawdy bits.

But Vanda's knack for bawdy was inversely proportional to the Minister's reaction. His first line of defence was invariably logic: What made her think he would leave the door open? Where did the Black women come from? How could they walk through the streets without any clothes on?

'Don't try to make sense of it, baby!' Vanda would explode. 'Lie back and enjoy it, OK? Use your imagination.'

Vanda would then pack the Minister's bed with a bouquet of black, yellow and white beauties. But for all their differences they always drank champagne.

'Can't they drink something else for a change, baby?' the Minister protested.

'Now you've ruined everything!' Vanda would explode. 'You haven't got a speck of imagination!'

She was right. He was constitutionally unable to fantasize. And she not to.

Once Vanda spun a particularly smooth yarn about a gorgeous skater (she must have just been watching a figure-skating competition on TV) who had glided straight into his bed (direct from the rink, all cool and fresh like a bottle of beer from the fridge), where they did double axels and other such stunts all night. And even then the Minister asked, Who is it? and Can I get you something to drink?

The strange thing was that whenever she dangled her verbal fish-hook in and around his ear, his sting ray refused to bite; if anything, the lure's bright colours put it to sleep.

Then there were the times Vanda demanded verbal reciprocity. The Minister knew no worse agony.

'So there you are, baby, lying in bed . . .'

'In my clothes?'

'No, baby, naked as the day you were born.'

'OK. What then, baby?'

'Well, you're lying in bed and tap, tap, tap – somebody knocks on the door. Who is it? you call out, and in come these two big, husky guys.'

'Naked?'

'What do you think? So you ask them, Who are you? And they say, We're the plumbers, lady. And you say, Can I get you something to drink? And they say, Got any champagne?'

By this point the story was far enough along for him to drop unobtrusively out of the picture. Though God only knew what she would come up with when she gave her imagination free rein.

Eventually she'd realize the Minister had tricked her. 'You're terrible, you know that, baby? All you care about is politics!'

But the Minister was always forgiven the moment his snail started crawling out of its house.

'You've been fooling me all along, I bet. You've been hard from the very start, haven't you, baby?'

Now he was standing at her door with a plastic bag full of meat products (Prša had forced it on him) and, even better, an ace of his own up his sleeve, a spanking new piece of gossip: Ivan Ljuština, the critic, had been raped by a group of women writers! The Minister didn't ring the bell; he went tap, tap, tap.

10

Sabina's climax was so light and airy that she might as well have been asleep. He pictured it as a bubble first lodged in the warm dark cavity of her nether regions, then gliding slowly along the smooth, mother-of-pearl walls and finally bursting open.

He thought of Vika, his second wife, whose idea of an embrace was like his of a half-Nelson: he could never be sure he'd get out of it alive. Vika. When he'd first proposed divorce, she spat in his face (once an actress always an actress) and said with all the pathos she could muster, I'll never fall in love again. But she had. Many times over. Her love-life was like a relay race, except she never passed on the baton. She would run as fast as her ample legs would carry her, picking herself up each time she dropped from exhaustion, pushing on – anything to maintain the illusion of youth. The last time he'd gone to see her, he was greeted by the Olympics bear-cub mascot grinning out from a plastic bag on her head. Kefir and egg-yolk, she said as she let him in. Nothing like it for the hair. Then, with no transition, genuinely desperate: I'll never fall in love again. Yet it was always the same. The kitchen table told all: an empty bottle of champagne and a half-empty box of chocolates, the sad detritus of a night of love. Strange to say, he loved her more at that moment than he had ever loved her before.

Sabina lay next to him breathing peacefully. Sabina . . . Sabina came from another world. Another planet. When he'd slipped out of her room the night before, he was certain that the set piece of their hotel affair had come to a close; even worse, he suspected she'd taken him on a whim or by mistake or as a stand-in for someone left behind in Moscow. In the morning they either would or would not nod at breakfast, would or would not bring up the interview, and that would be that. But in the morning she had knocked on his door

143

and *taken* him again in her cool, distant way, as if it were the most natural thing in the world.

Sabina was the last gift life had left for him and a gift he did not deserve. He had never had so young and beautiful a woman. So, yes, natural, so physically . . . well, precise. Every movement she made, every touch enhanced his desire. He derived great pleasure out of merely watching her. The way she ate, for one thing: slowly, painstakingly, with an almost feline fastidiousness. The way she drank: licking the rim of the glass with her tiny pink tongue, as if testing the contents, and only then proceeding to the daintiest of sips. He got great pleasure out of watching her move, walk over to the window, pull open the curtains, glide into the bathroom, take a shower, rub her wet hair; watching her smoke, position the cigarette between her thumb and index finger, raise it deliberately to her lips . . . Nothing else mattered any more, he didn't care where he was or what was going on around him, because he knew she would soon disappear and he needed to gather all his newly awakened sensations and concentrate them on his precious Sabina.

'Troshin,' she said with her soft German *sh*.

'What is it, Sabina?'

'Would you like to go to Vienna?'

'I . . . don't understand. I . . .'

'I have a passport for you.'

'A passport? For me?'

'It belongs to a friend of mine.'

'You must be crazy!'

'Hans, my friend, came into the country with me, but he's gone off to Bled for two weeks.'

'What's that got to do with me?'

'I took his passport with me because I thought you might need it.'

'I still don't understand.'

'I've taken care of everything: passport, train ticket. Here's my address in Vienna. I'll be leaving soon. Think it over.'

'But I can't possibly . . .'

'If you decide against it, just send the passport to Hans at his hotel in Bled.'

'Are you out of your mind? What kind of novels have you been

144

reading?' He could feel himself trembling. Where was the hitch in it all? Where was the flaw? He lit a cigarette and stared at Sabina's placid profile. She was absolutely immobile. A fine light seemed to be inching along her forehead, her nose, her mouth, her chin. Intentionally or not, Sabina had pushed a dangerous button. 'But why me? Why me?'

'I like you.'

'No lies, please. Just tell me. Why me?'

'But I *have* told you.'

'I don't believe you.'

'I want to give you a chance, Troshin. The only problem is, you need to make up your mind in a hurry.'

'Tell me, what kind of life do you see me living in the West?'

'We'll work out something.'

'God, why do you keep lying to me? Tell me the truth!'

'There is no truth! Leave me alone, will you.'

Troshin looked Sabina straight in the eye. A sphinx. A sealed book. He felt a combination of fury and panic rising in him, and before he knew it he had slapped her.

She looked back at him with her pale-grey, expressionless eyes and said with scathing equanimity, 'You are just . . . a Russian.'

'And you . . .' – he felt completely helpless – 'you . . .' – he rasped in a voice not his own – 'you are a bitch!'

'Well, that makes us a lot closer, don't you think?' Sabina said calmly, and pressing against him she ran her soft, childlike lips over his skin. Troshin thought he saw moist traces of mother-of-pearl glittering in the semi-darkness as Sabina's tongue, like a divine snail, slid tenderly along his body.

11

Pipo was all wound up, off and running. He was seated at the kitchen table, waving his hands in the air, choking on words, spitting them out like sunflower shells, while Marc rummaged through the cabinets, opened and closed the refrigerator, took out food and banged dishes together.

'Look at *our* faces and look at *yours*! The difference is staggering!'

'I don't see any difference,' said Marc, pouring water into a pot.

'What do you mean you don't see any difference? Look at these jaws.' He pointed to his own. 'See? See how tense they are?'

'I guess so,' said Marc calmly. 'Look, could you show me how to turn on the stove?'

Pipo stood up, turned on the stove absent-mindedly, and went back to the table.

'Well, now you see what I mean. *You* have open faces. Like open cans! And those mouths! Those American mouths!'

'American mouths?'

'You mean you don't see? You don't see how yours goes up at the end and turns outwards, while mine – look! – down and in, all tense . . . By now it's in the genes even!'

'Mouths?'

Pipo looked over at Marc, the picture of contentment, dropping a fistful of spaghetti into boiling water. 'You don't understand a thing, you know that? You know what makes me different? It's that I'm stuffed with history, the Balkans, folk dances, Europe, suffering, envy . . . I'm a walking spasm, man! A gunny sack of nerves!'

'I don't see what you're getting at,' said Marc, skilfully dicing onions and parsley on the cutting-board.

So Pipo did his best to explain to Marc why he was a walking spasm, a gunny sack of nerves, and Marc did his best to understand.

First Pipo went on about his 'ideological kindergarten' and the relationship between east and west and between north and south; about his first chewing gum and Mickey Mouse and Rip Kirby, his first banana and Radio Luxembourg; about living in a country that still had blood feuds and where practically nobody had heard of Niels Bohr but everybody knew Calvin Klein, where the natives had gone overnight from bow and arrow to trains and cars, from village to megalopolis, a country that had the highest infant mortality rate in Europe – and would have the highest rape rate if anyone bothered to keep count; about the prize he had won at school for a composition entitled 'A Ray of Freedom Pierced the Dark and Stormy Clouds' and about the novel *And Quiet Flows the Don* ('Tolstoy?' 'No, Sholokhov'); about Ben Bella, whose prison sentence had stood him in good stead for another composition, and the Vietnam War, which he had demonstrated against and then enjoyed in *The Deerhunter*; about learning 'The Internationale', 'The Marseillaise', and 'God Bless America' ('Know any or all? Bet you don't! See?'); about how you could be walking down the street one day, minding your own business, and get a knife in your gut (our Turkish heritage); about what it means to write for a population in which one out of ten (ten years and older) is illiterate, though no one has trouble making out 'Levi's', 'Benetton', 'Timberland', or 'White Horse' ('But they can see the horse on the label, Pipo!'), for a population that revels in newly composed 'folk music' with lyrics like 'A drop or two of blood upon the sheet/To show that you were first, my honey sweet' and boasts the lowest income per capita in Europe; about stretches of track where a driver may be ordered to stop the train at pistol point because the pistol-packer feels like a picnic ('Hey, that's cool!'); about how people don't mind wading through mud to their knees if they can have their nose in *Variety* and be up on the latest films in New York; about the *korzo* ('The *korzo*?' 'Something like the Mexican *paseo*.' 'Gottcha') and the May Day parade and the vows people take to uphold the achievements of the Revolution; about how people push lift buttons ten times because they have no faith in technology and how in foreign airports they are the first to run to the luggage conveyor belt, pushing, craning their necks, practically prostrating themselves on it for fear their suitcase will get lost or stolen; about what a musical people they are:

some yodel, others yelp, some wail, others weep, some screech, others stamp their feet and yet others sing in choirs and choruses; about what an ingenious people they are: selling foreigners the jellyfish that bit them on the beach, raising enough 'Canadian earthworms' to corner the world market, sniffing out three million kilograms of truffles for Italian gourmets; about air-conditioned tombs, complete with colour television sets and freezers, while the living, Gypsy children and *Gastarbeiter*, sell themselves abroad and fork out half their pay for a bottle of perfume; about heads of factories who disappear, vanish into thin air with millions in public funds ('Vanish?' 'Into thin air – 2,938 people were reported missing last year alone!') . . .

'Sounds just like America,' said Marc.

Pipo was devastated.

'Sorry, old buddy,' said Marc, straightening up, 'but would you happen to have some ketchup?'

'Just some tomato paste in that tube over there,' said Pipo absent-mindedly, drumming on the table with his fingers.

'Oh, that'll do fine.'

'This city really bugs me,' Pipo went on, somewhat more composed. 'It drains all the energy out of me. All I can do is dream. All day I dream I'm in an American movie, where the *action* is, while in fact I'm in one of our own, where the only action is a guy cracking a beer bottle over his head and pressing his hand down on the glass and crying, or a Czech one, where the only action is a bunch of country bumpkins dangling their legs in a stream and asking one another riddles like "Who is man's best friend"?'

'His dog, isn't it?' Marc said hesitantly.

'His bed, man, his bed!'

'Hey, that's cool.'

'So that's what you call cool, is it? Well, I'm a city slicker, if you know what I mean, and I don't need beds and streams; what I need is *action*.'

'Give this a good stir, would you?' said Marc calmly, putting a mixing bowl in front of Pipo. Pipo picked up a wooden spoon and began stirring the gooey mass. Marc took a pouch out of his pocket and rolled a joint.

148

'Here, try this,' he said after a few puffs. 'It'll take the edge off things.'

Pipo took a few puffs, passed it to Marc, and went back to his stirring.

'Hey, enough!' said Marc and took the bowl over to the stove. 'Now if I understand you correctly, you don't much like it here.'

'I don't know . . .' Pipo said gloomily.

'Well, what do you say we trade places.'

'What?' Pipo cried, staring over at Marc.

'Have you seen *The Passenger*? Antonioni.'

'No.'

'Well, Jack Nicholson plays this guy who finds a corpse in a run-down old hotel somewhere, and he gets this idea, see, of taking the man's passport and assuming his identity, living his life. The corpse's life, I mean.'

He took a few more puffs and handed the joint back to Pipo.

'And what happens to Jack Nicholson?'

'He gets killed.'

'But . . .'

'Look, neither of us is starting out as a corpse, so we don't have to worry about that kind of thing. We look enough alike. You be me, and I'll be you. I like it here.'

'But haven't you got . . .'

'A wife and children? Here, look.'

Marc took a wallet out of his back pocket and held out a picture.

'Wow! A real dish!'

'That's Jenny. And these are Burt and Thomas, our kids.'

'Well, I haven't got anybody. Except Mamma.'

'Nothing wrong with a mamma.'

Pipo looked at Marc and burst out laughing. Marc followed suit. But then Pipo turned serious and said, 'No, don't laugh. You know, there are times when I'm, say, sitting on the toilet, and I stare up at the light and think, Nikola Tesla – he's our great scientist, he invented the light bulb – Nikola Tesla worked his balls off to come up with that bulb and give me the chance to sit here and read if I feel like it. What sacrifice am I willing to make to better the lot of mankind or even a small fraction of it?'

'Write a novel,' said Marc, just as serious. 'A major novel.'

149

'How can I write a major novel when I live a minor life?' Pipo muttered, more to himself than out loud.

'Know what that minor life needs right now?' said Marc cheerfully. 'It needs to be fattened up with a little spaghetti and mellowed out with another good joint. What do you say?'

'Great,' said Pipo, feeling his whole body relax.

12

Sabina was asleep. A milk-white breast had slipped out from under the covers and nestled in a fold in the blanket. Hands folded under cheek, legs together and slightly bent at the knee, Sabina slept the way a chart illustrating 'Positions for Healthy Sleep' shows people how to sleep. Position No. 1. Standard.

Fate had drawn his name from a hat and sent him a sign. Sabina. Somebody up there had let down the silk cord and was waiting for him to decide. Old man Ginzburg standing in the middle of his empty room, one hand in his pocket, the other pointing to the ceiling. Who was that young girl in the picture on the wall? Or did it no longer matter?

Sabina stirred for a moment, then turned from side to back. Position No. 2. Innocence. Her breast slipped down under the covers. The veins in her gracefully thrown-back arms pulsed beautiful and blue under the fine, nearly transparent skin. Her eyelids were coated with the mother-of-pearl mist of repose. She slept the sleep of an angel.

Troshin was exhausted. He felt he had spent his life's assets: two failed marriages and a fifteen-year-old son. For fifteen years Lyuda used Alyosha as her main weapon, but that was over now: Alyosha had lost interest in him. What else was there? A few books. Could he have written more of them? Could they have been better? Not really. And it was all over now, all gone; life had nothing to offer him.

Sabina turned over on her other side. Her arms were now draped over his pillow. Position No. 3. Relaxation. Her straight soft hair flowed down her cheek. The skin on her arm fairly glowed from within. She was like a half-unravelled skein of the finest silk.

He had lived his life seriously, as if it served a predetermined

151

goal, whereas in reality it had been one chance event after another, glued together after the fact to fashion some semblance of a biography. The merest 'what if . . .' would have sufficed to tumble the entire construction and take him back to square one, a writer with a hero but no plot.

Troshin went over to the bed, carefully lifted the blanket and gently kissed each of her round, warm, innocent pink toes, his tongue dipping into the valleys between them.

Sabina's legs drifted lazily apart. Position No. 4. Abandon. Her pink pudenda open like a bitter young fruit. Troshin suddenly desired her passionately. Sabina, the faceless, scentless snow queen. Oblivion.

For some reason Troshin recalled a banal story about a man who was so panic-stricken about dying that he wore himself out keeping alive, and eventually jumped off a bridge from sheer exhaustion. Suddenly all the loose ends in Troshin's life began coming together and a magic magnetic field seemed to point them in one direction: Sabina.

Troshin kissed her all over. Sabina, still asleep, began whispering indecent expressions. Whispering them in Russian. Words spoken in a foreign accent create a kind of split. Troshin kissed Sabina more and more fervidly, as if trying to heal that split. Sabina kept saying the words and splitting open. Say them again, say them again, Troshin admonished her. And Sabina kept saying them, twisting, moaning in her sleep. In the flickering moment of intoxication between disappointment and pleasure he crossed the border and gazed into the depths, mirror-smooth and shiny, and before he leaped he whispered, 'Yes, Sabina, yes . . .'

JEUDI, le 8 mai

1

Troshin kept peering at the face in the passport photograph. It resembled his own in several basic respects: shape, hair colour, eye colour . . . But Hans Meyer was somewhat younger than he was, and Troshin couldn't for the life of him tell whether the man was stupid, clever, good or bad: someone seemed to have taken a magic cloth and wiped every distinctive feature from his face. Then Troshin glanced again at the train ticket and (though he already knew it by heart) the address Sabina had written out in her childlike hand. Argentinierstrasse 66, he repeated in a whisper, feeling his fear drift away on the tide of hissing *s*'s and tumbling *r*'s. He used it as an incantation, because each time his fingers travelled over the passport, each time his eyes lit on the ticket, the fear would return – rise from the pit of his stomach, lodge in his throat – ready to choke him.

He was awakened the next morning by the telephone. He hesitated a moment. The phone rang again. Argentinierstrasse 66, he whispered and picked up the receiver.

'Yura?'

'Yes . . .'

'Hey, you sound funny. What's the matter? Listen, can I come and see you for a second?'

'Well, actually I was just . . .'

'Look, Yura, things can't go on like this.'

'What things?'

'We're a delegation, aren't we?'

'What of it?'

'Look, I was at the consulate yesterday. They asked about you. It doesn't look good – you staying away like that.'

'I couldn't make it.'

155

'That blonde, eh?'

'No.'

'Look, Yura. Watch what you tell her in that interview. You know what they're like in the West. They'll twist every word you say; they'll put words in your mouth if you give them half a chance. Remember the problems Bondarenko had.'

'I didn't give an interview.'

'Is she . . . good?'

'Who?'

'The blonde.'

'Go to hell, will you!'

'I was only kidding!'

'Good.'

'You missed the factory visit yesterday too. I took an extra packet of samples for you. Your absence was noted, by the way. It doesn't look good.'

'Sorry.'

'There's a big reception today. I don't suppose I'll see you there. Just tell me when you want to meet for the airport.'

'At three. Down in the lobby.'

'Fine. Oh, and one more thing . . . You wouldn't have any . . . money left, would you? I mean, you've spent most of the time in your room and all, and I thought you might . . .'

'No.'

'OK. No problem. Just wondering.'

'See you later, Vitya.'

Troshin hung up with a sigh. He lay down again and lit a cigarette. *OK*, Vitya had said. Alyosha liked using English words too, but his crowd said *okayushki*. For the time being at least everything was *o-kay-ush-ki*. Suddenly the fear was gone. He could still change his mind. The plane for Moscow over the train for Vienna. After all, he'd made the choice once before.

It all began with Markov's heart attack the day before the delegation was due to leave. Troshin had been abroad often enough (that is, he could be presumed 1] safe, and 2] possessed of presentable – that was how they put it – English) to take his place. So off he went on a five-day trip to Washington and New York with Grushko,

Tyomin and Flora. Petya Tyomin vanished into the crowd on the last day, and that was that. The amazing thing was that Flora, who'd headed the delegation, didn't lose her executive position at the publishing house when she showed up without him. Of course having a respected war hero and war novelist for a husband didn't hurt.

On the first day they gave a reading at the Soviet Embassy in Washington, on the second day they had meetings in New York with two publishers, on the third day they saw Norman Mailer and John Updike in the flesh at the American PEN Center on Fifth Avenue, and on the fourth day Troshin, unable to withstand the temptation, pulled out a well-hidden scrap of paper with the address and telephone number of Sasha Liberman (who had emigrated a few years back on an 'Israeli visa') and called him from a public telephone. Only as he dialled did he realize he'd fallen into the Soviet trap of assuming the hotel phone was bugged.

'God, Yura! Is it really you? I can't believe it. Tell me again . . . Yes, yes, the gang's all here . . . Fine, just fine! . . . You'll never guess who's here, Ira! . . . Jump in a cab. This very minute . . . This very minute, you hear me?'

Sasha's patter had cast its spell. He waved down the first taxi he saw ('Madison Street, please!'), Sasha's *Fine, just fine* (he'd said it in heavily accented English) still ringing in his head. As the New York streets flew past, he caught himself superimposing their Moscow equivalents on them, and somewhere along the line he came to the most natural conclusion in the world: what mattered was not so much where he was as that he was off for a night with old friends.

Sasha and Ira were jogging in place at the entrance to a yellow-brick building very much like the one they'd lived in in Moscow. It was cold out, and Troshin's first glimpse of their faces was filtered through the warm steam of their breath. For a while the three of them stood there hugging and kissing, staring in disbelief at one another, then hugging again and jumping up and down like penguins to keep warm. Finally Ira, always the sensible one, ordered them inside, and they took a rickety lift (it too reminded Troshin of its Moscow counterpart) to the apartment.

'You remember my mother, don't you?'

He had seen Yulia Karlovna all of two or three times. She was a tiny, stooped old woman with thin grey hair gathered in a bun. Yulia Karlovna, who remembered Petersburg in its grand old days, had gone into emigration with her son and daughter-in-law at the age of eighty and was now writing her memoirs, thereby joining the ranks of those mistresses, wives, and friends with whom Mandelshtam had once exchanged a greeting, Bely once danced a waltz, and Akhmatova once drank tea, and who, having outlived them all, sought to give their own dwindling lives meaning in memory.

'Ira, you put on the water for *pelmeni* and start peeling potatoes. No, Mamma can peel the potatoes. You phone Dima, Valera – everybody! I'll take Yura to Brighton Beach and pick up some herring and vodka.'

As Sasha pushed him out of the door, Troshin was again reminded of warm steam, but this time it was thicker, the Russian steam-bath variety.

Riding along in the car, Troshin had time to examine Sasha's profile – the double chin, the wrinkles – and muse on the ageing process.

'Tell me, Yura, what made them pick you?'

'It was a heart attack, actually.'

'You had a heart attack?'

'No, Markov.'

'Oh, that arsehole. Who'd you come with?'

'Grushko, Tyomin, and Flora.'

'Pretty fancy company! Must be getting up there yourself! What are you doing here?'

'Talking to American publishers.'

'American publishers don't give a fuck about you!'

'Well, we've had some . . .'

'Don't tell me I've hurt your feelings! Your pride as a representative of Soviet literature! By the way, Tyomin's going to defect.'

'How do you know?'

'Everybody knows everything here. What about you?'

'Me?'

'Planning to join him?'

'Can't say I've given it much thought.'

'Well, when you do, I'm here. Get it?'

'Right.'

'So Flora's with you.'

'Uh-huh.'

'Nothing wrong with Flora that a good lay wouldn't cure – that's what I always said. Hey, what do you say we take it on ourselves, break into her room. You're still up to it, aren't you?'

'I'm older than I used to be.'

'Well, I'm not. We're in great demand here: Blacks, Puerto Ricans, Slavs. And the only Slavs who get more of it than us are the Poles – especially since Solidarity. They bank on politics; we sell our Russian soul. New World nookie's wild about soul. It's the only commodity that's in short supply around here, and we've got it coming out of our ears.'

'What about Ira?'

'Ira's Russian,' he said with a wave of the hand and announced ceremoniously, 'We have arrived! Brighton Beach. America's answer to Odessa.'

While Sasha parked the car, Troshin stared out at a small, gloomy street lined with stubby buildings and shops and crowned with an elevated railway, the famous El. The shops offered a large selection of fresh herring, well-aged sauerkraut, Russian sausages and smoked salmon, Hungarian, Bulgarian and Yugoslav vegetable and fruit preserves, Ukrainian *pertsovka*, Armenian and Georgian cognac, Russian vodka, Dalmatian wine, Georgian *sologuni* cheese and Soviet chocolates. Music came blaring out of all the shops: old Russian romances, recent *émigré* imitations, and some local, that is, Odessa fare. Troshin, obediently tagging behind Sasha, had the feeling that everyone knew everyone else – the salesmen seemed so free with the customers, often calling them by name – and that both salesmen and customers seemed not yet quite at home with the idea that everything everybody asked for was available and, nostalgic for shortages and queues, sometimes played at setting up obstacles before finally coming up with the desired product.

'Feast your eyes!' said Sasha, turning to admire a woman walking out of the shop with a bag full to overflowing. 'Only here and in Odessa can you see an arse as big and beautiful as that.'

The 'antique shops' were stuffed with junk that had a hideous, phantasmagoric, naturally messy order to it. They specialized in

159

icons (counterfeit and genuine), fans, rosary beads, costume jewellery, *matryoshka* dolls, small plaster busts of Lenin, strapping Pobeda-brand alarm clocks, electric samovars, amber in all shapes and sizes, brightly patterned Russian scarves, lacquer trinket boxes, rabbit-fur *ushanki*, miniature Kremlins (and one large one for use as a night-light), lorgnettes, souvenir badges, sheet music, works of Solzhenitsyn and works of Brezhnev, cassettes of Galich's camp songs and cassettes of the Red Army Chorus.

Waiting for Sasha to come out of the liquor store, Troshin leaned against an El pillar with several sacks of cabbage and meditated on what it meant for him to be in New York (America!) for four days and to be going home the next day, having seen almost nothing, yet here in Brighton Beach having come to see his own country in a new light. And even though the picture he had received was only a grotesque sketch, a caricature, a harum-scarum conglomeration of values, times and settings, it was none the less – and perhaps all the more – valid, bona fide, true to life. If he hadn't looked up Sasha, he would have been spared it all, but seeing Sasha wasn't the only reason to get in touch with him; no, he'd wanted to see the *other life*. Back in Moscow he'd been periodically obsessed by it, the thought of giving everything up, dropping out of sight and turning up on the other side, completely different . . .

Sasha emerged from the shop with a large bag of bottles. He stowed it in the car, but extracted one bottle, opening it in the street so they could each take a swig from it in Russian style. Then Sasha took Troshin to a nearby Uzbek hole-in-the-wall, where he ordered two portions of authentic Uzbek shish kebab. When the owner heard their Russian, he gave a malicious snort and said in his none-too-good best English, 'I am Uzbek and here you speak only Uzbek and English.'

Through the open kitchen door Troshin could see a tiny woman hacking away at a side of lamb and hear laughter and Uzbek music. Sasha's conspiratorial wink struck Troshin as a poor imitation of male bonding in action; in fact, he suddenly saw the two of them as overgrown schoolboys.

'Bet you've never had *shashlyk* like this before.'

'Right . . .'

Sasha looked over at Troshin, and the happy-go-lucky macho mask dropped from his face.

'You know, Yura, I could have taken you to the Empire State Building, but I brought you here. And look at you. You're scared shitless – it's written all over you – scared of what you've experienced here will force you to confront. I can tell exactly which detail presses which button in your memory. Well, you could have seen it all back in Moscow. Any day at all. But what you're trying to work out is why I left and what kind of life I lead and whether it's paid off. As if you were the one who'd left, not me. Or at least as if you had a chance to leave. Well, you haven't. Haven't now and never will. You haven't got the guts for it. By the way, things are a lot simpler than you think. A jar of caviare, say. Your caviare, Soviet caviare, the kind only the *nomenklatura* has access to. Well, there are plenty of people who leave just to buy that fucking jar. Maybe they think it has the answer. Maybe that's all freedom is. That or this *shashlyk*. Isn't that right, boss?'

'Right, yes, yes,' said the Uzbek, clearly in a better mood.

'There, you see?' said Sasha, standing up from the table after leaving a much too generous tip.

They drove home in silence, which Sasha broke only to ask when Troshin's plane was leaving.

'Eleven-fifty,' said Troshin, thinking with malicious glee of the panic he must have caused Flora by not showing up today for the scheduled sightseeing tour. 'A shame we didn't give her that roll in the hay,' he said after a long pause.

'Who?'

'Flora, of course!'

Sasha burst out laughing, and Troshin joined him.

That broke the ice and set the mood for the party that followed. The vodka flowed like water; Ira, pink with excitement, rushed around the table urging herring and pickled mushrooms on everyone. People seemed to have come out of the woodwork for the occasion.

There was Dima, sitting next to Troshin in an honest-to-goodness lumber jacket, the kind they'd first seen many years ago on Marlon Brando when they went to *On the Waterfront* together. Dima was now writer in residence at a college in the suburbs. (It's a great place, Yura. Every year I pull in a new grant and put out a new book!) Considered rather mild-mannered in his Soviet works, Dima had turned to themes virulently anti-Soviet in emigration, a particularly difficult transition in his case: not only had he never been near a labour camp, he'd lived high off the hog in Moscow and had to go searching for disaffected characters.

In the middle of everything Yasha phoned from Washington. (That's right, a reporter for the *Voice of America* . . . It's our job to know you're here! . . . Of course you'll stay! Don't be ridiculous! It's a once-in-a-lifetime opportunity! We'll take care of everything. *Goodbyushki!*)

Then there were two women in their thirties sitting opposite Troshin: Valya, a chemist, who was working temporarily in an old people's home in Queens to the tune of a thousand smackers a month, and Galya, the proud owner of her own bakery – Bubliki, she called it – on the Lower East Side. Next to Galya – Valera, a writer. ('You'll be hearing about him before long. He drives a taxi for a living. A good number of us have been that route, Yura.')

Then there was Vasya Punin. Punin had managed to smuggle in some icons and an oil or two. Enough for a start, in any case. Now he was into soc-art. (I invented it. Wait till you see the slides. People can't get enough of this stuff.) He would scale down socialist-realist sculptures and paint them in bright colours, his speciality being subtly bizarre distortions of Mukhina's muscle-bound shock-workers. Punin kept trying to foist off on Troshin a bright-pink penis with tiny hammers and sickles painted all over it. (Go on, take it, Troshin. Take it back with you and give people something to laugh about.) Punin so got on Troshin's nerves that he felt a sudden wave of sympathy for the authentic ugliness of Soviet monuments and started wondering whether some day, like so many things that were originally ugly, they too might not seem beautiful.

Meanwhile, Troshin felt the vodka going slowly but surely to his head, the faces merging, the voices . . . (What's Lyuda up to? How's Gena? Have you heard that Tsimerman showed up the other day? Tsimerman, the director. Did you know that Galochka Savelyeva had hooked a rich American businessman?) It was too much. The people, the vodka, the more-Muscovite-than-Moscow atmosphere. For long stretches he would sense a vague pale of woe among the guests, but then he'd think, was he any happier than they were? and in the next instant he would make up his mind to stay, of course he'd stay, that's why they were here, wasn't it? to celebrate his decision to stay.

At one point he finally stood – rather unsteadily – and raised his glass. 'Listen, everybody! I want to make it official! I'm staying! I've decided to stay! Cheers, everybody!'

His voice was soon lost in a chorus of whoops and hollers. Soon everyone was standing, clapping him on the back, kissing him, hugging him, talking to him and one another. Air, give me air! Ira was the first to notice. She grabbed him by the arm and dragged him off, pushing open a door as she went. Before he knew it he was alone on a bed in a dark room, the only light coming from the street. He was staying. Suddenly he was afraid. No, he wouldn't stay. Fear again. God in heaven, where was he? What was he doing here? How in the world did he get here? No, he couldn't stay, he couldn't even stay in this room! But as he turned to go, he saw a woman coming through the door.

'Psst!' she said, lowering herself on to the bed with him. Troshin didn't move. Her warm, moist, even breath loosed his tangled nerves, and suddenly, violently, he buried his head in her lap. He realized he was sobbing.

'Don't cry, my darling, don't cry, my sweet,' she murmured in the dark, stroking his head. 'Everything's going to be all right.' And then he took her, drunkenly, awkwardly, crudely.

'There, you see?' she whispered. 'Everything's all right.'

'Forgive me,' Troshin mumbled, hideously ashamed of himself.

The woman did not respond.

'Which one are you?' Troshin asked. The whole thing was so obscene.

'Valya.'

'Oh. Valya.'

'I read one of your books while I was there.'

'Why do you say *there*?'

'Why? Because I'm here now.'

Troshin took her hand and closed his eyes, and Valya told him her story, her words sliding and colliding along the walls of his ears, lulling him to sleep.

163

When Valya was twenty-seven (she was thirty-two now), she wanted to get married. Or, rather, her mother and grandmother wanted her to get married. They must have known why getting married was so important. Do you, Troshin? She decided to get a master's degree in chemistry at the Department of Food Sciences. Well, actually, it was her mother who persuaded her to do it. She said it would help her to meet people; she might even land a doctoral candidate. But during her studies Valya worked as an inspector in a chocolate factory. She liked her job. Making chocolate was an interesting process. Besides, the factory smelled nice and you could eat as much chocolate as you wanted. Then her grandmother told her mother she was putting on weight, and her mother wept and said, Look at you! Nobody will marry you now! Her grandmother wept too, though Valya was sure her grandmother didn't know why. The upshot of it was that Valya had to take a new job. But the new job didn't help. It didn't help trim her figure and it didn't help find her a man. It actually made things worse: it was in a distillery. Now we're really in trouble, said her mother, and she was right, because Valya started drinking. She still drank, but not the way she did then. So her mother pulled a few strings and got her another job. But by that time Valya was writing her thesis and spending most of her time with the dictionary. Every time she looked up a term she'd forget it on the spot. Now you'll never find a husband, her mother wailed. But Valya liked the Institute where she was studying. She liked the wide range of sleeping partners, and she liked falling in love. Not that she fell in love at first sight. No, she'd go to bed first and fall in love afterwards. Make believe you're not in love, her mother told her. That mopey, love-sick look of yours – it drives them all away. And then her grandmother came up with the coat. A special rabbit-skin coat to break the spell. Believe it or not, the first time she wore the coat to the Institute, she bumped into this Finnish guy. A Finn from Finland, not one of ours. He'd come to study grain production, though she couldn't imagine why – it was always winter up there. In any case, he fell in love with her and they got married. You see? her grandmother said and wept for days. Valya was here on a Finnish passport. The Finn was a bastard. No soul.

While Troshin drowsed, Valya soared high above the Kremlin

churches, then grazed the onion domes, then skimmed Chagall–like along the ground, waving a wand with a soul on its end. And the soul was white and it spun its wings like a pin-wheel and Valya would blow on it, take deep breaths and blow . . .

Troshin opened his eyes. The morning sun was streaming through the window. The woman next to him was breathing deeply, calmly, her kind, sad face half buried in the pillow. He got up slowly so as not to wake her.

Standing in the middle of the room, still groggy, he smoothed down his hair and clothes. Suddenly his eye, guided by the sun, lit on a corner shelf above the desk and he made his way over to it. The shelf housed a row of small, dusty objects: a bouquet of dried flowers, a small wooden icon, the reproduction of an icon on cheap paper, a set of rosary beads, a cross, a pair of Moscow theatre tickets, a packet of Belomor cigarettes, a child's clay whistle, some family pictures and some pictures of Moscow friends, including one of himself coming out of the Sokolniki Metro station. Troshin felt a lump in his throat. You still found them in peasant houses, these family museums, altars to the past. He carefully removed his own picture from the shelf – he couldn't remember the day or the occasion it commemorated – dusted it off, and returned it to its place. Then he tiptoed out of the room and closed the door behind him.

The living-room was empty. He peered into the kitchen. Yulia Karlovna, wearing a frayed housecoat, was standing motionless at the window. He went in. She turned, focused her faded, empty eyes on him, and said softly, 'Come and see.'

The window looked out on a courtyard with two or three bare trees and a couple of benches. An old man in a winter coat and fur hat was sitting on one of the benches, staring into space and tapping his cane on the ground with even strokes.

'Just like Moscow, isn't it.'

At that moment the tea-kettle began to whistle. Troshin turned to go.

'Can't I offer you some tea?' she asked with only a trace of reproval in her voice.

'No, thank you. And please thank Sasha and Ira for me.'

He went over to the telephone table in the living-room. The

165

notice board above it was covered with names and numbers: Zhenya, Dima, Vasya, Larisa . . . There was only one John, and it was written in Cyrillic. The largest piece of paper had MOI TELEFON printed across the top and Sasha's number scrawled underneath.

'There's no need to phone for a taxi,' the old woman said with stately grace. She was a withered monument, uprooted from one century, dropped into the next. 'You can hail one on any corner.' Troshin gave her an embarrassed nod and left.

In the taxi he reached for his cigarettes and came up with a folded sheet of paper. It was a hand-bill he had picked up at one of the Brighton Beach shops the day before. He lighted up and unfolded it numbly.

> NEW YORK'S FIRST ALL-RUSSIAN TALENT SHOW
> We haven't forgotten our great Russian soul,
> Our talent for laughter and tears.
> So come sing, dance, play for us. This is our goal:
> The best New Year's party in years.

The talent show was to take place at Edward R. Murrow High School, 1600 Avenue L (at the corner of East 17th Street), Brighton Beach. Tickets were available at the Black Sea (the shop where the advertisement had come from) and Mike's Video. The volunteers would be supplemented by a number of semi-professionals, whose pictures reminded Troshin of funeral announcements. Suddenly he flinched: one of the faces looked familiar. The text accompanying the picture, captioned Valentina Gribanova (Valya?), read, *Listen to her sing 'My Russia's Blue Sky' and you'll feel ten years younger!*

Troshin folded up the sheet of paper and placed it on the seat. Watching the streets of New York fly past again, he calculated exactly how many days it would be until Valentina sang 'My Russia's Blue Sky'. Just as he came up with the answer, Forty-Second Street flashed into view. He'd gone through the looking-glass, and it was all so similar, all so frighteningly the same . . .

Troshin closed the passport. Hans Meyer's expressionless face disappeared between the covers in a faint swish. That swish sealed

Troshin's decision. He looked up and saw the city dissolving in grey-pink hues. He stood, opened the refrigerator, took out the brandy, and went over to the window, where he toasted a Zagreb he hadn't seen, the living Hans Meyer, and the dead Yury Troshin.

When Anton Švajcer, a retired professor of French literature and the author of *Flaubert and the South Slavs*, walked into the Crystal Palace, he couldn't believe his eyes. The first shock had come two days before when a writer acquaintance of his, Pero Mark, had let fall in a conversation that one of the participants in this year's Colloquium was a bona fide great-nephew of Flaubert's, the second when Mark announced that the Frenchman was hosting a modest open house after the official closing ceremonies.

What had greeted the elderly professor's eyes, however, was far from a 'modest open house'; it was the most sumptuous spread he had ever seen. The spacious hall was filled with people strolling, clinking glasses, pausing at tables, chatting and chewing. The tables, all groaning with food, formed a large *U* in the centre. The first one the professor came to was laden with four roasts of beef, six enormous bowls of chicken fricassee, stewed veal, three sides of mutton and, in the middle, a fine roast suckling-pig flanked by four pork sausages in sorrel. There were decanters of brandy at each corner and bottles of sweet cider frothing round the corks. Large dishes of yellow cream quivered with the slightest shake of the table, and only old Professor Švajcer knew whose initials were drawn in the nonpareil arabesques on their surface. He also immediately identified the cake that had provoked loud cries of wonderment but that none of the guests had yet dared touch; in fact, his eyes filled with tears at the sight of it. At its base there was a square of blue cardboard representing a temple with porticoes, colonnades, and stucco statuettes in niches studded with gilt paper stars; then, on the second level, there was a donjon of sponge cake surrounded by small fortifications of candied angelica, almonds, raisins and orange slices; and, finally, on the upper platform, a green meadow with rocks and nutshell boats set in lakes of jam, there was a small Cupid swinging in a chocolate swing, the two posts of which rested in real roses. The elderly professor thought his heart would break when a fat man, all wavy arms and waggy behind, blithely plucked the Cupid off the swing, wrapped it in a napkin, and stuck it in his pocket. The boor. The professor was burning to go up to him and tell him he had just desecrated Emma Bovary's wedding cake, which Charles had ordered from the new *pâtissier* at Yvetot.

The professor's eyes wandered from face to face, hoping to find one appreciative of or at least touched by the magnificent literary and culinary feat. But the faces were all stupor, gluttony, vulgarity – nowhere a trace of the purity that should ennoble the features of the literati.

Sighing, the professor waddled over to the second table, which was undoubtedly the grandest. There were bouquets lining the whole length of the table; napkins in broad-bordered plates, each folded in the shape of a bishop's mitre and holding a small oval roll between its gaping folds; there were red lobster claws jutting out over the dishes, lush fruit piled high in wicker baskets on a bed of moss, quails dressed in their own plumage, the steam still rising from them. The professor could relish the quality and flavour of the food merely by inhaling deeply. On a separate table a few steps away there was an assortment of Spanish and Rhine wines, bisque and almond-cream soups, Trafalgar puddings, and all sorts of cold meats in aspic trembling in their dishes. There could be no doubt: it was the menu of the famous dinner to which Emma and Charles were invited at the château of the Marquis d'Andervilliers. Old Professor Švajcer pictured Emma's excitement, the grace with which she dropped her glove into the wine-glass; he pictured her eating the maraschino ice from a silver-gilt cup she held in her left hand . . .

Just then the elderly professor noticed a woman of about his age leaning over the Trafalgar pudding for a closer look, her eye-glasses travelling dangerously down her nose. The inevitable was not long in happening. Oh, how crude and ignorant they were!

Withdrawing in mild disgust, the professor came to a tiny table off by itself adorned with nothing but a large pyramid of plums on vine-leaves. The professor was unusually moved by the simple, plain pyramid. It was Emma's, of course; she knew how to look after her house and prepare tasty dishes out of nothing.

On the table next to it there was an equally simple, plain basket filled with apricots still moist with dew. It too the professor was able to identify: the famous basket Rodolphe sent Emma from his estate.

None of these people had any idea why certain food had to be on certain tables. None of them would recognize the *garus*, the aperitif so loved by the Léon the professor so hated.

The professor's last stop was a small table with nothing on it but a glass of hard cider, a hunk of rare mutton and a cup of coffee. Exhausted, he sat on the chair that had been provided. His hand trembling slightly, he raised the cup to his mouth and downed the coffee with great pleasure. It was the table of old man Rouault, who liked his coffee laced with brandy. Once more the professor glanced over the crowd, this time trying to guess which of them was Flaubert's putative great-nephew. The fat man who'd pocketed the Cupid was surely a local writer.

Silvio Benussi and the novelist Mraz were standing at the Marquis d'Andervilliers's table, cracking lobster shells with great gusto.

'Actually, I prefer a more Russian diet,' Benussi said and loudly sucked in the contents of a claw.

'What do you mean,' asked Mraz, between sucks on his own claw, 'exactly?'

'I mean in terms of literary fare. Tolstoy, Chekhov. Yes, Chekhov – there was a man with taste.'

'I think we should go in for more theme-oriented conferences, don't you?' said Mraz, still struggling to void his claw. 'What would you say to a Rabelais symposium?'

'Or Petronius,' said Benussi, inhaling the last drop of juice and then licking the claw clean.

'Right,' said Mraz, finally smashing the claw to bits. 'People used to eat a lot better in literature.'

'Literature used to be a lot better in every respect! Food and drink, love and hate, blood and guts . . .' And smacking a new claw against the edge of the table for emphasis, he splashed its juice all over a pale-looking young man.

If Davor Kukac looked pale, it was because with his every move he felt the knife in his back give another twist. It had been placed there three weeks before by his best friend Nino Kovač, a literary critic and theoretician, in the form of a review Kovač had written of Kukac's first novel. The fruit of two years of sun-up to sun-down hard labour in the university library, the novel consisted of a fine web of literary references, allusions and quotations conceived as a delicacy for the literary epicure and a tribute to the completely forgotten *fin-de-siècle* writer Kukac had rediscovered, in other words, a sophisticated game that both displayed Davor's talent as a writer and restored a neglected genius to the canon. And after Davor had carefully explained to Nino (that combination stuffed shirt and lightweight who after all his years at the university couldn't tell a classic from a hack) where it all came from and what he, Davor, had done with it, Nino scribbled off a long article in which he had carefully explained where it all came from and what he, Davor, had done with it, and – pronounced it the work of an incompetent plagiarist!

A glowering Davor Kukac went up to the sponge-cake donjon and heedlessly crumbled one of the raisin-and-almond fortifications. Just as it reached his lips, the following reached his ears: *When you steal from one author, it's plagiarism; when you steal from many, it's research.* Davor straightened up and flexed his shoulders. All that was left of the knife was a dull pain below his left shoulder-blade. He popped the fortification into his mouth and turned to see a group of two local writers and a foreign woman. 'Cheers!' he said, more to himself than to them, and downed the wine left in his glass. He had toasted Wilson Mizner, author of the aphorism, and Ranko Leš, who had just quoted it.

'That's why you won't catch me messing around with critics,' said Leš, fixing the toy poet with his glare. Both Ilona Kovács and the *garus* in her glass were having equilibrium problems, which were periodically exacerbated by the fact that she kept tugging at Leš's sleeve and craning to see what other people were doing: she didn't understand the language and was bored.

'I'm a man of the eighties, my boy,' Leš went on, 'and all this provincial, pseudo-intellectual *canaille*' – he flung out his arm, tottering dangerously in the process – 'means nothing to me. No, *Mitteleuropa* is my habitat, my spiritual and intellectual milieu.'

At that point Leš's Hungarian friend stood on her tiptoes and whispered something in his ear. Leš nodded and put his arm around her waist.

'Austria–Hungary is in, my boy,' he said to the toy poet, 'and it makes sense to start with whatever lies close at hand.' And with a roguish wink he gave Ilona Kovács a squeeze.

'*Kedvesem, gyere . . . Szívem, gyere,*' she mumbled, snuggling up to him even closer.

'Well, I'm off, my boy,' said Leš with a playful punch to the toy poet's shoulder.

The toy poet took a gulp of his *garus* and looked on with the contempt of insecurity as Leš and his Hungarian left the hall. His glance then lit on Sapozhnikov, the Russian, and Malgorzata Uszko, the Pole, who were huddled together in a corner like a couple of neighbours at a country tea party. Provincials! the toy poet thought, and drained his glass dry.

Victor Sapozhnikov was sitting in a corner next to the elderly Polish critic, eating heartily from a plate piled high with meat jelly. Never in his life had he seen such opulence. He'd have to record every detail and describe it in all its glory back in Moscow. What was that crazy Yura doing up there in his room all the time? He used to think he was a regular guy. Being on the road with people certainly taught you what made them tick. Well, he was having a good time at least: he'd been to three museums, had a good walk around the town, done a little shopping . . .

The Polish critic sitting next to Sapozhnikov paid him no heed; she was totally taken up with her glasses, which had slipped into a bowl of yellow cream and needed wiping. Sapozhnikov suddenly decided a glass of white wine would go well with the meat jelly, and as he rose to find some of the former, a large chunk of the latter rolled into the Polish critic's lap. For a few moments the two of them stared at the quivering mass as if it were a rare genus of snail, then Sapozhnikov lifted his fork, took aim, and . . .

The Polish critic gave Victor Sapozhnikov such a look that his fork froze in mid-air. 'What do you think you are doing, young man?' she cried. 'Are you drunk?' And she shook the meat jelly off her dress and on to the floor.

'*Izvinite*,' said Sapozhnikov, blushing apologetically.

'*Nie szkodzi*,' said Małgorzata Uszko, as if nothing had happened, and went back to wiping her glasses.

That made Sapozhnikov even more uncomfortable, and he stood up, clicked his heels (which he had never done before in his life), and moved off, bumping into the Danish writer, Cecilia Sørensen, as he did so.

'*Tfu, chort!*' he muttered, heading as carefully as he could in the direction of the d'Andervilliers table.

'First tell me how you got him into your room,' said Thomas Kiely, handing Cecilia Sørensen a glass of white wine.

'We had a few drinks together in the hotel bar, and I told him I was interested in his views on women's literature,' she said, nervously sipping the wine. 'He went on about literature of the kitchen and literature of the clitoris – your typical male chauvinist claptrap.'

'Yes, but how did you get him up to your room?'

'Simple. I proposed we resolve the clitoral vs. phallic literature controversy in bed.'

'And he accepted?' the Irishman interjected.

'What do you think?' the Danish woman replied, rather hurt.

'Sorry,' said the Irishman with a laugh.

'Immediately I suggested a little s-and-m action. I told him I interpreted his negative attitude towards women writers as a textbook case of sublimation, the sublimation of a masochistic strain in himself. In other words, the only reason he so challenged and insulted women was that he had a masochistic desire to be beaten by them.'

'Terrific! How'd you dig up all that on him?'

'Dig up? Crap! I *made* it up! All I wanted was to get him out of his clothes and find a way to tie him down.'

'How *did* you tie him down? He's a real bruiser, that bloke.'

'Sheets. And the sailor's knots I've learned from Peer.'

'What about the other two? Who are they?'

'Local writers. Tanja and Dunja. Great women!'

173

'What did you do to him?' asked Kiely, refilling her glass and his and practically trembling with excitement.

'First we went through all the ways we could torture him. Tanja suggested a series of ritual tortures by means of kitchen utensils.'

'Electric?' the Irishman asked in horror.

'Manual,' the Danish woman replied gravely. 'Then torture by grater, by cleaver, by mixer . . . He blacked out when we got to meat-grinder.'

'I should have done too.'

'I suggested a more standard rape, with all the brutality men use on women, but Tanja had a different idea: moral degradation. More in line with the Mediterranean mentality, she said. The most important thing here, apparently, is to make a fool of a person.'

'And how did you do it?' the Irishman asked eagerly.

'Tanja went out and bought some glue, and we poured it all over him; then we slit open the pillows and sprinkled him liberally with feathers.'

'Splendid! Couldn't be more traditional!'

'Tanja'd also brought back a large balloon, and we blew it up, tied it with a string to his penis, and left him there with the door open. A few minutes later I phoned the main desk and reported a maniac in my room.'

'Brilliant!' he cried, but immediately his eyes narrowed. 'You're not making this all up now, are you?'

Cecilia Sørensen frowned and took a sip of wine.

'Listen,' he said after a short silence, 'would you do me a favour?'

'What?'

'Would you let me use it in my novel?'

'Why not? What's it about?'

'Women. I'm calling it *It's Me, Molly Bloom*.'

Cecilia Sørensen did not respond. She was depressed. Her glance wandered off distractedly and fell on a familiar fat cigar.

Next to Jean-Paul Flagus stood a tiny old man peering up at him through a pince-nez with all but love-sick eyes. *'Mon dieu, mon dieu!'* he cried, shaking his head. *'C'est un grand jour pour moi! Vraiment, un grand jour!'*

Monsieur Flagus eyed the curious old man with impatience,

174

blowing one smoke ring after another and obviously seeking an excuse to get rid of him. Catching sight of Prša in the distance, he waved and started off, but the little man grabbed him by the sleeve.

'*Non, non! Attendez, s'il vous plaît!*' the man cried pitifully. 'Let me guess. Élise de Schlésinger?'

'I'm terribly sorry, monsieur, but I really must . . .'

'No, of course no, *quelle bêtise!* Wait a moment! You have no idea what this means to me! I consider your great-uncle the greatest writer of all time. Greater than Shakespeare! And now I have the unbelievable pleasure of standing face to face with a scion of the hermit of Croisset, *ce martyr de l'art, ce génie, cet esclave de l'art*, who sacrificed everything to it: personal happiness, career, success, life itself!'

'But I am not his great-nephew,' Jean-Paul Flagus said coldly.

'You're not? He's not your great-uncle?'

'My grandmother was Caroline Comanville.'

'*Caroline? Votre grand-mère?! Incroyable!* That makes you his nephew! *Mon dieu!* His very own nephew!'

Jean-Paul nodded and made another attempt to depart, but again the man latched on to his sleeve.

'Then where does the name Flagus come from?'

'It's a pseudonym. Flaubert, Gustave: Fla-gus. But mum's the word!' And with what was meant to be a conspiratorial smile he shook himself free and headed off in Prša's direction.

'*Comme ça, motus, bouche cousue,*' the old man whispered, looking around in a daze. Next to the plum-pyramid table he spied an unusually lanky, awkward-looking young woman standing with a plum in her hand. As he approached, he noticed that her eyes were the same deep blue as the plum. He took one for himself, careful not to disturb the pyramid and, looking up at her with the compassion of old age, said, 'Do you know what today is?'

'No,' said the woman.

'Today is the anniversary of the great Flaubert's death,' he said solemnly.

'Oh,' said Ena the Bell-Tower, absorbed in something completely different, and took a wistful bite out of her plum.

3

Prša threw open the door of the Colloquium's temporary head-
quarters to find Franka sitting at her desk admiring the chocolate
Cupid the novelist Mraz had pinched for her from Emma Bovary's
wedding cake. 'Don't think I didn't see it,' he said when she threw
the napkin over it and pushed it aside. Then he plopped into a chair,
said, 'Phew! I'm glad that's over' more to himself than to her, and
started drumming with his fingers on the desk. Now all he had to
do was make sure they got off safely. What a series of catastrophes!
First the stupid Spaniard who had nothing better to do than splash
around in the pool, then the crazy Czech who dreamed up a novel,
picked up his per diems, and packed up without giving his talk . . .
If it hadn't been for the Frenchman and his shindig, the whole thing
would have been a bust.

'I've finally got the list of foreign participants ready,' said Franka.
'Want to see it?'

Prša crossed his legs and took the sheet of paper. She'd done a
good job, even translated the titles.

> Benussi, Silvio (Padova, Italia), critic. Works: *Storia della
> letteratura italiana contemporanea* (A History of Contempor-
> ary Italian Literature), *La critica letteraria contemporanea*
> (Contemporary Literary Criticism).

> Espeso, José Ramón (Madrid, España), poet. Works:
> *Ciprés que crece del barco* (O Cypress That Grows from the
> Ship), *Los habitantes del alba* (Dawn Dwellers), *Poema
> madrileño* (A Poem of Madrid), *Redoble de memoria* (Mem-
> ory's Rumble).

Kiely, Thomas (Dublin, Ireland), novelist. Works: *It's Me, Molly Bloom* (in progress).

Kovács, Ilona (Budapest, Magyarország), poet. Works: *Kép* (A Picture), *Fénykép* (A Photograph), *Az ember a képről* (The Man from the Picture), *Tájkép* (Landscape).

Sapozhnikov, Victor Victorovich (Moskva, SSSR). Novelist, playwright, children's writer. Works: *Svoi chelovek* (One of Us), *Kolodets* (The Well), *Progulka v lesu* (A Walk in the Woods), *Mamka, babka da ja* (Mamma, Grandma and Me).

Sørensen, Cecilia (Århus, Danemark). Novelist. Works: *Danish Cookies, Levnedsbog* (My Life).

Stenheim, Marc (New York, USA). Novelist and screenwriter. Works: *The Revenge of Walter Mitty, Destry Writes Again, The Garbage Pail, Wonder-Woman's Lover-Boy, Play It Again, Mary!*

Troshin, Yury Vasilyevich (Moskva, SSSR). Novelist. Works: *Sluzhebnyi vkhod* (Service Entrance), *Gorodskaia zhizn'* (City Life), *Krasnaia luna* (Red Moon), *Korotkaia vstrecha v metro* (A Brief Metro Encounter), *Zhenshchina v sinem* (The Woman in Blue), *Vtoroi raz* (The Second Time), etc.

Uszko, Małgorzata (Kraków, Polska). Critic. Works: *Krytyka i dzieło* (Critic and Work), *Studie literackie* (Literary Studies), *Poezija i znaczenie* (Poetry and Meaning).

Zdražil, Jan (Praha, ČSSR). Poet. *Láska* (Love), *Den s andělem* (A Day with an Angel), *Holub* (The Dove).

Prša tossed the list back on the desk. He had a feeling the Colloquium's original international glitter had dulled a lot in recent years. 'How come the Frenchman's not on the list?' he asked.

'We got a telegram from him today saying he couldn't come. Here. Waited until it was over to let us know.'

'Hold on a second. This is signed Jean-Paul Joubert.'

'Jean-Paul Joubert. That's who we invited.'

'Yes, but isn't our fellow Jean-Paul *Flagus*?'

'That's your problem.'

'Insinuations, insinuations! You women are all alike. Look, one couldn't come, so another one took his place.' And he banged his fist hard on the table, missing Cupid by a hair.

'All I'm saying is I've heard of Joubert, I've read him, and I've no idea who this Flagus character is.' Her tone of voice made it very clear that the subject was now closed.

'She's heard of him, she's read him,' he mumbled, stalking out of the office. 'Big deal!'

4

The Minister tore open his belt, let out his breath, sank into a chair and started playing absent-mindedly with the slip of paper he had picked from Vanda's hat. He'd had too much of that suckling-pig. It was delicious, but he'd overdone it. That French guy had really shown them up: he'd all but come out and said, 'This is how you really do it, and if you're short on cash, I'm not.' Slimy frog. Prša said he was going to poke into his background, but he'll be gone before you know it. Who cares anyway? He wants to throw his dough around, that's his privilege.

'Know how much that Frenchman laid out for the party?'

'How much?' Vanda called in from the kitchen.

'At least five thousand dollars! Bring me some bicarbonate of soda, will you?'

'Heavens! What would Flaubert have thought?' Vanda was as concerned as if the sum had come straight from Flaubert's pocket. She loved *Madame Bovary*. She'd read it three times through and wept three times through. 'If I wasn't on sick leave,' she said, bringing in two coffees and the sodium bicarbonate on a tray, 'I'd go down there and give him a piece of my mind.'

'What would you say?'

'I'd say, "Shame on you for squandering your poor dead uncle's fortune!"'

'Who knows if they're even related?' said the Minister, reaching for the antacid. 'He could be a complete phoney, an imposter, a spy!' And he looked over at Vanda or, rather, at the ample, well-rounded breasts peeking through her housecoat.

'Have you been to the hat yet, baby?' she asked, following his glance.

Only then did the Minister notice he had something in his hand.

179

'What's this, baby?' he cried, unpleasantly surprised, and held out a blank slip.

'Let me see,' she said. 'Oooh! Baby!'

'Trying to put one over on me, eh?' he thundered.

'No, baby, I swear! I don't know how it got there. Really, baby! Pick another one. Go on. Pick another one.'

'Not on your life,' said the Minister with a frown. He had been thrown at first by the blank slip. It seemed a bad omen. But then he realized he could turn it to his advantage. He was too tired tonight for what Vanda was always raring to go for.

'But look at all the possibilities, baby!' Vanda whined, taking one paper after another out of the pink hat and unfolding them as if they were caramels. 'Look at this one, baby. See what I've picked for you? The see-saw!'

The Minister stood his ground or at least did his best to play for time. 'What a snake in the grass! Pulling a trick like that on your baby. Pulling a dirty trick like that on your baby.' But when her cheeks started glowing, her eyes shining, he knew what he had to do. 'So you thought you could get rid of me, did you?'

'No, baby, no!' said Vanda, playing along.

'Thought you could get rid of me with a blank piece of paper? Well, you've got another think coming.'

'And what might that be?' cried Vanda in mock horror.

'The cards!' he bellowed. 'The cards! And make it snappy!'

Vanda ran for the cards. 'The cards' meant strip poker! Her favourite foreplay.

The Minister loved his Vanda. More than all her predecessors. All but Dinka, of course. Though they had a lot in common. Big hearts, for one thing. Like all real women . . .

He'd been crazy about Dinka. She was the kind of woman no man could resist, a real beauty. True, all girls were prettier then, but she was special: jet-black hair, pearl-white teeth, and full of fun, the way a woman ought to be. She'd laugh at anything. He'd never heard a laugh like that since.

Damn those Russians! It was all their fault. Russians drove her wild. All you had to do was hum a few bars of *Kalinka* or *Ochi chornye* and she'd start twitching and whooping these passionate whoops from down in her gut, like a female Tarzan or something.

It was bigger than her, something the Minister never understood, and it was the key to her being. The moment she heard their *ei, ai, iyukhnyei!* her eyes would film over and she was gone. Of course, everybody loved the Russians back then; everybody read or saw *How the Steel Was Tempered*, and *The Young Guard*. The Minister remembered giving her a novel called *Alitet Takes to the Mountains* and inscribing it:

> I gaze on you, Dinka, through love's sparkling prism
> And cry, 'All hail to freedom!' and 'Death to fascism!'

But she went too far. In 1948 she married a Russian political officer and the Minister lost track of her. When the break with Stalin came, he turned his back on the Russians like everyone else. He often wondered what his life would have been like if she hadn't left him.

At least he got back at the Russians. Years later, but still. A group of dancers, singers, actors had gone to Moscow on one of those cultural exchanges, the kind that are supposed to cement friendly relations in a week. Well, after one of the performances the Minister had come out on stage to accept a gift from some Russian bigwig, a gigantic picture that took several stage-hands to bring on, and he gave the Russian this big round thing one of the sculptors here had made. Well, the Russians must have thought it was hollow, but it weighed fifty pounds if it weighed an ounce, and he didn't get a grip on it and it fell right on his foot! *Iyukhnyei!* Did they ring down that curtain fast! And while it fell, the Minister had thought of his Dinka.

'You lose, baby!' Vanda screamed, clapping her hands with joy. 'Take off your pants!'

'My pants?' said the Minister, disconcerted. 'I still have my socks on!'

5

'Come in! Come in, Monsieur Prša!' said Jean-Paul Flagus, ushering Prša into his suite. 'So glad to see you! Raúl! We have company!'

The swarthy Raúl appeared, nodded and immediately made his way to the bar. 'Gan I offer you something to dring?' he said in his strange accent.

'You gan,' said Prša, blushing immediately.

'How about a bottle of champagne?' Jean-Paul interjected in French.

'*Oui, merci*,' said Prša, lowering himself into a seat and raising his eyebrows. 'Actually, though, I came to thank you for the magnificent luncheon you put on. As hosts, we should actually have done the honours.'

'You mean the party? A trifle, I assure you.' He paused, then added with great lethargy, 'I'm a rich man, Monsieur Prša.'

Prša thought how wonderful it was to be so rich you could just say so.

'No, no. It was our duty,' Prša insisted, 'though the Minister . . .'

'I understand,' Jean-Paul interrupted. 'Everything will be different when *you* are Minister.'

'Pardon?' Prša gulped.

'You do hope to be Minister, don't you?' asked Jean-Paul, lighting his cigar.

'Well, I . . .'

'Then Minister you shall be,' he said calmly and without a trace of irony.

Prša's mouth dropped open. Here was a man whose age and dignity seemed incompatible with so wildly categorical a statement. 'I really don't know,' he said, shrugging his shoulders.

'The present Minister looks the perfect candidate for a heart attack, don't you think?'

'He's already had one,' Prša blurted out. 'How did you guess?'

'Experience, my boy. The experience that comes with age. One glance at a coeval tells all: burst blood vessels in the cheeks means clogged arteries, deep circles under the eyes – kidney trouble . . . Sorry for the physiological details. I merely wished to point out that I should be happier to see you in his place.'

'But I'm just an ordinary writer,' said Prša, looking modestly into his champagne. Flagus had gone straight to his weak spot. It must have been written all over him! He was sick and tired of the dirty old Minister, sick and tired of writing his speeches, listening to his inanities, toadying to him.

'Surely a man who truly loves books (I remember the talk we had at lunch), a man with so many books to his credit (including a brilliant new novel), can do much more for literature than a doddering relic.'

'In principle, you're right, of course . . .' Prša said cautiously.

'There, you see? That's precisely what I mean. All you need is a bit more élan, panache.'

'I repeat,' said Prša, even more self-effacingly than before, 'I'm just a writer.'

Jean-Paul trained his watery eyes on Prša and blew a few smoke rings. 'Do you know how many languages Agatha Christie has been translated into?' he asked.

'I'm afraid I don't.'

'One hundred and three,' said Flagus, waiting for Prša's reaction. Prša merely shrugged.

'Can you imagine your *Golden Finger* in even a third as many languages?'

'I'm afraid I can't.'

'Raúl!' Flagus called, turning towards the bar. 'Take out your little toy, will you?'

Raúl, who had been looking on in silence, went over to the desk and opened a black box. Soon Prša saw the flicker of a computer screen and heard the clicking of a keyboard.

'Raúl has a doctorate in linguistics. Slavonic linguistics, to be precise. He's a computer wizard besides. Did you know that the

Persian qadi Adul–Hasan Ismail had a library that he transported in strict alphabetical order on four hundred camels? He took it everywhere he went. Nowadays it would fit on a couple of Raúl's floppies.'

Almost immediately Raúl handed the bewildered Prša a print–out listing the words 'golden finger' in thirty languages.

'Nice gadget you've got there,' mumbled Prša, dropping the print–out on the desk as if it had scalded him, 'but there's more to it than that.' He had begun to wonder whether the Frenchman wasn't pulling his leg.

'Not at all, *mon cher*,' said Jean–Paul. 'A little well–placed capital, a few connections . . .'

'You must be joking, Monsieur Flagus,' said Prša, who was by now close to tears. 'Is this some kind of game?'

'If that's how you wish to look at it,' said Flagus affably. 'Yes, let's look at it as a game. You're a writer, you've got imagination. Try and think in broader categories, try and think globally.'

'Globally?'

'When most people look at a map, they think in terms of geography, politics, demography, geology, ecology. Well, when I look at a map, I think in terms of literature. I divide it into unmarked, uncharted areas and areas that on a more conventional map would be designated as rivers, mountains, cities.'

'I don't see your point.'

'My point is that I am a visionary. We live in an age of information, my boy, and the literary map I envision has its own reality. It won't be long now before anything not specifically entered into an information network will cease to exist. And that includes whole countries, cultures, languages. Our "spiritual map" is in for a sea change, wouldn't you say?'

'Oh, definitely,' said Prša, though he had not quite grasped Flagus's argument.

'And surely you'll agree that many realms of human activity are more or less controlled by information systems even now. Well, why not add literature? The total control of literature. Yes, the time has come to bring the whole of our literary heritage under control in one gigantic, yet to be designed and constructed computer, a wonder of technology that will show Raúl's lap-top up for the antiquated plaything it really is.'

'But how can you control something whose very essence is unpredictable? Literature is creativity, intelligence, genius, not data.'

'I didn't say it would be easy. But there are certain factors working in our favour. This is an era of Salieri rather than Mozart, a time in which literature is based upon production values, and production is something that, in principle at least, lends itself to control. Your objection goes back to the romantic myth of the originality, the unique, inimitable quality of each work of literature – nonsense like that. Obsolete as it is, it still has the power to attract. *You've* been taken in by it, if you don't mind my saying so.'

'No, no. Please go on.'

'What we need are effective methods of control, means of thwarting genius, the chaos of genius, if I may put it thus. Literary espionage, for instance. Imagine writer X, who for years has been slogging away at a novel he assumes to be brilliant, unique. Now imagine that someone finds out about the novel – its title, its concerns, everything there is to know about it – and then hires a ghost writer to beat X to the punch. Granted, it won't be so good as what X could have done, but it will certainly devalue, even destroy his original idea. This is war, psychological war, my boy! The survival of the fittest! No one has time today for works of genius. Besides, what do they do but spread discord and revolt.'

'Interesting,' said Prša, who never would have come up with the concept of 'literary espionage' on his own.

'I have been much influenced in these matters by the work of Señor Borges – scholar, transcriber and maker of models – who has done more than anyone to strip literature of its aura of inviolability, to quash the idea of the genius and originality of the written word (though he has unfortunately been carried away by the genius and originality of the *re*written word). Of almost equal importance are the bands of third-rate speed-writers who fill in thematic blanks as if they were crossword puzzles, thus considerably accelerating the pace of literary inflation and unwittingly but unswervingly undermining the myth of a great, unmatched, and unmatchable body of literature. Then there are those major writers who achieve the same result by swallowing the literary small fry, as it were, by the very

185

mass of their output. And a big fish bloated by a meal of little fish is an easy catch. No, production is the answer, my boy. Imagine a literary Andy Warhol producing a series of cloned stories, cloned novels. All one need do is make the reading public believe they represent "brilliant" cynicism, a "dazzling" recycling of everyday experience. By the way, have you noticed that writers are often more concerned with their literary trimmings than with their literary hamburgers?'

'But why should they even make literary hamburgers?' asked Prša, his head swimming with Flagus's eccentric turns of phrase.

'There, didn't I tell you?' said Jean-Paul with a smile. 'You're as burdened with the idea of originality as the rest of them. Have you ever stopped to think of what a great thing uniformity is? What are the things that unite the world as we know it, after all? You can count them on the fingers of one hand: Coca-Cola, hamburgers, the Bible . . . It takes an enormous amount of money and power to create a symbol of uniformity.'

'But what does it do?' asked Prša, who had clearly lost the gist of Flagus's argument.

'It furthers total control, for one thing, though, as I've already implied, that also requires a large army of . . .'

'Army?'

'A large army of literary critics and theoreticians, for example. A critic with a comparative background will always question the claim of a writer to be new, unique; he'll always throw him together with some group or other, some movement, some model. Critics can scarcely wait for a new work to come out so they can pounce on it, tear it to pieces, gnaw off every scrap of meat. And don't think writers don't know it. Don't think a writer staring at his PC in the heat of inspiration can't feel the critic champing on his tail; don't think he isn't scared he'll find it gone the next time he looks. Not even the greatest creator of all time, the Creator Himself, has fared better at the hands – or should I say teeth – of His critics. And His *magnum opus* took only seven days. No, my boy, I have no doubt that some day soon our position of total control will enable us to alter the very face of literature, to guide the efforts of its creators, create our own prefabricated works, award them prizes, make them bestsellers, raise up lowly writers and strike down the mighty, in other words, regulate the course of literary history, be its movers and shakers, so to speak. We live in a technocratic world, my boy. The total control of literature is a monumental idea, a milestone on the road to literary engineering. At last we shall be able to analyze the process of literary production in a scientific fashion and pro-gramme such models as we deem worthy. Global literary engineer-ing! A splendid goal, you must admit. Yes, it is the duty of all those who love and venerate literature to gather data for the computer of the future, for whoever presides over its data will have tremendous power: the hitherto unheard of power to bring forth new forms, a new literature, a new culture. Don't you agree, Monsieur Prša?'

Deeply ensconced in his armchair, Prša was doing some deep thinking. Hadn't he always felt more control was needed? What was his obituary file if not the perfect starting point for the type of information-gathering Jean-Paul had in mind? Should he tell him about it on the spot, or was this not the proper occasion? A map of the world flickered before his eyes. Flagus was right: anything that wasn't hooked into the information network would soon cease to exist. And if somebody at this latitude and longitude failed to take matters into his own hands, it would turn into one of those uncharted areas on Flagus's literary map.

'It occurs to me, Monsieur Flagus,' said Prša suddenly, 'that you must have some ulterior motive for telling me all this.'

'Whatever gives you that idea, Monsieur Prša? No, I'm simply dreaming out loud, fantasizing about how marvellous it would be if more writers with your inspiration were to toy a bit with the idea of total control. During our lunch together you spoke with such insight about literature and your colleagues that I had no qualms about exposing my vision to you. But let me be more concrete. If there were even an ounce of control, would that poor Czech's manuscript have been stolen?'

'You mean you believe him? You believe there *was* a manuscript?'

'That's not the point.'

'Wait a second. The people you were talking about, the writers – they'd be what you might call literary spies, wouldn't they?'

'What is it about the word that bothers you? Dante, Marlowe, Milton, Defoe, Marvell, Byron, Kipling, Somerset Maugham, Graham Greene, John Le Carré – spies all. Wouldn't it make sense for a writer to spy for his literature rather than his country? Tell me, how do you like the idea of an ATCL?'

'ATCL?'

'Agent of the Totalitarian Control of Literature.'

'I can't say I find it very . . . attractive,' said Prša, frowning. 'It reminds me a little of science fiction.'

'Yes, we have indeed been skirting the realm of the fantastic. Though there's nothing unusual in that. We're writers, *ergo* dreamers. But let's forget the whole thing, shall we? Let's raise our glasses to literature, literature just as it is.' And he raised his glass.

'To literary production!' Prša responded nimbly and emptied his glass.

'Let's not go overboard, now,' said Jean-Paul with a wink. 'Did you know that an American poetess by the name of Nancy Luce was known for composing poems about the hens on her farm and copying them out on their freshly laid eggs? She signed each poem with the name of the hen who'd laid the egg.'

6

Vitya Sapozhnikov glanced nervously around the airport restaurant, drumming with his fingers on the table. 'Not here yet,' he sighed, his eyes coming to rest on the girl opposite him as if requesting an explanation.

'He'll come,' she said calmly.

'And if he doesn't?' he said, staring into her face. 'He wasn't in his room!'

'Don't worry. Maybe he took an earlier plane and he'll meet you in Belgrade. Coffee?'

'Vodka, if they have it,' said Sapozhnikov, and started in again: clock, runway, restaurant entrance, girl.

The girl looked on, smiling. When Sapozhnikov's glance came to rest on her, she lowered her glasses from her forehead to her nose.

'Those glasses were in style in Moscow ten years ago,' he said, watching his face in the lenses.

'That's just the point,' she said with an even broader smile.

The waiter brought an espresso for her and a vodka for him. Sapozhnikov grasped the glass with his chubby fingers, traced a few invisible circles on the table, then knocked back the contents in one gulp.

'Cheers!' he said. Then all at once he added, 'You wouldn't happen to have a needle and thread on you, would you?' and pointed to a button hanging by a thread from his jacket.

The girl burst out laughing and shook her head. Sapozhnikov sighed again and reached down into his bag under the table. He pulled out a book and a small bundle, both of which he placed ceremoniously on the table.

'For you,' he said.

The girl picked up the book and gave Sapozhnikov a questioning look.

'Yes, mine.'

'*One of Us*,' she read out loud. 'Will you autograph it for me?'

'Oh, sure. I forgot. Got a pen? I'll give you my address too. You must look me up when you come to Moscow. My wife makes the most fabulous bortsch.'

Next she unwrapped the bundle. Out peeked the heads of three wooden dolls. '*Matryoshkas!*' she cried. 'But why three?'

'Well, I bought three. For souvenirs. In case I met people.'

'And you didn't?'

'Well, you . . .' he said, frowning and looking back at the runway. 'How much time have we got till take-off?'

'Plenty. He'll make it.'

'You don't think something's happened to him, do you?'

'No, of course not. If he doesn't show up here, he'll certainly meet you in Belgrade.' She glanced down at the inscription he'd written and said with as much sincerity as she could muster, 'I'm looking forward to reading it.'

Sapozhnikov reached down into his bag again. 'Listen, Anja . . .'

'Yes?' she said, laughing.

Sapozhnikov took his hand out of the bag and drummed with his fingers on the table again. 'Why are you always laughing? Look, are you sure you haven't got a needle and thread?'

'Positive,' she said, shrugging her shoulders, blowing on the long lock over her forehead, rolling her eyes and sputtering laughter.

'Go ahead and laugh,' Sapozhnikov muttered, and reached back down into his bag. This time he came up with a longish rectangular parcel, which he laid down carefully in front of her with two fingers. 'This is for you too.'

'More?' she cried gaily, extracting a box with a man's wrist-watch in it. 'Thank you, but I have a watch,' she said, and, clicking a nail against the dial, added, 'It even works.'

'Take it anyway. I bought it because I thought I'd meet some . . .'

'. . . people. I know,' she said, and then felt the need to buck him up. 'You're a real magician, Vitya. What else are you going to pull out of your magic bag?'

But Sapozhnikov only frowned again and sighed.

'Hey, what's wrong?'

'Nothing,' he said, looking back at the runway.

'Cheer up, cheer up,' she said. 'How about another vodka! My treat!'

Sapozhnikov nodded, touched by the offer, but went back to his own thoughts. The waiter soon brought the vodka, and again Sapozhnikov engulfed the glass with his hand, twisted it several times on the table as if preparing it for take-off, then raised it high into the air and poured it down his throat. 'We're human too,' he said in the direction of the runway, thus getting four days of protest off his chest. Then he yanked the button off his jacket with such passion and finality that it might have been his heart. For a moment the girl thought he was going to place it before her, but in the end he stuck it in his pocket.

Just then they heard the 'first call for the flight to Moscow via Belgrade departing from gate four', and Sapozhnikov bent down to pick up his bag. But the girl suddenly flicked her glasses up on to her forehead again and said, 'Wait here.'

She was back in a flash with a little bundle of her own. 'This is for you,' she said with a peck on the cheek.

'Anja! Really! You shouldn't have!'

'Now let's go,' she said, giving his arm a friendly nudge. And off they went.

The girl ran out of the airport building and raised her arm to hail a taxi. When she noticed the two watches on her wrist – a woman's and a man's – she burst out laughing and began waving her arm madly, as if the watches were bracelets hung with tinkling baubles.

'I see you! I see you! You don't have to wave your arm off!' the taxi-driver grumbled, opening the door for her.

Victor Sapozhnikov stood obediently waiting his turn at gate four, still keeping an eye out for Troshin. 'Maybe he *will* turn up in Belgrade,' he thought with a sigh, and at that moment his eye lit on a public telephone. He hesitated for a moment, then left his bag, and went over to it.

'That's right. He's not at the airport . . . I don't know . . . I think he was with an Austrian reporter . . . Sabina something . . . Right

'. . . I don't know . . . Don't mention it. Only doing my duty . . . Right . . .'

Sapozhnikov hung up and went back to his bag. He looked around again and then remembered the girl's present. He reached into the bag and peeled the paper off a large, thick sandwich.

'What a girl!' thought Sapozhnikov, and took a big bite. The sandwich tasted delicious.

7

After Jean-Paul Flagus and his companion Raúl passed through customs, Jean-Paul turned and gave Prša a hearty wave. Waving back, Prša felt the waiterly mask of reserved cordiality drain from his face for the first time in the past four days, and for the first time he allowed himself to feel tired. He collapsed into the nearest plastic chair and sat there, gawking at the travellers in the artificial orange-yellow light of the airport and enjoying the sweet numbness enveloping his body.

Jean-Paul Flagus was an odd bird. Maybe he had a private income and literary ambitions, maybe he was an agent for a foreign power, maybe he was just a brilliant practical joker or a literary theoretician gone over the edge or a devil from a novel in disguise. In any case, his identity could be checked into. That wasn't the point. The point was that Flagus had *power* (which might be another way of saying *money*, but that wasn't the point either), and Prša had a good nose for that kind of thing. A nose like a wolf. They say that wolves never attack anything stronger than they are; their victims are always puny and frail. That is how Prša operated. For as long as he could remember. Ever since he'd had a ball stolen, a tooth knocked out, and ever since his father, once a strong, vibrant man, had been made a living relic at the whim of an informer, at the hands of torturers. His father had come back from prison with a face that was all weakness. Prša knew its every wrinkle, its every twitch: fear never leaves a man; it even grows with efforts to hide it. He'd seen its tell-tale signs in others as well, and he vowed never to let himself be victimized by a wolf. He would be a clown, a chameleon, a parrot – anything but a victim.

His eye fell on a fashionably dressed young woman breezing through customs without a care in the world. He noticed the leather

193

strap of an elegant travelling-bag on her slim wrist and wondered what would happen to her self-confident mask if he went up to her and for no reason whatever gave that strap a tug. The thought excited him. He remembered having been excited in the same way by the sudden turn in his relationship with his wife (a high official's spoiled-brat daughter, whose self-confidence depended wholly on such external factors as the latest fashions and Daddy's dollars) the first time he walloped her across her much-pampered face and the façade fell like the façade of a building under fire. She'd run off for a while now, but she'd be back. He could go straight over to that public telephone and blackmail her back: he knew everything there was to know about her father's import–export racket. Blackmail was a racket too, of course, but you had to fight fire with fire. And she would come crawling back to him. She'd justify it as a sacrifice for her father and her children, but she'd be driven as much by fear or humiliation. Things were going to be a lot simpler now. His parrot days were over. The time had come to show some teeth. To spit in the Minister's face, for example. He who spits first spits best. *The Golden Finger.* The golden finger was now pointing at him. He had to take it and make this latitude and longitude on Jean-Paul's literary map his own, stamp it with his golden fingerprint.

Prša stood and headed for the telephone.

The elegant young woman had finished with customs and was now waiting listlessly for her flight to be called. Her eye was caught by a small middle-aged man with an exciting intensity in his moody, sullen face. The man put a coin in the telephone. It got stuck. He gave the telephone a whack. Out poured a handful of money. The man's lips parted in a smile.

Golden finger, zlatan prst, digitus aureus, zolotoi palets, doigt d'or, goldener Finger, arany ujj, zlatý prst, złoty palec, dedo de oro, dito di oro, gishti i artë, χρυσους δακτυλος, gouden vinger, gylden finger . . .

8

The Minister lay on the couch, staring dully at the television set. He felt rotten.

'Baby-y-y! Want some garlic in it?' came Vanda's voice from the kitchen.

'A little,' the Minister called back. He was just tired, that's all. He'd have to put in for retirement. He'd start the ball rolling tomorrow. And move in with Vanda. The only person who cared. He'd have been a lot happier if he'd met her early in life. He might even have had some decent children. His wife – God, she was awful. Always so *genteel*. At first he'd been stupid enough to see her coldness as a kind of virginal modesty. He even found it attractive – like cool, clean sheets after a hard day's work. But she had the soul of a secret agent. She never let him out of her sight. And that look on her face! Like somebody picking up a dirty sock. For a while he thought he could re-educate her, but then she took off on her own, studied law, took a doctorate, and the dirty-sock face got worse and worse. She was smarter than him, better educated, but she stuck to him like a leech. He couldn't understand it. Now he saw it as a kind of Prša-like streak in her, the kind of slimy stick-to-it-iveness Prša had shown through the years. Of course with Prša there were extenuating circumstances: he shouldn't have sent Prša's father to Goli Otok back in '48, but those were hard times, bloody times – some people were guilty after all – and he never dreamed of 'repenting'. What he had done was keep Prša junior out of gaol in '71 during the next big round-up. And he hadn't found a way to shake him loose since. The funny thing was, Prša didn't really need him. Neither did his wife. But Vanda – Vanda couldn't live without him. If he lived into old age, he wanted to live it with Vanda and Vanda alone. Like Cousteau's salmon on TV. Vanda would be his she-salmon in their nice, warm ooze, mating and mating, scale to scale, tail to tail, until they fell apart and sank into the deep, piece by piece, bone by bone, rotting there slowly, sweetly, one on top of the other in a heap, settling into the rich dark mud, while billions of silly minnows and polliwogs scurried about over them, eager to have their day as big fish before they too fell apart and sank into the ooze.

'What kind of potatoes do you want with your fish, baby? Boiled or baked?'

'Boiled!'

Just then a short feature about the Literary Colloquium came on the news. The Minister looked up to see a ten-year-old photograph of himself on the screen. *We have just learned of the sudden death today in Zagreb of* . . . and the Minister heard his own name, there could be no mistaking it . . . *long an active figure in the political and cultural* . . . Wait a second! What's going on here?! . . . *He was born in* . . . and the Minister heard the date of his birth . . . *and after the war he occupied important positions in* . . . Sabotage, that's what it was! Who would play such a dirty trick on him? . . . *rising quickly through the ranks to* . . . The Minister felt a sudden stabbing pain in his heart. . . . *He succumbed to a heart attack while taking part in the Colloquium* . . . Sabotage! Quick, Vanda! The telephone! he tried to shout, but by now the pain had slithered into his left arm and he could scarcely breathe. Vanda! he tried again, but all that came was a hoarse rattle. When Vanda wandered into the room a few moments later, she froze – a knife in one hand, a potato in the other – at the sight of him. The last thing that flashed through his panic-stricken mind was a couplet that went:

> The fearless Comanche then raises his bow
> And I, a lone ranger, ride on.

Then darkness descended upon him and he lay there motionless, his face bright red, his eyes rolled upwards, his hands gripping his crotch.

'Baby-y-y!' Vanda screamed at last.

Next to the typical scene of a coronary victim stretched out on a couch, the paramedics found the highly atypical scene of a woman in a fur hat, winter coat and thick gloves sprawled on the floor, shivering as if in a fever and sobbing uncontrollably.

9

The moment the NO SMOKING sign went out in the first-class cabin, Jean-Paul Flagus laid his head back and lit one of his thick cigars.

'Tell me again, *mon cher Raúl*, how you managed to get back at Jan Zdražil even after the unfortunate disappearance of his novel.'

'I stole into his compartment just before departure time and slipped a few anti-regime pamphlets into his bag.'

'Are you sure they'll do the trick?'

'I believe I am well enough acquainted with the current political situation to state without compunction that he will be arrested at the border.'

'My old friend Kolář will be very happy to hear it,' Jean-Paul Flagus said and puffed a few smoke rings.

'Might I ask, monsieur, why your friend is so intent on revenge?'

'It goes back a number of years to the time when Kolář still lived in Czechoslovakia. Apparently, his brother there wrote a fine novel, which Zdražil, its putative editor, did everything in his power to mangle. When the novel came out with Zdražil's "corrections", Kolář's brother committed suicide. Kolář is now more than wealthy enough to afford a minor satisfaction like revenge.'

'By the way, monsieur, I read the novel before it . . . disappeared.'

'Well?'

'Zdražil wasn't lying. It *is* a masterpiece.'

'Damn!' said Flagus with a snort. 'Don't tell Kolář.'

'Oh no, monsieur! One more thing, monsieur. Who do you think could have known that we stole the novel? Who could have stolen it from our room?'

'Perhaps the person who erased the data from your disk at last year's PEN Congress in New York. Which reminds me, when does

197

that "Literature in the New Europe" symposium in Amsterdam open?'

'Tomorrow, monsieur.'

'What do you say we pop over and have a look? I have a suspicion or two about who that person is.'

'Very well, monsieur.'

'Tell me, how did you handle the Flaubert situation?' Jean-Paul asked, changing the subject.

'I used Monsieur Prša's recommendation and library card to take out all editions of Flaubert in the city's libraries; then I bought up everything I could find in the bookshops.'

'Did you make a decent haul?' Flagus asked bitterly.

'Enough for a goodly number of boxes, though I can't say I got very much for them.'

'And did you watch them actually throw the books in the pulper, as I requested?'

'I did, monsieur.'

'Thank you, Raúl.'

Raúl let a few moments of silence elapse before venturing his next question. 'Might I ask, monsieur, how one can hate someone who has so long been dead. It's like hating a . . . statue.'

Jean-Paul turned and fixed his watery eyes on Raúl. 'Flaubert was the writer who made me aware of what true talent is and thereby injected me with a virus of hate. His shade has followed me ever since; it chokes me like an invisible noose. Flaubert is merely a name for talent, Raúl, and talent is something I loathe and despise. Some people build rich lives on love; I have built mine on hate. Every Mozart must have his Salieri, don't you think? And remember: the Mozarts die young; the Salieris have their way.' All at once Flagus cheered up. 'But let's leave motives aside for the moment, shall we, Raúl? Motives may have a certain truth to them, but they limit truth as well. Think rather of the power to have one's own way. Which is the power a writer has when he assigns his characters their fortunes, incidentally. But my satisfaction is greater, because I do the same with *living writers*. The creativity involved is the same, you see? I design their fates and then make them happen. Of course, each of them wants what none of them has – a life full of excitement and adventure. But I give one a melodramatic death and another a new lease on life. Which reminds me, did you take care of our new friend Prša?'

'I timed the death notice to arrive at the station just before the evening news.'

'And you're certain they'll put it on the air?'

'I have no reason to doubt it, monsieur.'

'You've done a good job, Raúl. You don't mind my quizzing you like this, do you?'

'Might I ask *you* another question, monsieur?' ventured the diffident Raúl. 'Would you tell me your opinion of Monsieur Prša? Do you really think he grasps what you wish of him?'

'Enough for my purposes. He's smarter than he looks, actually. A writer, Raúl, is half parrot, half priest. He is a poll parrot in the loftiest sense of the word. He speaks French if his master is French, but if sold to a Persian he'll say his "Polly's a fool" and "Polly wants a cracker" in Persian. A parrot has no age; it cannot tell day from night. If it bores its master, it is covered with a black cloth, and that, for literature, is the surrogate of night.'

'A fine quotation, monsieur.'

'You're turning into an insufferable know-all, Raúl,' said Jean-Paul Flagus, shaking a finger at him in jest.

'My apologies, monsieur.'

'Though isn't everything a quotation in the end, *mon cher Raúl*? The very world we live in – is it not the quotation of another world, our lives quotations of other lives? Not that our pleasure diminishes thereby. Quite the contrary.' Jean-Paul smiled and laid his hand on Raúl's. Raúl's hand was sinewy and warm.

10

Everything went smoothly, painlessly. At the Yugoslav border, which he had actually feared more, as well as at the Austrian. He held his breath while fate in the person of a young border guard stamped the green passport page and said, '*Willkommen in Österreich!*'

As soon as he closed the door, Troshin drew the curtains, turned off the light and listened to his own heart pounding. He took a deep breath and was surprised to hear a whistlelike sound escape from him. His fear, he realized. He switched on the light above his head and opened the passport, his hand trembling. He examined the various stamps as if they could be read like palms.

The train began to move. Troshin shed his jacket, stretched out otherwise fully dressed on the berth and flicked the switch again. He closed his eyes, breathing in the chlorine from the pillows and listening to the clickety-clack of the wheels. In a few hours he would be in Vienna, his head in Sabina's lap, forgetting, forgetting.

He tried to breathe in rhythm with the train. It didn't work. His heart beat too fast or too slow. He opened his eyes and felt a shiver run down his back: there was a mirror on the underside of the berth above him, and his own reflection stared down at him in the semi-darkness. His body looked smaller than natural, truncated somehow; it fitted too neatly into the narrow coffin of the berth. Troshin let out a curse, lit up a cigarette and stepped into the corridor.

The dimly lit corridor was empty except for a small man standing at the window, looking out into the dark. The man turned, nodded and moved to the next window. Troshin leaned against the door to his compartment and inhaled. He suddenly felt unsure of himself, as if engulfed by a thick mist of loneliness.

The man stood there immobile, stock-still, his back a bit too straight, and either his bearing or his dark suit put Troshin in mind of a waiter. He recalled having had a similar sensation of 'waiterliness' back in Zagreb, and now it had followed him into the train.

'Are you going to Vienna?' he heard himself ask. Moreover, he asked it in French and immediately blushed, French being a language he spoke poorly. The man nodded pleasantly, and then, as if Troshin's question had reminded him of something, took a newspaper out of his pocket and disappeared behind its pages. Troshin noticed a black umbrella hanging from his elbow. It had a striking handle in the shape of a dog's head. But even more striking was the man's large silver signet ring, which sent a cold sparkle in Troshin's direction.

Troshin met his own face again in the dark glass. It looked old. God, did this whole thing make sense? Maybe he should have given up the idea. Maybe he should give up the idea that things make sense. Though what difference did it make now that he'd cut the umbilical cord? What difference did it make whether he lived a new life or died? All he knew was that he'd burned his bridges behind him and that his only guide through the darkness ahead were those two pale-grey, expressionless eyes.

The corridor was impossibly quiet. The man was still buried behind his newspaper. *Die Literatur-Zeitung*. Wasn't that the one Sabina worked for? Troshin yawned more out of uneasiness than a need for sleep and, putting out his cigarette, nodded to the man (who couldn't see him) and went back into the compartment.

Again he lay down and closed his eyes. A series of images unfurled beneath his eyelids the way landscapes succeed one another in a train window. They opened with Sabina, then moved back through his life as in a film. Troshin felt helplessly bound to a seat in an imaginary cinema, aware, as so often happens in dreams, that he had no choice but to watch the evening's absurd feature to the end. One scene stood out: a child (a boy named Yura) is standing in the middle of a deserted Trubnaya Street courtyard clutching a ball in both hands, hunching his shoulders. Go on, play, his mother motions to him from a closed window on the third floor. There is a glass of gooseberry compote on the window-sill. The glass has a label on it, and the label reads 'Gooseberry Compote' in his mother's hand. Go on, Yura, play, play! his mother motions, smiling through the dull glass. But the boy stands motionless, still hunching his shoulders, still clutching the ball to his breast. It is very cold out. He is alone in the courtyard. A bird may fly into the picture and fly out again. All of a sudden Troshin sees someone emerge from the darkness or, rather, a hand, an invisible hand setting fire to the live picture. He sees his mother's face turning yellow and slowly fading, her hand pausing in the air, then it too fading; he sees the compote glass (now for some reason enormous) and the individual gooseberries go up in flames and fade away, until soon there is nothing left but wispy scraps of ash.

Then Troshin has the feeling it was all just a dream in a dream and he is now being awakened from the dream by the man from the corridor. Troshin can see his face plainly. He bends over him, raises his black umbrella, and aims the point of the stick at his chest. It's only a dream and dreams don't hurt, Troshin thinks, but then he thinks better of it and covers his heart with his hand. The point enters right between the thumb and index finger, and Troshin feels a sharp pain. *Je suis un parapluie*, he mutters. It was a sentence he had memorized in his French-language kindergarten. The film starts up again for a time: the courtyard returns to the screen, and the boy with the hunched shoulders nods, tosses the ball into the air and fades from the picture. *Hey . . .*, Troshin wheezes with the same hint of reproach that his mother's voice used to have and, just as he thinks again how amazingly absurd it all is, he loses consciousness.

11

Sabina Pluhar gave a satisfied stretch after typing the final sentence. 'Pushkin!' she called seductively, on her way to the refrigerator. She poured some milk into a bowl and called again. 'Here, Pushkin!'

An enormous Siamese cat slithered down from the window-sill and landed at her feet in a single noiseless bound.

'Pushy-pushy-pushkin!' she lisped, scratching the cat behind one ear. Both had their eyes half shut – the cat with pleasure, the girl with fatigue.

The phone rang.

'May I speak to Sabina Pluhar?'

'Speaking.'

'Yury Troshin will not be coming.'

'What?!'

'He passed away just after crossing the border. Heart attack, it appears . . . Mademoiselle Pluhar?'

'Yes?'

'Your cheque is on its way.'

'Thank you.'

'Incidentally, we learned only ten minutes ago that as the result of an error . . .'

'An error?'

'. . . it was actually Sapozhnikov who . . .'

'Sapozhnikov?'

'Mistakes do happen, Mademoiselle Pluhar. You are to forget the whole affair, is that clear?'

'Yes, Monsieur Flagus.'

Sabina hung up. She sat by the phone for a while, then went over to her desk. She pulled the last sheet out of the typewriter and placed it with the others. She took a bottle of correction fluid, whited out each 'Yury Troshin' in the text, and typed 'Victor Sapozhnikov' into the spaces page by page. Then she went back to the telephone.

'Yes, the interview is ready . . . His name is Victor Sapozhnikov . . . That's right, a young Soviet writer. I'm sure you'll find it interesting. I can drop it off in the morning if you like.'

While she spoke, the giant cat leaped up noiselessly on to her desk and stretched out over the papers. One of its paws pointed to the following statement made by Victor Sapozhnikov:

> *Sie fragen mich, wie ich das sowjetische System erlebe. Was soll man über ein System sagen, in dem die Menschen innerhalb nur einer Generation Krieg, Hunger, Gefängnis, Konzentrationslager, Lügen, Übergriffe, Korruption, Demagogie, Massenvernichtungen, Sklavenarbeit, Armut, Angst kennengelernt haben? . . . Ein Draculasystem . . .*

'Down, Pushkin!' Sabina shouted, noticing the cat on the desk. The cat jumped down with supreme indifference and headed back to the window-sill. Sabina was shivering. She sat in a chair and rubbed her chin against her shoulder. Her pale–grey, expressionless eyes were open wide and large tears trickled down her cheeks.

12

Dear Peer,

I'm not coming home. I'm on my way south with Ivan. I'll write you more about him later when I have time for a letter. I feel like a ball of wool that has started rolling and has no idea where it will end. It's a wonderful feeling.

Yours,
Cecilia

13

Pipo Fink sat deep in his armchair, absent-mindedly fingering Marc's binoculars in the semi-darkness. He was desolate, undone. The stupid Yank. Blows into town for four days complete with binoculars and bird book, has a look-see, and poof! he's gone. Just like that. Without so much as a *ciao*. Screw you, Pipo!

He pictured Marc (in T-shirt and tennis-shoes!) making his way through the international jungle of Kennedy Airport. If they'd taken their game to its natural conclusion, he, Pipo, would have been the one pink-panthering his way through the crowd. And beyond. Marc would have been sitting in this moth-eaten armchair, in this ridiculously high-ceilinged flat, all yellow with age and as steeped in stench and dust and smog as eternity itself. Hm . . . It wouldn't get Marc down, though, and Pipo knew why: lack of experience. Marc hadn't spent years in this stinking menagerie, deaf, dumb, blind and doomed to solitude, he hadn't lived the life of a reptile, of a snail . . .

Pipo absent-mindedly patted Marc's binoculars and lifted them to his eyes for a look-see. What was left for someone like him, who instead of hanging out in international airports (one of his metaphors for life) hung around in a musty apartment? What were the screenplay possibilities? If he were sitting in the Russian Tea Room on Fifty-Seventh Street and training his binoculars on Zagreb, what would he feel nostalgia for? A novel entitled *The Life and Works of Pipo Fink*? A bunch of TV scripts about bear-cubs and ants and why the wind blows and the rain rains, which his mother had arranged in neat files? His mother?

'*Pipili!*'
'*Yes?*'

'What are you shouting for?'
'You're the one who's shouting!'
'I am not! I just wanted to see if you were awake.'
'Well, I am.'
'Want some coffee?'
'Yes!'
'You're shouting again! I thought I gave birth to a child, not a monster!'
'I didn't choose my parents! Only monsters can spawn monsters!'
'What a terrible thing to say about your poor, dead father!'
'I meant you, not him!'
'I know what you meant. You meant you wish I was dead!'
'I did not!'
'Well, I do. At least I wouldn't have to worry about you.'
'Worry about me?'
'Well, look at you! No wife, no children . . .'
'That's enough, Mamma!'
'. . . only me. I'm all you've got.'
'Are you going to make coffee or aren't you!'
'There, you see?'
'There I see what?'
'The way you treat me.'
'Hey, switch channels, will you?'
'What's that supposed to mean?'
'It means I'm sick of your educational TV.'
'Well, I can't get you on any channel!'

Pipo aimed the binoculars at the bookshelf. Long rows of identically bound white volumes. *Five Centuries of Croat Literature*. Mamma bought it on the instalment plan. For no reason in particular at first, then for Pipo. (*If it wasn't for me, he'd never have gone into literature, which might have been a lot better for everyone concerned!*) Five centuries! Though, of course, every country, large or small, has its five centuries. The Gutenberg galaxy and all that. And why shouldn't the Croats have as many volumes of 'great works' available for sound-proofing a living-room wall as the Danes, Flemings, Walloons, Andorrans, Luxembourgers, Icelanders or Irish? They all had their time-honoured ways of determining who was to be included in the canon, who excluded, and how much and what of the lucky few was to be preserved. Five centuries! Five centuries of hard-bound, indispensable, representative, accredited classics. Should you devote your life to assuring yourself a volume? Was it worth it just to spend your afterlife squeezed between two random authors (authors you may have spent your current life avoiding) in a living-room bookshelf?

Still, it was better than wasting your imagination on those bears and ants, on idyllic goo that didn't fool even the tiniest of tots. If by some miracle you were given something decent to work on, you might be unable to rise to the occasion by now.

'This script of yours, Fink . . .'
  'Yes?'
  'It'd cost a fortune to make. It needs a lot of work.'
  'Any suggestions?'
  'Well, you can get rid of the puppets, for one.'
  'That's easy enough.'
  'And why so many actors? It's only television.'
  'But don't you think . . .'
  'I don't think, I know. One is enough.'
  'Fine.'
  'And those stupid sets! Nothing beats a nice clean backdrop.'
  'All right.'
  'Then the pies. I mean, can't you ever be serious?'
  'But it's for children!'
  'For children, not a hungry tech crew, OK?'
  'OK.'
  'As for the hot air, the poetry stuff, leave it to the theatre. This is television, man. Keep it simple!'
  'Right.'
  'Oh, and that sequence at the zoo is out. Location costs are astronomical!'
  'But I thought kids would . . .'
  'Kids know what an elephant looks like. They don't need you to show them.'
  'Fine.'
  'And have it ready for me by tomorrow.'
  'Fine.'
  'By the way, I spoke to one of your writer friends this morning. Pusić?

*Kusić? Gave me a whole pile of scripts. They're breaking down the doors,
Fink. Ph.D.'s too. You got a Ph.D., Fink?'*
  'No.'
  'Just wondering.'

It was hopeless. All you could do was hate it all, negate it all,
trample it all underfoot. What else could you expect in a place where
everything was stupid, dirty, sick, where anyone with talent was
doomed to failure or living-corpsehood? It had become a tradition
over those five centuries: a writer would make a running jump and
a big splash and then sink to the bottom and get stuck in our
mythical Pannonian muck, mud, mire, in unremitting provincialism, ignorance, madness, drunkenness – you name it. What was left
but to give in, give up, stop dreaming – that was the worst of it –
renew old friendships, discover new interests, take up a hobby,
climb the Sljeme at least once a week, renew your membership in
the American Library, sign up for a language course, go to the
mountains in winter and the coast in summer, save for one trip
abroad a year – four days were enough, a four-day trip was not to
be sneezed at – sneeze at as few things as possible, adopt a positive
attitude, make sure nothing slipped through your fingers, rewrite
your big script and resubmit it, start work on a novel, start to jog,
learn survival techniques, stop dreaming, get with it, get married,
have a family, defend the virtues of day-to-day existence, make it the
basis of *your* existence, wave it like a flag, it was all there was . . .

  'Hello?'
  *'Hi! Remember that side of pork I told you we might lay our hands on
through union connections? Well, it's ours.'*
  'Have you bought the onions to go with it?'
  'Two fifty-pound sacks.'
  'Good.'
  *'I'm going to drive it all home now. Would you pick up the boy at
school?'*
  'I can't. I've got a meeting and then an appointment at the bank to see
about that loan.'
  'All right. I'll do it.'
  'And would you stop off at Mamma's for the laundry?'

'What laundry?'
'I had to use her machine. I couldn't get anyone in to look at ours.'
'All right. I'll do it.'
'Good. See you.'
'Bye.'

It was hopeless. Day-to-day existence was all there was. It was the most efficient formula for survival. Life with cloven-hoofed ruminants may be stuffy and smelly, but solitary confinement is both solitary and confining. Stop dreaming. Or at least reprogramme the dreams.

Pipo hoisted himself out of the armchair, binoculars in hand, and realized he felt weak. He might have a fever. He went into the kitchen hoping to find something to drink in the refrigerator, but the refrigerator was empty. In the pantry he found a dusty bottle with some slimy dark-green herb floating in it, clearly one of Mamma's high-alcohol medicinal concoctions. He opened the bottle, swigged, shuddered and staggered to the kitchen table.

The kitchen was a godawful mess. Only the night before, Marc had been sitting there at the table. The things he'd said to him, the way he'd played himself up! A wave of shame came over him and he took another swig from the bottle. He brought the binoculars up to his eyes and suddenly he was in another world, an aquarium, swimming along the walls, the cabinets, the dishes. In Marc's binoculars Mamma's day-to-day existence took on its own sad beauty.

On the table he spied a glass jar labelled PLUM JAM 1983 in his mother's handwriting. Pipo focused on the label, reading it over and over as if deciphering a hieroglyphic text. Then he put down the binoculars and picked up the jar, turning it reverentially in his hands like a priceless *objet d'art* whose existence was the sole remaining proof of human life prior to a nuclear explosion.

After their third joint they'd felt the need for something sweet. They took the jar off the pantry shelf and started spooning the contents directly into their mouths, choking with laughter. The feeling of lightness now returned to Pipo, the feeling that everything just is, everything co-exists, there is no cruel order of things. He remembered the exhilarating feeling of things and images flowing

210

one into the other (Flash Gordon in the old comic book on the window-sill reciting Hamlet's monologue), the warm, iridescent feeling of the brotherhood of all things. Everything was right somehow and great fun.

But what happened next – outside the kitchen, after the kitchen – Pipo could not remember. How did he get to bed? When did Marc go? And why had he forgotten to leave a note or at least a short message at the hotel? (Pipo had phoned there the moment he got out of bed.)

Gathering up the jam jar and the booze bottle on the way back to his room, Pipo noticed Marc's Talking Heads cassette lying on a shelf. So he'd forgotten that too. Softened by the thought, he added the cassette to his booth and, after dropping into his chair and taking a gulp from the bottle (avoiding the slimy green stuff as much as possible), he slipped the cassette into his new Sanyo and turned it on. Instead of the Talking Heads on came Marc's voice. Pipo's mouth fell open.

Hey there, Pipo old buddy! You can close your mouth now. The reason I turned on the tape is I didn't want to wake you. So while you catch up on your shut-eye, I'm sitting here with Mom's preserves (yum!) and talking on top of the Talking Heads. You were high as a kite, old buddy, and on three joints! I know why: lack of experience. You think too much. You're not Dostoevsky, you know . . . Don't worry. I won't chew your ear off. I have to get back to the hotel and pack. I've got an early flight for Amsterdam. There's another literature conference there – something about the New Europe – and I thought I'd check it out for a day or two on my way home. I left you my address in the fridge (I knew you'd open it the minute you got up). Oh, by the way, I'm the one who pinched the Czech's manuscript. You can close your mouth again. Want to know how? Simple, my dear Pipo. I lifted it from the French guy's room. How did I know it was there? It all began at the PEN Club Congress in New York last year, but that's a whole nother story. The upshot of it is, the guy's a real nut. Like, certifiable. The Dr No, no, the Lex Luthor of literature. Rich, powerful, obsessed and as nasty as they come. Want to know

211

how I got into his room? Heh-heh. Wait till you hear this. Once I needed to learn how to crack a safe for a novel I was writing. I was heavily into Realism at the time, so I took some lessons from a professional. A professional safe-cracker, I mean, not a professional writer. Anyway, I turned out to have the knack. The wife and kids get a real kick out it: I never use a key to open a door. It's like this Clark Kent/Superman thing. But now I'm running off at the mouth and erasing your new Heads. There's only one more thing I wanted to say . . . I left you my tennis-shoes, my T-shirt, and my binoculars. In case something happens to me, you dig? Best to your mom. Tell her the jam was yummy. Hey, I have an idea! Why don't you hop on a plane and meet me in Amsterdam! It'd be great! My number there is 233 456. *What's faster than a speeding bullet? It's a bird, it's a plane, it's* . . . Come on, Pipo, you old stick-in-the-mud. Action, Pipo! Action!

Pipo played the tape again twice. Then he went into the kitchen and opened the fridge. Sure enough, Marc's card was sticking out from between two eggs. Then he closed the fridge, leaving the card in place, and went back to his room. He took another swig out of Mamma's bottle and switched the cassette-player on. This time for the music.

That Marc was an incredible guy. His story, though – it was so garbled. Like a quick first draft. A French maniac steals a manuscript from a Czech maniac who seems to have stolen it from himself, whereupon Marc steals the stolen manuscript from the French maniac. And then that conference in Amsterdam. 'Come on, Pipo, you old-stick-in-the-mud.' Easy for him to say. That was just the point he was trying to make about the difference in their speeds and (another of his metaphors for life) screens. Pipo would have to see whether there was anything left in his account, borrow the rest from Mamma (*All right, lazy-bones. But will I ever stop footing your bills?*), negotiate a few extra scripts, phone the airport and find out whether there *were* any flights to Amsterdam (you could never be sure in this country) and then work like a beaver for the next six months to break even . . .

What's the matter, Pipo baby? Is your *Side of Pork* script any more true-to-life than Marc's Superman story? With a flick of the lens your pork will look phantasmagorically surreal and as far removed as the planet Pluto. Action, isn't that what you wanted, Pipo? Maybe a quick trip to Amsterdam (to give Marc his binoculars back) will give you something you've never had: a plot. What are you standing there for, blinking like a lizard? What you need is a trip to Amsterdam, not a Hamlet trip (the latter – in its oversimplified 'To be or not to be' version – being culturalogically coded to produce spiritual diarrhoea at the press of a button). Come on, you old stick-in-the-mud. Flick the lens. You can do better than life if life is so low in talent. Action, Pipo! Action!

INT. PIPO'S FLAT. NIGHT.
Pipo sits in his armchair, deep in thought. He is smoking nervously. Suddenly, as if having come to a momentous decision, he stands and strides over to the window. He contemplates his own image in the dark glass. Then he returns to his armchair, sits down, takes a swig from the bottle beside it and dials a telephone number. Then he changes his mind and hangs up. His head falls back to the head-rest, his legs go up on the table, Close-up on his tennis-shoes. Blackout.

> TALKING HEADS
> *And you may find yourself living in a shotgun shack.*
> *And you may find yourself in another part of the world.*
> *And you may find yourself behind the wheel of a large automobile.*
> *And you may find yourself in a beautiful house with a beautiful wife.*
> *And you may ask yourself, 'Well . . . how did I get here?'*

14

Even though he did not get back to his flat until very late, the young Spanish consular official did not go to bed immediately. He had spent the evening with a beautiful student of Spanish literature, eating crayfish and drinking wine by candle-light, and was too aroused to fall asleep. All he could think about was the walk they had planned for the following afternoon. So he picked up the latest *Vjesnik* and was immediately drawn to a short article that read:

> Today marked the conclusion of the Zagreb Literary Colloquium, a biennial symposium that brings together local writers with their foreign counterparts. The theme of this year's meeting was 'Contemporary Literature: Its Trends and Tendencies in the Dialectics of World Events'. The exchange of opinions benefited greatly from a lively, friendly atmosphere.
>
> The tone of the conference, which began on Monday, was set by the French delegate, Jean-Paul Flagus, nephew of the famous Gustave Flaubert. Among its highlights was yesterday's tribute to Vuk Prša on the occasion of the recent publication of his novel, *The Golden Finger*. The event, which took place at the Sljeme Meat Packing Factory, was of special interest to the workers, who for the first time in their lives had a chance to meet and chat with so distinguished a group of artists.
>
> At the final session, Mr Prša, who organized this year's Colloquium, expressed his gratitude to the participants for the unusually high level of scholarly and creative discourse and announced that the papers would appear in a special issue of the literary review *Republika*. After

wishing everyone present success in his or her literary endeavours, Mr Prša brought the Colloquium to a close with the words, '*Au revoir* in two years!'

E.B.-T.

The Spanish consular official put down the newspaper and immediately jotted ¡*Protestar!* in his diary. He found it unseemly, to say the least, that the article had omitted all mention of the tragic death of José Ramón Espeso. It was *their* hotel, after all, *their* pool.

The article reminded him of the unsealed envelope still in his desk, and he took it out and reread both the letter he had written to Luisa Gonzales and the postcard José Ramón had written to her (with its gruesomely out-of-place GREETINGS FROM ZAGREB on the front). The message of the poem was so tender that anyone unaware of José Ramón's biography would have associated it more with, say, a glove of the finest leather than – bricks. At this hour of night the Spanish consular official was particularly taken with the last two lines and, thinking again of the beautiful student and suddenly brimming with happiness, he read them over in a hushed voice:

> *En las puertas del Oriente*
> *Se esconde mi suerte . . .*

II

999   The accident at the Chernobyl nuclear reactor took place in late April 1986. We learned of it several days later. The front-page headlines read DANGER OF RADIOACTIVE RADIATION! and NATIONALISM – OUR GREATEST DANGER! My friend Nenad closed the window and said, *We have come to the beginning of a new age.*

1000   I had a letter from J. in America. *How's your back? Have you had it in traction yet? You really should. I'm working on a new novel. It's called* Sing, Bird, Sing! *Drop me a line.*

1001   Late in June I went to Munich. Munich was like Zagreb or like the Zagreb that could be. *It's got our low atmospheric pressure, and people talk to themselves in the street*, I said in the postcard I sent to Nenad. I spent a long time with some paintings by Gabriele Münther at the Lenbachhaus Gallery. I like her better than Kandinsky.

1002   On my way back to Zagreb I shared a compartment with a girl named Ankica who works as a barmaid in Munich. We drank beer from the bottle instead of talking. Someone in the next compartment kept shouting curses. *This is the first time I've been home in three years*, Ankica said sadly.

1003   In July I went to Mljet, where I ran across a Dutch literary theoretician named Rainer who didn't recognize me and a Belgrade writer named Radoslav who did. We sat on the beach talking about literature and life, and when we were tired, Radoslav asked me what time it was. I couldn't tell him because I had no watch. *You should have a watch*, said Radoslav. *Every writer should have a watch. When I get back to Belgrade, I'm going to take up a collection among my writer*

217

friends and buy you a watch. To which I replied, *Thanks, but I don't wear a watch*. To which he replied, *No problem. Now look how well I swim*.

1004 I got another letter from J. in America. *How's your back? Had it in traction? I'm working on a novel called* Sing, Bird, Sing! *Drop me a line*.

1005 In August I had a bad attack of sciatica on Korčula and spent ten days in bed completely immobile, having injections, reading the novel *Pulp* by the Polish novelist Jerzy Andrzejewski, and underlining the passages in which he complains of his sciatica. He can be extremely delicate. For example, he writes: *Despite a recent increase in irritation in the crural nerve and the ill effects it has had on my motor skills* . . .

1006 I spent ten days in September at a spa, swimming in a heated pool, doing exercises and reading the papers, which were all inflation, strikes, foreign debt, embezzlements, frauds, legislative measures, etc. At lunch and supper I shared a table with a man named Borut, who was taking a slimming cure. When I told him what I'd found in the papers, he said, *Why do you think I look like this? Instead of protesting, I sit in a corner and stuff my face with cake!* I said I was in complete sympathy.

1007 I got another letter from J. in America. *Tell me how your back's getting along. You really ought to go to a professional and have him give your spine a stretch. I'm working on a new novel called* Sing, Bird, Sing! *Drop me a line*.

1008 A dull but continuous ache in my left leg kept me at home for most of December. Helga sent me a card from Brazil. My friend phoned from Finland, where he was travelling. *You'll never believe this*, he said, *but I'm in a Helsinki hotel room with five feminists*. And when I said, *So what?* he said, *They're all pregnant!* I didn't quite know what to make of it.

1009 Early in January I went to Havana for a symposium on literary theory. At the deserted airport in Gander, where we changed planes, I killed time studying a map of Newfoundland flora and fauna. It was twenty below out, and for some reason I could not come up with either the day of the week or the time of day.

1010 Havana – with its wonderful pastel pink, blue and green houses, corroding from the salt and humidity and peeling like cardboard boxes – reminded me of a) a tropical fruit on the verge of rotting, or b) already rotting de Chiricos. I couldn't decide which.

1011 I had a room on the ninth floor of the Habana Libre Hotel, where I could watch the city change from yellowish pink to dark blue as I sipped a *cuba libre* and breathed in the sweet, sticky, warm, wet air.

1012 The room next to mine was the room of Professor L., the world-famous semiotician. We often met on our balconies, stretching our necks a bit to smile and say hello, then looking out at the sea-birds (Cuban or American as they might be) against the fickle sky. *Birds of prey have the most sophisticated flying techniques*, Professor L. remarked. I told Professor L. about the flying techniques I had developed in my dreams. First I flew straight up, the way angels do, but no matter how hard I tried I never got more than a few feet above the ground. During those early flights I often got caught in trees – if there happened to be trees in the vicinity. In time I gained height and flew horizontally, like a bird or a plane. *Interesting*, said Professor L., stretching his neck a bit. *Tell me*, he said, after a moment's thought, *do you flex your head and knees before taking off? I mean, like this*. And he demonstrated what he had in mind. *No*, I said. *Strange*, he said. *That's your basic starting position, the one used by . . . everybody who flies.* Then he sank into thought.

1013 Walking through the streets of Havana, I saw old American Chevvies and new Soviet Volgas. At Copelia I patiently waited half a mile for an ice-cream. The whole queue swayed in time to the calypso coming over the PA system. I swayed too. At the Bodegita del Medio I sampled Hemingway's favourite cocktail, a *mojito*, with

219

a fresh, dark-green sprig of mint. Then I went back to the hotel and watched television. It consisted of long speeches by Castro, which I didn't understand, and American movies.

1014   At the Café Habañero, Professor L. and I had a *Mary Pickford* cocktail and talked about sea-fish. *The latest research shows that crustaceans have quite a stormy emotional life, that they have the capacity to fall in love, and that they tend to be faithful. Only people are swine,* Professor L. remarked.

1015   My sciatica returned. As the aches in my left leg increased, I cut down on my walking as much as possible. The symposium participants were very sympathetic: they immediately offered me the remedies they swore by. My bag was soon a blaze of Czechoslovak, Hungarian, American, Soviet, German, Belgian, Spanish and, of course, Cuban pills.

1016   In the Plaza de Armas, the Plaza de la Catedral, and all the other *plazas* of old Havana, old Professor L. would bend and pet every stray dog that crossed his path. There were an unusually large number of stray dogs about. *I have the same weakness for women in tears*, he said, taking out his wallet and showing me his bevy of grandchildren.

1017   Havana reminded me of a papaya or a mango. I couldn't decide which.

1018   Over lunch the professor and I discussed human intelligence and how it is basically determined by humour, play and unpredictability; drunkards and how unpredictable they are; and films. The professor had another weakness: writing screenplay treatments. They sounded weak to me. *More often than not, good literature comes from trash*, he said. It sounded profound to me.

1019   The best part of Hemingway's house was the bathroom. It had a scale in one corner and a series of handwritten figures running up the wall: his weight. *I sometimes think we love people more for their weaknesses than for their strengths*, I said to Marla, the interpreter.

1020   One day the professor and I gathered pink and white shells on the deserted Santa María beach. At one point I looked up to see him in a mist shimmering up from the burning sand and turquoise sea. *Do you realize we're in what once was paradise?* he said, cracking his knuckles for some reason. I had the feeling he could vanish at any moment.

1021   From over-ripe Havana I flew to Madrid the severe. In Toledo I saw an exhibit featuring instruments of torture. The ache in my leg grew more acute.

1022   In Madrid I saw Picasso's *Guernica* and was amazed to find it black and white. I had always assumed that it was in colour and the reproductions were in black and white. It was a great discovery and a great disappointment.

1023   Late in January I came back to Zagreb and went straight to bed with a bad sciatica attack. *What you need is more action*, my friend Grga said over a cup of coffee.

1024   I spent February, March and April in bed. I read Luis Buñuel's *Mon dernier soupir* and reminisced about Madrid, which now seemed much more beautiful. I underlined the passage in which Buñuel talks about his sciatica. Like the time he and his mother and his sister Conchita and his brother-in-law went to the opening of *Yerma* and the pain got so bad he had to stretch his leg out on a stool. After the third act he hobbled out of the theatre supported by his sister and convinced that Lorca was a bad playwright.

1025   Of course I told my friends the stories about Dalí and Picasso and the Café Gijón and all as if they were my own memories of Spain instead of Buñuel's.

1026   Late in April I went back to the spa. I exercised daily and swam in the pool. Sometimes there was a heavyweight boxer swimming with me. *The minute I saw you I knew you were – how shall I put it – gentle*, I said. *Boxers* can *be gentle*, he said, *though many people* *think we're not.* The day he left the spa, he told me, *I like being a boxer. All I do is punch, punch, punch. I never think and I always win.*

1027   I've decided to write a novel, though I don't know quite what it will look like. *What you need is more action*, my friend Grga said while we were having coffee together. My friend Snježana dropped in one day and asked what I was planning to write about. *Oh, I'd like to use circular action*, I said rather vaguely. *Circular action makes no less sense than action in a clear-cut direction.* And Snježana said, *Sounds pretty boring to me.*

1028   I got a letter from J. in America. *How's your back? You've let them put it in traction, haven't you? I'm giving up on* Sing, Bird, Sing! *I've started a new novel called* Bird Poison. *Drop me a line.*

1029   I got a small parcel from Radoslav. *We bought you a very nice watch*, he writes. *You can dive into water with it, and it shines in the dark.*

Author's Afterword

The novel you hold in your hand was originally published in 1988. Since then, many things have changed—even the country in which it was published no longer exists. Today, only five years later, many things are different. I have changed, as well.

This novel recently appeared in a Danish translation. One Danish critic, forgetting to check the original date of publication, harshly criticized me for writing "a satirical novel" while my homeland is in "a bloody war." That angry Dane has inspired me to write these lines.

This novel appeared in 1988. Many things have happened since: some episodes in the novel are today ancient history. Who would seriously believe today, for example, that the Czech Jan Zdrazil cannot return with his novel to Czechoslovakia (which, by the way, is split into two republics today) or that the Russian Trošin intends to emigrate secretly to Vienna. The only ones who would take this seriously are employed in the ever-lazy Russian bureaucracy.

Many things, I repeat, have happened since: some episodes in the novel, which then seemed absurd, might take place in the near future. Mr. Flagus's insane idea about the total control of literature seems less insane when we see the same ten titles and the same ten authors in the bookstore windows of Amsterdam, Paris, Stockholm, or London. Did Mr. Flagus have the *publishing industry* in mind when he passionately developed his ideas about "literary hamburgers"? On the other hand, my new small state (in which, by the way, there are fewer books every day!) exercises the tried and true strategies of ordinary totalitarianism. I doubt that this is what the nasty visionary Mr. Flagus had in mind.

"Whole countries, cultures and languages will cease to exist . . . the spiritual map of the world will change," said Mr. Flagus. In just a few years, the spiritual map of the world has really changed. Having destroyed its walls, Eastern Europe (at least that part in which I live) has moved farther away from Western Europe. Today, I can imagine my hero Pipo in Amsterdam only as a refugee. I can also imagine him in the New York about which he daydreamed, but only in a story which East European literature has already used up, a story of exile.

New walls have sprung up in Europe in just a few years. The Belgrade writer Radoslav now lives in a different state and speaks a different language. Trenches have been dug out between us. The telephone lines have been cut; letters are not carried; the roads are blocked. The watch that *shines in the dark* arrived several years ago. Today we both live in darkness: Radoslav in his, I in mine. Our darkness smells of gunpowder.

As far as the local characters are concerned, they are the same—after five years and in spite of the war. The ministers and their servants have changed, but, surprisingly, everything remains the same. The Pršas of today diligently compose their dossiers. The only difference is that now the innocent are accused publicly. The political system has changed and so have the political accusations. Most frequently encountered today are: *Yugo-zombie*, *Yugonostalgic Jerk*, *Nationally Colorblind*, and the like. They are linguistically more attractive than those which were thought up by Prša, the hero of my novel, I admit. In the literary world, little has changed. Ivan Ljustina, the critic who was raped in my novel, has changed for the better and has subsequently become a defender of women's rights!

I would write a different sort of novel today. It would be less breezy, I am sure. Nonetheless, to the Danish critic and to all others who like books to grow from reality rather than imagination, I can say that together with the war there is a parallel life which still has its charming moments. For example, T. Z., a well-known Croatian critic—one of those who stoke moralistic fires from his columns, one of the many who in the name of the "homeland which is in a bloody war" accuses his fellow writers, one of the Pršas of our age—was recently mentioned in the press himself:

> After three unsuccessful attempts, in a court of justice, two prominent Croatian writers finally met—Tvrtko Zane alias Branimir Donat and Predrag Raos.
>
> If we recall, the object of disagreement is Predrag Raos's finger which, according to the testimony in the accusation, Tvrtko Zane broke at the annual conference of the Writers' Association more than two and a half years

ago. It is the difficult task of the court to confirm whether Mr. Zane really broke that finger and committed a criminal offense which inflicted upon Mr. Raos a serious physical wound or not.

In answer to the accusation, Mr. Zane said that he was empowered to throw Mr. Raos from the hall where the Writers' Association's conference was being held for the simple reason that he, quite unlike Mr. Raos, was a member of that Association. Mr. Zane added that "Raos impeded the work of the conference by jumping in from the public and seizing the microphone." When asked how he could remove him from the hall, Mr. Zane claimed that "this was not possible to accomplish metaphysically," but that Mr. Raos would have to be carried—"as you normally carry out a garbage can."

Mr. Raos demanded that Mr. Zane say whether he still considered him mentally ill. The judge forbade the question, considering it irrelevant for this criminal case. Mr. Raos countered that between the mentally ill and a garbage can there is a fundamental difference. "A garbage can can be easily lifted," asserted Mr. Raos, "while it is necessary for six orderlies of Zane's size to remove a mental incompetent." This is, according to Mr. Raos, "obvious proof that Zane did not think only to carry him out but to knock him out first, which indicates premeditation."

To the judge's question as to why he held Mr. Zane by the neck, Mr. Raos answered, "when a man of 308 pounds lies on top of you, you probably will not be able to caress him."

The discussion was put off until February 19, 1993, when two expert witnesses—a doctor and X-ray technician—will attempt to shed light on this affair. They should confirm whether Mr. Raos's finger was broken in a fight with Mr. Zane or whether the finger in question was broken in some other, still unconfirmed, manner. (*Slobodna Dalmacija*, 28 December 1992)

As I said, literary life goes on. I would finally add that my novel's German translation has the title *Der goldene Finger*. I took the title of my hero's novel. And now I think that it is lucky that I did not write about the war, although that would probably satisfy my Danish critic and all those who force poor East European writers into their own—western—cultural stereotypes. Others have written about it, about the last war, indeed. And the new war has taken place. I wrote about a finger. And a finger has also taken place.

Dubravka Ugrešić
ZAGREB, APRIL 1993

225